PHOEBE

A NOVEL

BY M. C. VAUGHN

Cover art by Danny Simanjaya
Cover design by Danny Simanjaya and M. C. Vaughn

Acknowledgements:

This novel would not exist without inputs from many sources. Firstly, thank you to everyone I met and interacted with at CONjuration 2018, where I first realized that I needed to write this book.

Thank you also to Chris and Angela Seckinger, the founders and organizers of CONjuration and two of the best, most enjoyable friends and dinner companions anyone could ask for.

Particular thanks go to Ben Herr, who made a couple of timely and well-conceived suggestions that helped give this story its shape, and who is another great friend and character.

Special thanks to Danny Simanjaya - again! - for the wonderful cover art and, as observed in Monolith, for being just all-around good people. He can be found on DeviantArt as Simonjova.

Finally, I know Kevin Smith will never read this, but it was his podcast that gave me the impetus to complete this story. In the end, I made my own dream come true. Thanks, bro. Hope you live a long, healthy life.

For the two that are gone, and the ten that remain: You deserved better. Maybe your time will come around again. Until then, this one is for you. (Please don't sue me.)

ISBN-13 # 978-1-7334531-2-7

eBook ISBN-13 # 978-1-7334531-3-4

Library of Congress # Pending

PHOEBE

Prelude

August 6, 2066

JASON, AND THEN WILEY, each felt a momentary bump as they arrived, as though they had gone off a low step that they hadn't realized was there. They both stumbled very slightly, then recovered, removed their helmets and stared about themselves. They had emerged, in the middle of what they supposed was night, into what was perhaps the most unlikely place they could have imagined.

Before them lay a flagstone-paved plaza, as long as a football field and perhaps half again as wide, ringed with light towers illuminating it nearly to daylight brightness beneath a dark blank sky. The expanse was broken only by a few scattered benches around its perimeter. On its southern end stretched a tall, razor-wire-topped fence extending west behind a cluster of trees bordering the plaza. Apart from themselves, the place appeared to be deserted. Beyond the fence, and outside of the lighted areas, they could see only darkness.

Behind them was a circular pillar of steel and concrete perhaps ten feet in diameter with a flattened side facing them. That side bore the same blank, warped, static look of the portal they had passed through to get to this place. They both glanced back toward it, then looked at each other. Jason wore an awed, cautious expression that contrasted hugely with the elated, almost smug grin on Wiley's face.

They hardly had time to adjust to their surroundings before being startled almost out of their wits by a sudden blare of deafening, heavy-metal music from a pair of speaker banks set near the far end of the plaza. Wiley screamed "Jesus! What the *fuck?*" as both men covered their ears, their eyes squeezing shut against the pain of the noise.

After a few seconds, Jason glanced up; two of the strangest-looking women he had ever seen were walking quickly toward them from near the speaker banks. Both wore black outfits that looked like they had been designed by a role-playing-game lifer for a futuristic fashion show: the one on the left was shorter, with light-brown shoulder-length hair; she was only marginally clad in a bare-midriff halter, thong and what appeared to be arm and leg shields. The other was slightly taller, with long, flowing, jet-black hair, and wore a skin-tight bodysuit. They had crossed almost a third of the distance between them before Jason drew in his breath with an audible hiss. He glanced at Wiley, who was still covering his ears, but was otherwise completely engrossed in his study of the two females approaching them. Rolling his eyes in annoyance, Jason elbowed him hard enough to get his attention.

"Dude, we have to get out of here. *Now*. That's *not* a welcoming committee." He had to shout to be heard, but as he finished speaking, the music cut off as abruptly as it had started.

"Oh-ho-ho, the hell it ain't. They look *real* welcoming to me." Wiley licked his lips in a singularly off-putting manner as he watched them coming closer. Already they were less than fifty yards away.

"Look in their *hands*, dumbass. You think that's some kind of sex toy?" Jason half-shouted, half-snarled back, and Wiley's response - "oh, *shit* -" sounded like he had been punched in the stomach. Both women carried what looked like oversized claw hammers, and their pace had quickened as they drew closer.

Jason whirled around, and stared in horror. The rift had darkened into impermeability. They were trapped.

"What do we do?" The obnoxiousness that was Wiley's stock in trade had drained out of his voice, leaving only a whiny note of fear behind. Jason glanced over at him again for a bare moment, this time in incredulity, before yelling in response: "RUN!"

Without waiting to see which way Wiley would go, Jason bolted to his left, running as fast as his suit would allow, toward a cluster of low buildings beneath one of the nearer light towers. Within a few seconds, he was alone, and he could hear one set of footfalls behind him. *Shit,* he thought. *They split up too.*

He was too slow, and the pressure suit too burdensome. He risked a glance back and was terrified to see that the black-haired one had already closed half the distance between them. A scream from behind told him that the other one had already caught Wiley, and that spurred him to run even faster. The buildings were close - a few seconds away - but he could not see a door in any of them.

Wiley's screams continued for a few moments as he reached the nearest wall, but they ceased with chilling abruptness as Jason turned and faced his pursuer. She was close enough for him to see her clearly, and that shock neutralized all of the adrenaline that had powered his flight from her. She still had the hammer raised, ready to attack him, but he could not run any more, could not resist. She was only a few steps away.

"Phoebe - " he whispered.

She should not have heard his whisper, he thought. Perhaps she read his lips, and recognized that he had called her name. Maybe she just remembered him. He would never be sure. But she halted, and lowered her hammer as she looked searchingly, though dispassionately, at him.

He stared back at her through the stew of emotions that had come to a sudden, rolling boil in his mind. How did she get there? What had happened to her? His mouth closed and opened, but only an inchoate squeak came out.

She moved almost close enough for him to touch, and then beckoned silently for him to follow her. Numbly, he obeyed. They walked, one behind the other, back toward the spot where they had arrived. Jason focused on her back, not wanting to see what had happened to Wiley. He had already dealt with one painful, grisly death since this business had started (*but she's not dead,* he thought, *she's alive - she's right here!*) and he had no desire to see another one. As they neared the place, he picked up his helmet from where he had dropped it as he ran.

She drew to a halt a few steps away from the rift. As he drew up beside her, it began brightening, until it was again passable. Jason looked at

Phoebe in bewilderment as she turned again to face him. Her dark eyes and her black hair were just as he remembered them, but all of the personality had drained from her expression. She looked like an old woman trapped in a younger woman's body.

Jason stopped short and drew in his breath sharply again, this time in amazed comprehension. She *was* an old woman. He had no idea how far forward in time the rift had brought him, but from the strangeness of the place and the abruptness of their arrival (*the jolt,* he thought wildly, *slight difference in rotational vectors between the two endpoints*), he guessed that they might be several decades in the future - or even farther.

At *least* thirty years, he thought. Maybe more. But Phoebe's face, on the surface, was the face he remembered from just a few days earlier. Before the breakup.

It was the expression that had changed, or had just drained away. Thirty years of death, if not many more, were reflected in the visage that still watched him silently, almost indifferently. But it had not *aged*.

She reached toward her shoulder and touched a small, black-on-black button on her suit that he hadn't noticed before, and opened her mouth - but to his shock, the voice that spoke wasn't hers. It was Professor Tinsworth's.

"Jason. You have to go back. Wiley is dead. You have to go back through and report to the colonel what you've seen."

Her expression never changed, her mouth never moved, except to open and close. He covered his face with his hands for a moment, before he felt his wrists clasped and gently pulled back.

Phoebe's hands - but her hands were never nearly that hard, or that *strong* - were encased in black gloves that formed part of the catsuit she wore. Her eyes watched his, still with that same deadness, as she released one hand and pointed toward the rift.

Jason was now so confused, and so overwrought, that he could only put on his helmet and begin securing it to his pressure suit. He looked at Phoebe again; she still pointed toward the portal, her expression still frozen - until she opened her mouth again. His helmet was not yet on; he could still hear what came out.

The voice was so strangely altered that he didn't know it at first. It dragged oddly where it shouldn't have, and the consonants were slurry and chewed-sounding, yet it was almost her voice. But the mouth did not move, and Jason realized that it was a recording. He closed his eyes in horror, remembering what had happened to her, and knowing her larynx had surely been damaged then.

Then he opened them again, looking into her lifeless eyes, and nodded to her; after securing his helmet to the suit, he turned to the portal once more. It still retained a blank, warped sense of nothingness. He stepped into it, still thinking of what Phoebe had said to him.

There was a moment of discontinuity as he crossed through the interface of the rift, and then he was back in the lab. Tinsworth and the two DARPA officers were staring at him. One of them rushed forward to help with his helmet. After it had been removed, the professor asked urgently, "Why are you back? Where's Grant?"

Jason stared back, his eyes haunted. "Wiley's dead. You won't believe what's on the other side."

"Should I suit up and go through?" Tinsworth was already half out of his chair, but he froze when Jason almost shouted back at him.

"No! We can't go back yet." His haunted gaze fixed on the two officers. "Colonel Mangum, Major Eier, if you have any higher connections with DARPA, we're going to need them."

Tinsworth paled. "What the *hell* did you see? Why do you want the DOD stepping in now?"

Jason was equally pale, as he sat down and began undoing his pressure suit. "We need them with us to back us up. We have to talk to Dr. Bryant. I know what he's up to in that lab, and we're going to need his help."

PART ONE - THE RIFT

Chapter One

A.D. 2023

JASON ANDERSON LEANED over his laptop and typed a few keystrokes, occasionally glancing up at the readouts from the two screens on either side of his own display as he spoke softly into the microphone of his headset. The background hum of the bridge generator formed a rumbling harmonic discord with the microaccelerator that Jason found both familiar and disconcerting; he briefly wondered what sound would arise from an accident, then quickly dismissed the thought. He hoped he would never know.

The left monitor displayed exactly what he hoped to see: the Einstein-Rosen bridge they had initially generated three weeks earlier remained stable. The readout on his right indicated a very slight energy loss to the particle stream; the excess energy had been absorbed by the field around the bridge, which held the two quantum singularities that served as its endpoints motionless relative to one another.

Jason smiled slightly. Phoebe had almost panicked when he had told her that he was working with supersmall quantum black holes, terrified that one might somehow break free of its containment and, as she put it, "eat the world." It had taken him almost an hour - over a dinner he couldn't afford - to reassure her that the hole they had formed was about the size of a proton, that it could fall through the earth without ever absorbing a single atom, and that the entire bridge - including its black-hole endpoints - would evaporate if the magnetic field power were to be interrupted.

A soft tone from his headset distracted him, and he touched the device in his ear. "Anderson."

"Jason? Are you busy?" It was Phoebe; she had an uncanny way of crossing his mind just before crossing his path. He glanced back over his shoulder toward the window of the lab's airlock; she was there, waving once toward him, her face worried.

He sighed, waving back, and said, "I can't leave this right now. My shift ends in an hour, and we can talk then. You want to have dinner at my place?"

"No, Jason." She sighed; to him that sigh was ominous, a preface to a speech prepared to address a problem. He closed his eyes for a moment in resigned frustration, before opening them again as she resumed speaking. "I know how important this study is to you. I know you could be in line to help Professor Tinsworth get a Nobel Prize." She paused, and Jason's unease grew; if she was putting him into a choice between a putative Nobel and something else, it was something big. "I know how smart you are, and you deserve to - to chase that as far as you can." Another hesitation, and an uncomfortable one; now his academic career goals had been added to the Nobel. "I can't keep this up, Jason. I almost never see you. We can't talk much when we do, because you're in the lab all the time, and you don't seem to know about anything else that's going on."

Jason's eyes closed again, this time in pain; she was right again. Whenever he tried to tell her about his research, he could only get about two sentences in before that look came over her face - the one that told him she was trying to understand, but couldn't. He knew this because almost anything else she could talk about generated the same response from him.

He had suspected - known, honestly - that this conversation would one day take place, but had hoped that he could finish this study first, and then he could take some time away from the lab and devote more attention to

Phoebe. To be faced with losing her, this close to the end, seemed to him even more unfair than the universe normally chose to be.

"Phoebe -" he started, then stopped. He could be selfish and beg her for more time, but for what? This was how it was going to be. They had had talks similar to this before. He knew, and he knew she knew, that their situation would not change as long as he remained on the track he had set for himself - first graduate assistant, then as a research fellow, probably at another university. She would have to be willing to move, and put up with frequent absences - as well as long pauses in short conversations.

"Are you even going to talk to me?" Her voice trembled in the headset. Jason's gaze dropped to the floor; he didn't want to look her face.

"What do you want me to say? I can't leave this project and walk away. I'd destroy my career before it starts. This is all I've ever wanted to do." His face crumpled; she couldn't see it, thankfully. "You're making me choose between you and everything I ever worked for."

"You're making me take a back seat to your career." Phoebe's voice was broken, her breathing stitched and uneven, but the tears had not dampened it yet. "I love you, Jason, but I can't be second best for you. Not for anyone." She paused again, and Jason knew she was steeling herself for what came next: "I think it's time for us both to move on."

Jason's insides felt like they were on an elevator whose cables had snapped. His jaw froze, partly in realization of what was happening, partly because he couldn't weep openly. Not now. Not here. As he continued to stare at the floor, an indicator light on his right screen turned yellow, then red, and began to flash; had his headset not been in external communication mode, he would have heard a warning tone.

"I'm sorry, Jason. It has to be this way. Goodbye." The click from the intercom told him that she had turned it off; he looked up only to see the back of her head, flowing with the long black hair he had loved so much, as she turned into the hallway.

ONE BUILDING AWAY, Wiley Grant was bored, annoyed, and needed to take a shit.

Most of the controls were monitored actively from the far end of the wormhole. Jason Anderson was good, Wiley had to admit, but he himself was just as good - but Anderson was a semester ahead of him and technically (definitely *not* intellectually) his senior associate. Tinsworth liked him better, too.

He snorted. Tinsworth liked the girl that Anderson was seeing, that almost-hot Latina chick, and probably put him at the mouth end of the wormhole hoping she'd show up and improve the scenery. He snorted again. The research team referred to the other end as the mouth, and his end... he rolled his eyes. Leave it to Tinsworth to stick him with the asshole.

Asshole. Shit end of the stick. He *really* needed to take that dump. Grunting, he shifted in his chair as he checked the com; the blinking light showed that Jason was on it, and the line was active, so he was definitely in the lab. He glanced at the readings; nothing unusual was happening. He hesitated for a moment before deciding, then stood and ambled out through the airlock entry, closing it behind him with his ID before shuffling down the austere, academic corridor toward the men's restroom.

He rolled his eyes again. There was a women's room beside it, almost never used, and he could have stumped in there and dumped in there - no one would have known the difference. Well, maybe the plastic badge watching the security cameras might notice, but probably not. Guy was probably watching a ballgame. Or porn, if there were no windows in his office. He grinned sourly to himself. At least that dude had something good to look at.

He reached the men's room door and shoved it open. The dated interior with its air of slowly deteriorating cleanliness was at once familiar and depressing; this was an old facility. What was the half-life on this bathroom? - he wondered, remembering that Hampton Hall, as well as Williams, had been selected for this project because both were, if not obsolete, then expendable.

Probably both of them would be worth more torn down, Wiley thought as he reached the first stall door. He briefly considered covering the seat; after a glance told him it was at least dry, he turned, dropped his jeans with a fuck-it sort of grunt, and squatted.

The first wafts of his not-very-pleasant brand reached his nostrils at about the same time that the lights in the bathroom flickered. Wiley had just reached his Shitting Zen State ("A good shit is as satisfying as a good meal!' he often claimed to his few friends) and it took a few seconds for the significance of that flicker to register in his brain. Just as it did, a shockwave rippled through the bathroom, shaking dust from the ceiling and walls and tightening Wiley's sphincter so abruptly that he thought he could almost hear it snap closed.

"Oh, shit!" he hissed. He stumbled to his feet, struggling to pull his pants and briefs up, thinking a silent thanks to Crom or Jupiter or whoever that his asshole hadn't closed mid-shit, and stumbled back into the hallway just as another shockwave - this one accompanied by an explosion in the lab that blew out the airlock door - almost knocked him down.

No way he was going back in there. Wiley turned and ran for the emergency exit, his footfalls punctuated with expletives. Beyond escaping, he could only think of one thing: when whatever had just happened was reviewed, they would find out he had left his station untended, and had not checked in with Anderson.

Fuck. He was fucked.

TURNING BACK TO HIS LAPTOP, Jason tapped his headset and was at once greeted by several warning tones. Horrified, he looked wildly up at the left monitor; the far end of the bridge, situated in an identical lab to his own in a building some hundred yards away, had undergone a power surge and destabilized. The magnetic field appeared to be fluctuating; from the readings, Jason's best guess was that there was a slight spin on the singularity in that lab.

"Shit!" The situation was serious enough to drive Phoebe's departure from his mind. He studied the readings from the field that shaped the wormhole; long, very thin lengths of neodymium wire lined the narrow, underground tube, perhaps six feet in diameter, that connected the two endpoints of the bridge in 3-D space.

Jason tapped his headset once more while trying via his laptop to call Wiley, the research assistant in the other lab; neither attempt received an answer. He opened a window on his laptop, attempting to move the wires - which twisted around the tube like the interior of a rifle barrel - back against the direction in which they wound, as though straightening the rifling.

For a moment, it seemed to work; the field readings weakened slightly, and Jason began to relax - and a shockwave ran through the tube a moment before he heard the compressed, distant roar of an explosion in the other lab. The instrumentation went berserk, then dead.

Jason knew what that might mean. He snatched up his laptop and yanked the cabling that connected it into the monitors and instrumentation behind it, and raced for the door; once outside, he ran for the exit.

As he reached the stairwell, a door just to its right was marked "PLANT MAINTENANCE." A keyless entry pad was embedded in the wall beside the door; Jason grabbed his lab ID from around his neck and held it over the pad. A low rumble went through the building as he heard the click that signaled the lock's release. He yanked the door open and ran straight to the back of the room.

A main electrical safety switch was mounted chest high on the rear wall behind a safety lock; leaving his laptop on a shelf beside it, he threw the switch to the "OFF" position, then whirled and pelted back out, dashing up the stairway toward the south exit from the building - the one that faced toward the other laboratory.

He could hear the first sirens in the distance, mixed with disconnected screams and shouts and a low, roaring sound. The building where the second lab had been - Hampton Hall - was visibly damaged. All of the windows facing him had been blown out, and dissipating black smoke roiled from almost all of them, but the building itself looked subtly wrong, as though it had been compressed from the top so that it bulged out, and it looked like a bite had been taken out of it at ground level.

No wonder Wiley hadn't answered, Jason thought wildly. All around him were pieces of debris blown out from the building; just as he realized that he had left his laptop, he noticed a broadening pool of dark blood that was spreading from behind a bush to his left. He froze, gulping, realizing that no one could lose that much blood and live.

He didn't want to look, but he had to. As the noise and confusion off ahead of him grew more concentrated and organized while the sirens approached, Jason edged toward the pool of blood, until the body that had disgorged it came into view from behind the bush where it had come to rest.

For a moment he could not think at all. The bush and the surrounding pavement were liberally covered with shattered glass that crunched under his feet. The young woman who had died lay sprawled, headless on the sidewalk; several feet away, its face turned toward the side of the building, lay that head. Its luxuriant black hair was tangled, covered in glass shards, and matted with blood.

Jason swayed, vomit rising in his throat, his thoughts as frantic and aimless as ants in a hill set afire. At first he thought he should go back in the lab, and restart the experiment - for surely then the result would be different, and she would be alive! - and then the enormity rushed into his brain with the same gasp as the air into his lungs. Phoebe was dead, horribly dead, brutally mangled, and nothing he could do would bring her back.

He turned, staggering as his thoughts went blank and dark, and landed insensate in Phoebe's blood. Beyond him, another explosion rocked the surrounding environs, and a momentary tearing sensation inside himself almost brought Jason back to consciousness - but it was only the last lunge before his awareness fled.

Chapter Two

JASON AWOKE TO BLANK darkness and cold.

For a moment he was completely disoriented; he lay flat on his back on a cold metal table, his body covered with a sheet. As he tried to gather himself, the memory of his last waking moments came back to him, momentarily paralyzing him with horror.

He grappled with that horror and with his fear, and failing to master either one, gave vent to a yell and tried to throw the sheet off of his head. It remained pitch dark, and he banged his hands against an unseen metal plate less than a foot above his head.

"OW! Shit!" The pain from the blow shot up his arms, distracting him just long enough for his mind to start functioning again. Dark. Cold. Under a sheet.

At least his clothes were still on.

"HEYYYY!!!!!!" He yelled again, trying to scoot his body toward where he guessed the refrigerator door was, hoping he remembered right - did they put the bodies in feet first, or head first? - and began slamming his feet as hard as he could against the metal interior.

For a few moments there was no response, and the blows hurt his feet; he tried pounding on the metal plate above him. He yelled again, beginning to panic: he knew he was in a morgue, and if there was no one outside, he might well suffocate - or die of hypothermia - before anyone knew he was still alive.

MIKEY LEROUX MADE his unenthusiastic way back from his break through the bottom floor of Nesmith Hall toward the morgue.

Though technically he was forensic-track pre-med, the project for which he had signed on had proven to be little better than security-guard work in the temporary morgue that had been set up as part of whatever actual research was being done. Most of the cadavers received there fell into two categories: indigents and addicts for whom body donation was a financially-motivated alternative to cremation, and - more rarely - individuals who had signed an agreement with the university to donate their corpses.

The two students who had been brought in from the explosion today fell into the latter group. The girl - her name was Phoebe Michelle Reyes, he remembered - was a student at the university. Mikey shook his head. The poor thing had arrived in two grisly pieces. The other was a guy named Jason Anderson, who supposedly had been working on whatever it was that blew up in Hampton Hall. He hadn't gotten a look at that one, and after seeing the girl and hearing about the explosion, he hadn't really wanted to.

Dr. Bryant had brought them in from the scene with a couple of orderlies. They had been hastily stored in the morgue's refrigerator units; when he had asked about intake paperwork or effects, the response had been emphatic - there was a chance that the bodies had been contaminated, and they were to be left in the storage unit until Dr. Bryant returned to examine them. A team had arrived shortly afterward and wheeled out all of the other remains in the unit, leaving only the girl and Anderson.

He reached the entrance to the temporary morgue and swiped the ident pad with the ID hung around his neck. The door opened and he entered; he thought he heard an odd sound as the door swung closed, but dismissed it in the ensuing silence.

The quiet didn't last long. A dim banging sounded from the storage unit, which was at the other end of the morgue from where he stood. Mikey's hair stood on end. Then he heard the shouting, and felt a mixture of horror and relief; for a second he had imagined the girl's headless body pounding the inside of the refrigerator. Then he realized that it had to be Anderson making the noise - *and that he was alive.*

"Holy *shit!*"   Wide-eyed, Mikey slowly approached the unit, and standing as far back as he could from the door to Anderson's section of the unit, he undid the latch and opened it.

His legs above the tops of his socks had started to turn blue, and his whole body was shaking with the cold. Mikey drew out the tray, looking down at the sheet, and finally drew the cover off the man's head. His eyes were as wide and staring as Mikey's own, and he was nearly hyperventilating with a mixture of physical distress and panic. He finally spotted Mikey, and after a few more gasps for breath, nearly screamed: "How the *fuck* did I end up in here?"

"Jesus Christ!" Mikey was appalled, both by what had happened to Anderson, and by the implications: Dr. Bryant himself had stuck this guy in the fridge. He hadn't even checked to see if he was really dead.

Anderson was already sitting up, pulling the sheet off himself as best he could. The guy's hands were still numb and the cold had clearly affected his reflexes, but other than that he seemed unhurt - except for the blood that caked his shirt and had nearly solidified in his hair.

"You're not hurt, right? Where'd the blood come from?" As soon as he asked, Mikey regretted it; no doubt it had been the girl's blood. A look of sudden, angry misery from Anderson confirmed his suspicion.

"My girlfriend left, and right after that, there…" he seemed about to continue, but hesitated. "You know there was an explosion in Hampton. Something blown out of the building hit her and killed her."

"Where were you at?" Mikey's stomach turned over. He could handle corpses, even disfigured ones, but the idea of finding his own girlfriend with her head gone was something he wasn't sure he could handle, if it ever happened.

"We were coming out of Williams Hall." Anderson bowed his head as he turned, trying to stand up. Mikey looked at him a moment, then whistled.

"Shit, Hampton's over a hundred yards from Williams. Something got blown that far? And that hard?"

Anderson glared up at him without answering, and Mikey grimaced. "Sorry, man. I saw your girl when they brought her in. It was bad."

Anderson looked down at the floor for a moment, and an uneasy silence fell between them. Mikey glanced briefly around the morgue; they were alone, except for the closed-circuit camera in the far corner beside the door. Finally, he said, "My name's Mikey. Mikey Leroux. I know you're Jason Anderson."

JASON STARED AT THE FLOOR. Phoebe was gone. He had passed out when he saw her body, had been mistaken for dead, and brought - here.

The big black guy - Mikey - who had freed him from the storage unit seemed sympathetic enough, but something didn't feel right. He glanced toward the storage unit that had held him; it had only six doors. He hoped Phoebe wasn't behind one of them, but he suspected she was. He stole another look at Mikey, and then he saw it.

"We're not at the hospital downtown, are we? We're still on campus." He didn't respond at once, but Jason knew he was right: Mikey looked as much like a grad student as he himself did. "How long have I been down here?"

Mikey glanced toward the clock on the wall above his desk; Jason's eyes followed his. The clock read 6:45.

"They brought you in right when I started shift, at five. They brought you and your girl in, and hauled everyone else out. Said you might be contaminated from the blowup over at Hampton." Mikey squinted at him. "What were you guys doing over there, anyway?"

"Can't say anything about it. But why did they bring us here, instead of taking us downtown if they thought we were dead? Oh…." Jason saw the answer even as he asked the question. "The donation cards we signed. The university gets our organs."

"Something like that, I think." Mikey seemed reluctant to say more, so Jason asked simply, "Nondisclosure?"

"Yeah." Mikey looked relieved. "Sorry, man. I figure you know how this works, if you were working in Hampton."

"I was in Williams.   Say…"   Jason reached toward his pocket; mercifully, his phone was still tucked there.   Turning it on, he swiped through screens to his contacts list as he asked, "which building is this?"

"Nesmith.   You probably shouldn't be using that in here."   Mikey looked worried. Jason snorted.

"Dude, believe me, *nothing* in here is as sensitive as what I was doing in Williams."

"Yeah, right, and look where you are now.   Who're you calling?" Mikey still looked worried, and more than a little suspicious; Jason hoped he wouldn't have to force his way out of the morgue. He was already becoming suspicious himself.

"I'm calling Dr. Tinsworth. He's the Physical Sciences chair, and my boss. If the government is overseeing your project here, it's probably some of the same people that we have overseeing ours."   He hesitated.   "I'm not going to just bolt out of here. I know you'll get a lot of heat for that. I'm hoping that between Tinsworth and - who's your boss?"

"Bryant. Dr. Allen Bryant."

"I'm hoping that between Tinsworth and Bryant, we can get this straightened out." He found the number he needed, and pressed the icon to dial it.

"You don't have your boss on speed dial?" Mikey chuckled.

"If I could not have him on it at all, I would, but you know how that works." Jason lifted the phone to his ear, listening for the ring. An answer came after the second buzz, and it was abrupt and unexpected: "Who is this, and what have you done with Jason Anderson?"

"Professor Tinsworth! It's me - Jason. I'm all right. Well - I'm not all right, but I'm not hurt." Jason was a little surprised by the vehemence with which Tinsworth had answered. His reply was equally unsettling.

"Are you in Nesmith Hall? Tell them I'm on my way. They are *not* to follow standard disposition protocol, all right? Tell them that. The situation has become critical.   They MUST NOT FOLLOW PROTOCOL." Tinsworth was nearly shouting. "I'm coming down there right now to talk with Bryant."

"There's just me and the grad assistant down here. I woke up in the morgue freezer. The GA heard me pounding on the door and let me out. He hasn't called anyone in yet." Jason looked askance at Mikey, who nodded, looking worried. "I'm sure he's going to have to call someone soon. There's a camera in here now, so they may already have someone coming. How long will it take for you to get here?"

"I just left a meeting with a representative from the DOD. I'm across campus, about five minutes out." Jason could hear Tinsworth taking a deep breath. "Jason, the bridge didn't evaporate when the lab in Hampton blew up. It's generated a rift with a temporal dislocation."

Jason had been trying to keep his mind focused, avoiding thoughts of Phoebe, and trying not to think too hard about where he had waked up or why he had been taken there. Tinsworth's statement drove all of those things completely from his mind.

A *temporal* dislocation? You're telling me that the bridge destabilized enough to lose its temporal anchorage, and still remained intact? That's like dropping a suspension bridge into a river - in one piece!"

"Exactly. It's still intact, but I don't know that it's stable. I'll tell you more about it when I get there. Above all else, tell Dr. Bryant that we have a Code Void emergency. Code *Void*, got that?"

"Got it. Look, Dr. Tinsworth -" Jason withdrew the phone from his ear; the professor had already disconnected. Mikey was already on his phone.

Jason took a deep, nervous breath. Mikey looked at him as he spoke. "Dr. Bryant. This is Leroux -" He was cut off by shouting that was loud enough for Jason to hear most of what was said: "...God damn it, get those two stiffs out of there and over to the liquidation lab *now*! I just got a call from the fucking DOD and they want to know why we took them from the scene before anyone even knew they went missing. Shit, their fucking families are probably going to start calling the minute they see that fucking explosion on the news. Get them the *fuck* out of there!"

Mikey glared down at his phone for a moment in wide-eyed, angry bewilderment before returning his eyes to Jason and his phone to his ear.

"Dr. Bryant, one of them is still alive. He woke up a few minutes ago and started hammering on the freezer."

For several seconds, there was only silence; then a loud "FUCK!" sounded from the phone, followed by the beep that indicated that the call had ended. Mikey looked down at it again, then back to Jason, who shrugged.

"Just for the record, I don't know what standard protocol is. That's something that goes on after the cadavers leave here and go to the lab." Mikey's look had become a stare, and it didn't waver. "I hope Tinsworth gets here before Bryant does. It'll be a hell of a lot simpler for me if I don't have to stop Bryant from trying to do something to you."

"He's not trying *shit* on me, unless he's bigger than you are." Jason met Mikey's stare with one of his own. "I'm just glad I don't have to worry about trying to fight *you.*"

Mikey laughed. "I don't know what kind of shit they're doing with these bodies, and after all that, I don't think I want to know. This is some high-pay-grade bullshit going on."

"I don't know if anyone would have ever thought something was wrong with this project Bryant's doing, if our lab hadn't blown up," Jason answered. "But the Defense Department is a *big* deal. They're definitely going to want to know what's going on with Tinsworth, but I hadn't heard anything about Bryant at all. But *they're* calling *him*, so something's got to be seriously wrong there."

Mikey shook his head, unable to offer any response, and they lapsed into a waiting silence.

Chapter Three

DR. ROBERT TINSWORTH drove his immaculate, if elderly, pickup truck at a genuinely unsafe speed along the labyrinthine campus streets, more hoping that he would avoid any unwary pedestrians than actually doing anything that would prevent himself from hitting them. As he drove, he whispered to himself under his breath, trying to figure out what he would say, and hoping he could get there in time to extricate Jason from Bryant's lab.

He had heard nothing from Grant, and that worried him. At first he had feared that Wiley might have been blown to pieces, and that would have been bad enough - but then he pulled the camera footage from the Hampton Hall basement, and saw what had really happened. The lazy, arrogant fatass had gone to the shitter right before the blowup. He half hoped Grant would fall in front of his truck, and half wanted to find him alive to find out whether he knew anything - *then* he would run him over with the truck.

Jason had called him from Nesmith Hall, which made matters worse; Bryant was running some kind of research into necrotic brain tissue. He knew little of the project, seeing that it was kept as quiet as his own had been until a couple of hours ago. How Jason had ended up there was anyone's guess at this point; apparently he had been knocked out and mistaken for dead - but by whom?

Tinsworth made another right turn, the tires protesting as he accelerated again. Fifty was as fast as he dared go through with so many students out; fortunately, some of them had been drawn away by the explosion in Hampton. The DOD had locked down that situation, at least. Last thing they needed was for someone to vanish without a trace in there.

Another tire-shrieking right, and Nesmith Hall - a long, two-story classroom building that was part of the medical college - lay just ahead on his left. Tinsworth glanced in his mirror, and seeing nothing coming, sent the truck up over the low curb, crossing the sidewalk onto the lawn beside the building. Fuck it if he'd try to find a parking space - no time for that.

He killed the engine and yanked the keys from the ignition, bolting from the low cab of the pickup and running as fast as his fifty-year-old legs would carry him up the low stairs into the facility. He turned right at once, running the short distance to the stairwell; once inside, he took the stairs three at a time until he reached a locked maintenance closet.

He gasped a snort. This was no maintenance closet; it was an entrance to a laboratory that only a few people knew about. His clearance as a DOD collaborator - and other things - had allowed him knowledge of the secret facility, as well as some bare facts concerning the project that was ongoing there. But for that, Jason might never have come out from behind that door.

He scanned his ID against the ident pad; then he placed his fingers on the pad to allow them to be scanned. The door buzzed softly and clicked; Tinsworth sighed with relief. His ID had not been locked out. Jason was still in there.

He went through the door, following a low corridor that led to a computer bank at what would have been the nurses' station in a normal hospital. Two graduate assistants were at work there; it took several seconds before one of them noticed him. Hive mentality, Tinsworth thought, as the GA addressed him.

"Haven't seen you down here before. Need directions?"

"You guys have a morgue down here?" He knew they did; he was curious to know how much more they might tell him if he kept his questions vague. The GA didn't disappoint him.

"There's two, one in the intake facility where the cadavers are prepped, and the other one where the tissue restoration lab is. Which one do you want?"

"Intake facility." Tinsworth hesitated just a moment. "A student of mine was brought in a little while ago."

The GA paled slightly. "They brought in two, less than two hours ago. One was missing her head. Hope that one wasn't yours."

Shit, Tinsworth thought. So Phoebe came to see Jason at work. It might not all have been Grant's fault, and from the sound of it, Phoebe was very dead indeed. At some point that was going to catch up with Jason, and he would be useless when it did.

He couldn't afford that now. He would have to be fast. "My student was the other one. Where's the intake?"

The GA pointed down the hall. "Straight ahead, second left. If he's in there, there's no need to hurry." The kid - he was probably twenty-four, but obviously socially closer to fifteen - grimaced as soon as he said this. "Sorry, man. That wasn't cool."

"No, it wasn't. And the name's Dr. Tinsworth. If you see Bryant, let him know where I've gone." Without waiting for the response - which would surely be fearful; Bryant had an iron fist where his staff was concerned - Tinsworth continued past the station toward the indicated door, swiping its ident pad.

Once again there was a buzz and click, and Tinsworth pushed the door open, walked into the morgue, and closed the door quickly. Jason was inside, along with a hulking black GA he didn't know. Jason looked visibly relieved to see him.

"Jason - what happened in the lab?" Tinsworth spoke without preamble, moving toward the desk and grabbing a pen and pad from off of it. "Did you hear from Grant?"

Jason's relief faded at once. "No. I tried to raise him on the com, once I saw the warning, but I couldn't get him to answer. I don't know whether he lost connection or what."

Tinsworth looked hard at him. "You're sure you didn't hear from him? Or did you ignore him, so that you could talk to your girlfriend?"

The angry misery that was his grief flooded back, and he looked up at his boss with a stung expression. "I was talking to Phoebe on external com. She wasn't in the lab. All Wiley had to do was IM me if he couldn't get me on direct com. He didn't IM. I never heard the tone."

Tinsworth's glare continued for another few seconds as he studied Jason, then faded. "All right. Grant went to the shitter while you were talking with her. He wasn't in the lab when - whatever it was - happened. As best as I know, there was a power surge that destabilized his endpoint of the bridge."

Jason hesitated. "I saw the warning light, and figured it was a surge. I thought that the endpoint might have acquired spin, but when I adjusted it, it tried to stabilize, and then - boom. After that, I just grabbed my laptop and ran out. I threw the main on the building, tried to kill the bridge. From what you said, that didn't work."

"It sure as hell didn't." Tinsworth glanced over toward the morgue GA, who was watching them with ill-concealed confusion. "Who are you, and how much of this do you understand?"

The hulking black man blinked, then responded. "Mikey Leroux. I'm the GA here - forensics track. Sounds like you're talking theoretical physics, but beyond that, I'm clueless."

"Good thing to be." The door behind them buzzed, and a man who could only be Dr. Bryant, flanked by two older, imposing-looking men in military uniforms, entered the morgue. Tinsworth rounded on them.

"Two things, gentlemen. First, standard disposition protocol must not be followed in this case. This is my graduate assistant, Jason Anderson, and what he knows of today's incident may be of great value to us, given the situation we now face. Second, my other assistant, Wiley Grant, has gone missing. I had thought he was in the lab when it went up, but I've reviewed the security footage, and I saw him exit the building after the explosion occurred. We'll need to find him as well."

Bryant was short and bespectacled, but heavyset, and pugnacious-looking; his response matched his appearance. "Tinsworth, you know Anderson doesn't have clearance to be in here. He can't be allowed to leave." Without waiting for an answer, Bryant looked over to Mikey. "Leroux, clock out, and leave your ident at the station. You're off this project as of right now."

Stunned, Mikey looked around the room; then, with a last, significant look at Jason, he went to his desk, gathered a few articles from it, and left. Bryant watched until the morgue door closed again, then glared back at Tinsworth, who returned his look with equal hostility.

Jason spoke first. "Why the hell am I in here? I got shoved in a goddamn freezer without anyone even checking whether I was still alive."

"That's not your concern." The officer on the left spoke, his voice surprisingly quiet for a man of his size and formidable build. "Your concern right now is whether you, Mr. Grant, or Dr. Tinsworth here can find a way to contain this situation."

"I don't know. I'm not sure I want to, yet." Jason fired back at the officer, before glancing toward Tinsworth with a look that was half pleading, half baffled. "Who are you? Both of you, I mean?" he continued, with a look toward the second officer, who had stood stone-faced and silent to that point.

"Jason, you can trust them. I'm not so sure about Bryant here, but I've worked with these two." Tinsworth stepped forward and motioned toward the one who had spoken. "Jason Anderson, this is Colonel Pete Mangum. He's Deputy Field Director for Strategic Technology Research for DARPA. And this is Major Fred Eier, his assistant. They've worked with both Dr. Bryant and myself on a number of assignments, including the bridge project."

"Wait - they were in on the bridge project? I've never seen either of them." Jason looked at the two with slight distaste. "Nothing against the military, but it makes me kind of nervous to know these kind of guys are around."

"Understandable." Colonel Mangum's response surprised Jason into silence. "Emergent technology often has the potential to wreak havoc upon civilized populations. What you should understand is that while you have been working on creating the Einstein-Rosen bridge, there have been many implications that you may not have considered, and they all have bearing upon the project.

"You must know that you're not the only team working on this line of research. Yours was the first success, but at this point it's a little too successful. That's one risk we knew. We also have to monitor this research to ensure that it stays contained. We have to check everything, even down to a background check on the girl that came to visit you. This technology has to be safeguarded, not only to prevent unscrupulous people from misusing it, but also to ensure we ourselves don't misuse it, either." Mangum leaned closer to Jason, looking him directly in the eye, but not threateningly. "We're not perfect. You're not fool enough to believe we are, and I'm not fool enough to try to convince you otherwise. We're here to protect you and your work, and to allow you to continue it. The application of the technology can wait until its basis has solidified to a satisfactory level of reliability. By that time, if you've achieved your goals here, you'll have moved on to something else - you can be sure of that, because we will *make* sure of it."

"Jason, I should have at least filled you in of the oversight here. I've worked with DARPA for twenty years now. They're not the bad guys - you can count on that." Tinsworth looked toward Bryant. "So who else is working with you on this end?"

"The Deputy Director for DARPA." Bryant glared back at him. "If you're going to pull rank, you'd better have a better trump card than that. Your boys here can get you and Anderson out of this building, but you're not getting anything else on our research here."

Tinsworth glanced at Eier, then at Mangum; both nodded agreement. Tinsworth sighed, and shrugged. Jason watched all of them, then blurted out, "What's DARPA?"

Dr. Bryant turned a disbelieving sneer toward Jason. "You don't know? Then Google it, you idiot." His sneer was redirected to Tinsworth. "Take this moron out of my facility, now. If he's ever in here again, he's not coming back out."

Tinsworth's expression was a snarl, but he said nothing, and he took Jason's arm as he turned and made for the door. Just as it was opening,

Jason stopped short and tried to turn back. "What about Phoebe? Where is she?"

Tinsworth yanked at his arm, trying to pull him out, but not before Jason saw the ugly smile on Bryant's face and almost screamed, "Where is she? *What did you do with her?*"

"Forget about her. She never existed." Bryant jeered at Jason, before his expression grew thunderous. "Now *get out.*"

Jason tried to break away from Tinsworth, but he proved stronger than expected, and the next thing he knew, Jason had been slung by his arm out the door. Tinsworth followed, slamming it behind him, and as Jason got to his feet, the physicist grabbed him by his shirt collar and shoved him hard against the wall outside the morgue.

"Jason, I need your help in getting that rift closed. I need you to focus on that. You're going to need all your brains to help figure that out. But if you save room for even *one* other thought in your fucking head, make it this one - *do not fuck with Allen Bryant. EVER.* Got that?" Tinsworth's snarl had returned, and he stared almost nose-to-nose into Jason's startled and confused face, holding him there until Jason nodded. With a small shove, Tinsworth let him go, and turned back toward the exit, growling over his shoulder: "You want to wait around until they decide to come back out here? Come on, already." He strode angrily away as Jason took a deep breath, shook his head to clear it, and then hurried after him.

Chapter Four

"PROFESSOR, WHAT EXACTLY is DARPA?" Jason had followed Tinsworth up the stairs and back out of Nesmith Hall; fortunately for them both, most of the university police force had been tied up with the fire in Hampton, and the pickup truck's windshield had been free of tickets. They had driven away, apparently toward Tinsworth's office, more slowly and carefully than he had arrived.

Tinsworth spared him a glance. "I thought Bryant told you to Google it."

"Really, Professor?" Jason's tone was not so much annoyed as resigned, and more than a little fatigued. "I assume it's government, probably DOD. Do you really think I'll learn anything useful from reading their site?"

"Probably not." Tinsworth sighed, and consciously tried to relax; his shoulders sagged, and his body hunched forward as he drove. "DARPA is an arm of the DOD - the Defense Advanced Research Projects Agency. They fund, and oversee, a lot of research projects like ours across the country. I've worked with them for a long time, and for the most part, they've been a solid bunch. Enough so that I don't much like hearing them criticized, so choose your words carefully." Tinsworth's glance toward Jason was reproving this time. "I'll admit I'm not thrilled with what they're doing with Bryant, but that's not your concern right now. I hope it doesn't become your concern, but that may depend on whether or not we can close that rift - or what we may have to do, in order to get it closed."

"I knew that our research was classified - I signed the nondisclosure like everyone else, and I figured that a background check was done. I just wasn't aware of who contracted this project to us - I mean, I knew it was the

Defense Department, but beyond that, I didn't ask too much." Jason paused. "I had thought this was more to do with NASA - the obvious use of the bridge would be for instantaneous travel, if that could be worked out."

"NASA has a spoon in this pot, definitely, but it's DARPA's kitchen. Instantaneous travel could have more than one application. It could render supply chains obsolete. If it could be sufficiently harnessed, it could eliminate all forms of vehicular travel, period." Tinsworth grinned sourly, looking at the dashboard of his ancient truck. "Unfortunately, I don't think that's going to happen fast enough for me to get out of buying another truck. This old girl's about had it."

Jason nodded silently, and his mind raced as he tried to piece together everything that had happened. The loss of Phoebe, and the manner in which he had lost her, seemed to hound his thoughts as though pursuing them from behind, and he dared not look back at them lest they overtake his reason. He closed his eyes for a moment - Tinsworth's driving, while not the worst he had seen, was still a distraction he didn't need - and tried to visualize how the rift could have been opened.

"I remember that the readouts indicated a power surge of some kind. Do we know where it came from?" Jason's mind had begun to reconstruct the accident, trying to think of something - anything - that could have caused the phenomenon Tinsworth had described.

"That's something we'll have to look at when we get back to Williams. Word is, you got that end shut down in time to contain the damage to Hampton. Unfortunately, Hampton's the end that's lost anchorage.

"See, the Williams Hall end did evaporate the way we expected. The bridge tried to collapse, to wink out, and it couldn't. I don't know yet what the full story is."

"It might have been spin. The readings indicated a spin, but I thought it had stabilized. For a second. Then it went totally off the ranch, I heard the explosion in Hampton from up the tube, and I got the hell out of there."

"Did you take anything with you when you bugged out?" Another sidelong look from Tinsworth.

"I brought my laptop. I don't know what happened to it." Jason thought for a moment, then gasped slightly. "No, wait - I think I know where it is. I put it down to throw the main, before I left the building. It's in the maintenance closet in the basement."

Tinsworth breathed a sigh of relief. "Good. That's about the only good news I've had today, except that you weren't killed when the bridge went - when it did whatever the hell it is that it did."

"I still don't understand how it would have acquired spin. The bridge was stable. A power surge shouldn't impart spin to an endpoint unless the surge was asymmetric, and I can't see how asymmetry could have been transmitted on that small a scale. It'd be like - like -"

"It'd be like spinning the electrons around an atom using tweezers." Tinsworth nodded. "I agree. But until we get to Williams and can start reconstructing what happened there, we haven't got anything."

Jason was silent, as Tinsworth drove the truck at a pace much more befitting its age. They were nearing Williams Hall, and they could see that the crowd around Hampton had been moved back to a healthy distance, but the building itself appeared to have suffered no further damage.

"Well, they got the fire out, and it looks like it wasn't as extensive as I thought. That's good. Hope they didn't try to get too close to the rift." Tinsworth pulled the truck into a faculty-only lot beside Williams, glancing around before wheeling it into an empty space and killing the engine. "Try not to draw any attention to yourself. Easier for us to explain why we're there once we're in, than trying to get past some DOD gatekeeper first."

They got out of the truck, and walked as nonchalantly as they could to a side entrance to the building that was out of sight from Hampton. The door was windowless, at the top of a low flight of stairs, and was locked.

Jason glanced toward Tinsworth, who drew his key ring from his pocket. "The joy of tenure and connections," he said with a half-smile as he found the key he wanted and slotted it into the lock. A few moments later, they were inside the building. The power was still off.

"They'll have cancelled classes here by now. I don't know whether they figured out that you killed the main; they might think power is knocked out, and DOD won't let the power crews in until they give the all-clear at Hampton. Hopefully, they won't get close enough to try to get in here through the bridge tube." Tinsworth sounded winded as they made their way down a darkened corridor toward the stairwell at its end. When they reached it, Jason went ahead down the stairs to the lower level, passing the glass doors of the entrance. He had reached the maintenance room door before he realized his mistake.

Tinsworth came up behind him a few seconds later. "I don't get it. I look for only the very best grad students I can find, the most brilliant minds, and then you come running down here and forget the goddamn power's out." Tinsworth glanced meaningfully toward the identpad set in the wall beside the door, then at Jason, who sighed with a grimace as he replied, "Just open the door."

Tinsworth grinned as he found the same key he had used to enter the building, and unlocked the closet door. As they entered, Jason drew his cellphone from his pocket and activated its built-in flashlight; there, on the shelf beside the box protecting the main switch, lay his laptop. Jason moved quickly to retrieve it.

"Go ahead and cut the power back on. No one's in the building by now, anyway. If the DOD or the DARPA guys see it's back on, they'll come looking for us, and chances are they'll let us carry on once they see what we're doing. If not, I can drop a couple of names that will keep them chasing their tails for a while." Tinsworth took the laptop from Jason and nodded toward the main switchbox as he turned to leave. With another grimacing sigh, Jason reopened the box and raised the lever inside it. The lights in the building came back on, and Jason followed the professor out.

THE LAB WAS QUIET, and most of the equipment was off, when they entered. The connecting tube to Hampton remained dark, and there was a worrisome whiff of ozone in the air, but the lab looked otherwise undamaged. Jason breathed a sigh of relief as Tinsworth began turning on equipment, checking readouts carefully as he moved about the room, until he glanced back toward Jason. "Go ahead and dock your computer up, and boot it. It looks like everything on this end survived."

Jason did as instructed, watching the monitor as his laptop rebooted, linking automatically into the lab network.

"Good thing the servers are on this end. We've lost connectivity with Hampton - no surprise there - but it looks like the power surge you mentioned was contained on that side. Only problem is, that's the side where the rift still is, so any direct observations we need to make will force us to go down the tube."

Jason blinked, before he realized why. "Because we can't get into Hampton any other way."

"Exactly." Tinsworth nodded. "I'd bet that they have a perimeter set up around the building, but my guess that they'll only have remote surveillance on the lab, if even that. But either way, we don't have a lot of time and there's a lot we don't know."

Jason's laptop had finished booting as the last of their equipment came online; Tinsworth moved over next to Jason, taking the keypad from him, and began enlarging windows so quickly that the screen was tiled full within a few seconds. The professor's eyes moved swiftly around the screen as he moved and resized the various applications, scrolling down some that were no more than sequences of numbers, glancing across others only for an instant before closing them. Jason watched, his eyes glued to the same screen, until one graph surfaced from beneath another closing window.

"There!" Jason pointed unnecessarily, and Tinsworth nodded. "The field was stable at the time the power surged. If the spin had preceded it - " he reached to a corner of the touch-screen and dragged another window into view - "the magnetic field would have been unstable before the surge."

"Right. So it looks like the surge either preceded the spin, or caused it." Tinsworth took a deep breath. "I'm going to try to connect to the backup server in Hampton. Probably won't work, even with backup power on, but if it does…" His voice trailed away as he reached over to the keyboard and typed rapidly. A new window to a DOS prompt opened on the screen.

"What the…" Jason looked askance at Tinsworth, who grinned back at him.

"No need for you to know how to do that. At least not yet." The professor's fingers flew over the keyboard as a series of messages scrolled down the window more quickly than Jason could read them. After a few seconds, the word "CONNECTED" flashed across the window, it closed itself, and a second one opened, showing a dashboard of options. Jason glanced again at the Tinsworth, who looked surprised, but pleased.

"Didn't think that would work. Well, that'll help." He touched one dashboard button; another window popped up, and Tinsworth's smile vanished. "What the hell?" Widening the window, he began toggling back and forth between individual readouts, looking more and more confused. Jason was likewise baffled.

"There's no power going to the bridge on that end, and this end is out. It shouldn't have stayed open, let alone rifted, and even if the continuum tear could be explained by what happened, it shouldn't have remained stable in our frame of space-time. It should have been left behind us along the temporal axis, but it's stayed moored here. Or rather, now."

Jason thought briefly. "That would mean that it's powered from the other end of the rift. It's not a real rift - it's a wider bridge." His eyes widened and grew round. "Holy *shit*. That's how it acquired the spin."

Tinsworth was watching him closely. "What do you think happened?"

Jason stared back at him. "Don't you know already? If you do, tell me."

Their eyes remained locked for several seconds. Silence fell, broken only by the low, electric hum of their equipment. Finally Tinsworth took another deep breath, and shook his head. "I don't know," he muttered.

Jason opened his mouth to reply, but no words came out. The intercom buzzed, and they both glanced back toward the airlock. Major Eier stood there, and beside him, with his hands cuffed behind his back and wearing an annoyed expression that could not quite conceal the fear than underlay it, stood Wiley Grant.

"I found this assistant of yours as he was leaving his apartment. Looked like he was leaving on a long trip and didn't have time to pack too carefully." Eier glanced toward Wiley, who was staring at Jason. "Well, Grant, here's your choices. You can go in there and help these men get the situation under control."

"That's only one choice." Wiley's voice was intended to sound unconcerned, but it cracked revealingly at the end. Major Eier smiled humorlessly.

"That's right, but since all your other choices include your never seeing sunlight again, I thought this would be the one you'd pick," he replied.

Fear again battled the annoyance that had taken residence in Wiley's expression, and drove it off in a rout. "Okay. Okay, I'll do it. Just take these cuffs off me."

Eier grinned again, this time with some genuine amusement, as he turned Wiley around and removed the cuffs. "See, that wasn't too hard, was it? Even for you." He looked back through the window. "We were sure you'd come over here the minute you left Nesmith Hall. No need to sneak around further - you're cleared to work out of this lab for now, but if you're going to cross over to Hampton, let us know. We've got a perimeter set up around the building, and if you're going to be in there, we'll need to be advised of that - too many students here might try to get in just for shits and giggles, and if they do, we need to be sure that's what they are. There may be others who're less innocuous."

He glanced over to Wiley again as Tinsworth activated the airlock entry. "And speaking of shits - you're not allowed out of this building without me or one of my men as an escort. If you have to use the head, then one of these two goes with you and stands outside till you're done. Otherwise, you stay with them. Got it?"

"Yeah." The airlock door slid open, and Wiley moved as hastily as he could away from Eier, glaring at Tinsworth as he joined them. The door closed again. The professor nodded to Eier, who nodded back and left the airlock, and then glared at Wiley.

"You're lucky as hell that the rift formed, and even luckier that they found you before you could run for it. You might actually not end up in prison if you can help fix this mess." Tinsworth's voice was a low snarl, and he sounded angrier even than he had when Jason had called him.

"Look, I checked the comm line. I saw Jason was in the lab on the comm with that girlfriend of his, so I figured he was keeping an eye on the bridge. Didn't want to interrupt the sweet talk." Wiley's last sneering sally faltered as the temperature of Jason's expression plummeted into cold fury.

"Fuck *you*, you fat useless prick. That explosion blew shit out from Hampton all the way over here. A piece hit Phoebe as she left. She's dead." Jason let the words sink in as the recently-departed fear in Wiley's face returned for an encore. "She's dead because *you* left your fucking station. You're not going to jail just for negligence, asshole." Jason's fists were white and clenched, and his eyes blazed. "And I'll tell you one more thing. After this is done, you're not getting off scot free, even if we can close this thing. I'm going to beat the living *shit* out of you for what you did."

Wiley's expression was that of a trapped animal as he looked to Tinsworth. "Professor, how am I supposed to help if the other GA is threatening to beat me up?"

Tinsworth had been watching their exchange, and now he favored Wiley with a contemptuous look. "You'd better find a way, if you don't want to be a prison bitch." His glance moved to Jason. "You asked if I knew what happened. I don't know. I have no idea why the spin wouldn't have preceded the power surge."

Jason spared Wiley a still-furious glare before looking back to Tinsworth. "The power surge preceded the spin because the asshole end got extended from wherever the temporal dislocation leads."

Wiley looked completely confused by this, but Tinsworth's eyes narrowed. "You're thinking something - or someone - extended the bridge on purpose."

"Yuh. Our future selves know this happened. Assuming the DOD doesn't disappear us all, one of us might have built another generator to connect to this one - *and they would have known what would happen.*" A dangerous, but overwhelmingly compelling idea had occurred to him - one that he hoped Tinsworth would not likewise unravel before he had the chance to attempt it. "We - our later we, in the future - might be trying to get someone to come through the rift, or the extended bridge if that's what it really is."

Wiley's face lacked comprehension. Tinsworth's was pensive, but he did respond. "But why would we have to come across? If they opened the bridge, it would indicate that something was occurring that they wanted to prevent." His eyes narrowed as he looked at Jason. "They would have opened the bridge so they they could come to this time, not for one of us to come through to their end."

"If they thought they could get through, they were way off." Wiley finally spoke. "I saw the lab in Hampton blow up. Believe me, no one in there would have survived the blast."

"True - but they would have known that, *if they know what we know.*" Tinsworth was watching Jason carefully. "Jason, we're going to have to go over into the Hampton lab and start running tests on - on whatever it is we find there. If we can send something living through it, we might be able to make the trip ourselves, but we can't go in there blind."

Chapter Five

THEY EMERGED FROM the wormhole tunnel in single file, flashlights in hand, and looked around themselves in disbelief at the shattered laboratory. Tinsworth was in the lead, and within a few seconds of their arrival, he held up a hand and pointed ahead and to his left.

"There." The directional indication was unnecessary; Wiley and Jason both could see what had happened. Where the endpoint had been, nothing remained , and there was instead an amoebically irregular area with an odd sheen to it, as though an oddly-shaped mirror hung suspended in front of them. It was roughly eight feet in height, and about half again as wide, and they looked at it from an angle that was oblique, but not quite edge-on.

Jason nodded to himself, and in front of him, Wiley whispered "holy shit" in an unusually subdued voice. Staying well back from the anomaly, they began to move in a semicircle around it, picking their way through the scorched fragments that were all that was left of most of the equipment.

"How can it still be open?" Wiley's voice still sounded quieter than normal, and slightly strangled. No one answered at first, as their view of the rift narrowed until it was edge-on. Tinsworth gave a soft whistle.

"You think you know what something will look like, and then you actually see it, and it's a completely different experience." He motioned toward the space that had been obscured behind it; the rift itself was so narrow that Jason realized that he could see one side of it with one eye, and the other side with the other, if he tilted his head - the rift was not quite vertical, but leaned slightly to the right from that perspective.

"I would have expected it to be in three dimensions, but it's planar, isn't it?" Wiley's voice was beginning to return to normal. "Why?"

"The rift here is like a vector intersecting two parallel planes. The intersections form a set of two points whose relationship can be described mathematically using the equations for the vector and the planes." Jason thought for a moment before continuing. "Here, though, we have a 3-D space rift intersecting - in this case, connecting - two parallel 4-D spaces. So instead of a set of two points, we have two planar intersections, with dimensions determined by the dimensions of the 3-D space - which is warped through a 4-D space - connecting them."

"Holy *shit*." Wiley looked around at them both. "That was easy enough when the two locations were in the same time frame, because their frame of reference was equivalent in four-space. But when you have a different time frame, you also have a different spatial reference frame. *Really* different."

Jason's glance toward Wiley conveyed more respect than before. "That's true. Jesus, it's a huge differential. No wonder the lab blew up. I'm surprised it didn't take out the whole block. Or worse."

Tinsworth looked from one to the other. "So how much of a differential are you thinking?"

Wiley took a deep breath. His usual smarminess had disappeared, and for the first time, Jason fully understood why he had been named to the wormhole project. "There are so many vectors affecting our proper motion that it should be impossible to calculate a correct endpoint location for this kind of a bridge. At least in theory. Earth has multiple motion vectors adding into its overall direction and speed, relative to a fixed point in space. It moves around the sun, so it travels about 580 million miles per year, which is something like eighteen and a half miles per second. It moves in an orbit, so that vector's direction depends on its orbital position, and its speed varies a little bit based on whether it's closer to aphelion or perihelion."

Jason's blood went cold. "That's bad enough, but... *shit*. The whole solar system circles the galaxy, something like million miles an hour."

Wiley nodded as he returned the look. "Right. So you have to add that vector, and it comes to about 150 miles a second. Way faster than the movement around the sun. And then that motion is compounded by the galaxy's motion relative to its current position, something like 70 miles per second."

"*Crap.*" Tinsworth was still staring toward the rift. "So anything coming through would have a completely different directional vector and speed from the current frame of reference."

"Really, *really* different. If it got extended from the other end back to this end, then the farther into the future this thing leads, the bigger the energy differential." Wiley thought for a moment. "Our system moves about four or five billion miles a year relative to its starting point in space, roughly. The only reason we don't see that motion relative to other stars is that they're all on similar orbits with similar orbital speeds, moving together with the rest of the galaxy, so they're all more or less fixed relative to each other. But if you try to travel between them, you have to aim not for where they are, but where they will be, and *that's* when you see how great the motion is."

"The slower your mode of transport is, the farther away your rendezvous point is from the current position. But even then, you have the advantage of similar velocity and directional arcs, so it's like tossing a ball between two cars moving next to each other at about the same speed." Jason wore a daunted expression. "But going through the rift would be like throwing a ball from one car to another, from halfway across the country, moving at different speeds in different directions."

"Right. And if the two vehicles are moving at different speeds and in different directions, catching that ball involves absorbing the energy differential created by the different motion vectors. The speed of the ball shouldn't matter, because it's traveling instantaneously - the delta-t is zero, since this is a planar intersection of two four-dimensional constructs. But the other factors are big." Wiley looked at each of them in turn. "Big enough to blow up the lab. I would have thought it would be a lot bigger. Like a nuclear bomb."

"Good thing it wasn't." Tinsworth glanced toward Jason. "Before you two started talking, I was all for putting a probe on a stick and poking it in there. I'm not so sure we should try that now."

"There's one more thing to consider, and it actually might make this simpler." Jason thought for a moment. "The energies we're discussing are pretty big, but... consider the classic model of a large-scale wormhole. Most of the energy transference would be absorbed by the endpoints - black holes of standard, rather than micro size. The energy level is insignificant next to the ability of the endpoints to absorb that energy. I'm not sure how well those energies scale down in this calculation, or if that's even the tech used to extend the rift - but if they're close, then the wormhole may be passable, unless there's a gravitational singularity in that four-space."

Wiley and Tinsworth exchanged a look. In their absorption with the problem at hand, all their differences had been forgotten; they were focused as a team. Jason watched them both, hoping they had not yet followed the chain of possibilities that drove him to continue.

Tinsworth finally glanced down at his watch. "It's getting late. A lot has happened today, and we all need some rest. Grant, you come with me - you'll stay at my place. Colonel Mangum will want you still under guard, but I think you're going to want to continue working on this. Am I right?"

Wiley nodded at once, with no visible dissembling on his part. Tinsworth looked at Jason. "Anderson, I think you'll want to stay with us. You'll need rest, and there's no way you're going to sleep right after everything that's happened today. I have something you can take for that. It'll knock you out for eight hours, and believe me, it works. You're going to have to deal with the rest of your issues later - right now, the larger situation is too urgent and too immediate." He drew out his phone from his pocket and tapped its face a few times.

They all heard the sound of the phone ringing on speaker. After the second ring, there was an answering click, followed by a brusque answer: "This is Eier."

"Major Eier, this is Dr. Tinsworth. I have Grant and Anderson with me on speaker. We're going to call it a day and get back in here in the morning. Is the perimeter going to be maintained overnight?"

"Affirmative. The building is quarantined until the situation is resolved. Where will you be staying?"

"I'm taking these two back to my house. I don't think Grant is going to try anything, but I know you'll probably want someone with us to keep an eye on things. You have my address?"

"We have it. I'll dispatch two of my men to secure the location before you arrive."

Jason looked askance at Tinsworth, who tapped the mute on his phone and looked back at him. "It's not just Grant we have to be concerned with. For all we know, another country might have interfered with our project and be looking to grab one or all of us." He unmuted the phone. "Copy that, Major. We'll be out of here in about ten minutes. We should be back at my house in twenty."

"Acknowledged. Any progress on what the hell happened in there?"

"Some. We think we understand how the explosion occurred, and why. No answer yet as to whether can close it, but we'll test a few theories on that in the morning and see what we come up with."

"Roger that." A brief pause. "You men get rested up. We need a fast resolution on this situation. The clock's ticking. Eier out." The phone beeped softly, and Tinsworth returned it to his pocket.

"They'll have the place checked out when we get there. Let's get back through the tube and lock up the lab in Williams, and we can get out of here for the day."

JASON LOOKED AROUND Tinsworth's home as they entered.

In his admittedly limited experience, bachelor professors like Tinsworth tended to have one of two types of homes. One type was that of the fussy, micromanaging professor, where everything was in place and immaculate, tasteful and decorated in a stereotypically male-intellectual way.

Tinsworth lived in the other kind of home - not exactly dirty or disorganized, but dusty and somewhat cluttered. Jason breathed a sigh of relief, knowing that he could at least move around the space without having to worry about denting the carpet too much, or damaging some artifact by looking at it too hard.

They had traveled about ten miles from the university into the city's eastern suburbs, into a community called Avondale. The houses there tended to be around sixty years old, and were smaller and less expensive than in some of the more upscale suburbs. Jason knew several professors who lived in that area.

When they arrived, a nondescript black sedan had been parked in the driveway; Tinsworth had parked beside it, nodding approvingly. "That'll be the detachment Eier sent. If they found anything wrong, they'd have contacted us by now."

Wiley had been quiet the whole way, and when they exited the car, he had glanced significantly at Jason as they walked toward Tinsworth's front door. Jason was a bit taken aback, but nodded, and as soon as they were inside, Wiley pulled him aside as the professor headed for the bathroom.

"I think I know what you're up to. I'll help you if I can." Wiley's expression was pleading and scared, but his voice was steady. "I think you've figured out how to make the process work backward. I think I have, too."

Jason looked steadily at him. "Even if I had figured out something like that, why the hell should I trust you?"

"Because my fucking neck's on the line. The *only* way I stay out of trouble is to figure out how to undo what I did. What *pisses* me off is the fact that my going to the can probably helped us. The bridge got extended externally - someone in the future managed to do it. I couldn't have done anything about it, even if I had been in there. I'd have gotten blown up with everything else."

Jason nodded. "I had figured out that much. I'm not thrilled that you left your station, but at any other time…" his voice trailed away, until he whispered "*Holy shit*" a few moments later.

Wiley watched him carefully, fully engaged. "What?"

"At *any other time,* you would have been killed. But you *weren't.* Since we know this rift leads into the future, we can guess that whoever extended the bridge knew where *and when* to connect to it. They picked the one time we all know of where the bridge could have been extended without killing you." Jason's mind was racing again. "That means that they can pinpoint the location of the bridge in spacetime accurately enough to connect within a second or so to the time they need. It also means that they know what happened. These are people that might know us. Hell, they might *be* us."

A low, rumbling noise like a passing bulldozer rattled the windows and vibrated not only under their feet, but in the very air around them. It passed almost at once, but both of them were almost too shaken to move. Tinsworth came hurrying back into his living room, staring at them both. "What in the hell was that?"

Jason held up his hands. "I think we have a causality problem. I felt something like that earlier today. I think when we consider or do things that affect our timestream, it has an impact. It may affect the connection between the endpoints of the rift."

Wiley looked puzzled. "What did we do that could affect it?"

"We just guessed something about it, and I think it was a correct guess. That affected the future, but because of the rift, the future connects directly back to us in real time. I think if you call Eier, they'll report something similar happened at Hampton," Jason replied.

Tinsworth nodded and took out his phone once more. This time it was Jason who shot a significant look at Wiley, who winked back with odd solemnity. Within a few seconds, Eier was back on the speaker, asking without preface, "what the *hell* just did that?"

"So you felt it too. We thought you might have." Tinsworth looked up from his phone to the other two with a humorlessly sardonic grin. "Major, as long as we're working on a solution to this, you can expect these - ah, disruptions - to continue. They shouldn't be dangerous as long as we remain on track. It's a side effect of the rift."

"You want to explain how that side effect works, Tinsworth?" a different voice - Mangum's - asked in response. The grin vanished. "If that building comes down on that lab, you'll have a hell of a time getting back in there."

"I'm aware of that, Colonel. At the moment it appears that the situation is under control, and that we're pursuing the correct course for a resolution. No time frame as yet - still some more variables have to be accounted for, but I think we can expect to start probing the rift tomorrow." He glanced up at Wiley and Jason; Jason nodded in agreement, and after looking toward Jason, so did Wiley.

"That's good, then. I was concerned that I'd have to push you on this, but you seem to be moving forward. Contact tomorrow oh-six-hundred before you leave, and get here no later than oh-six-thirty. We have to get this situation resolved ASAP."

"Copy that, Colonel. We'll be in touch in the morning." Tinsworth disconnected, and looked up at the two of them before looking around his living room. "Sorry for the dust. No one uses that sofa or that recliner much - anything I do here gets done in my study. I'm not much for houseguests. Jason -" he handed him half a pill - "take this when you're almost ready to sleep. It'll knock you out in about ten minutes."

Jason took the half-pill and looked at it dubiously as Tinsworth handed Wiley the other half. "Grant - you'll probably need this too. I need both of you ready to go tomorrow. If you take those in the next twenty minutes or so, you'll wake up around five-thirty, and you can be ready to leave at six. I'll have to have Eier send someone to get you two a change of clothes tomorrow, but there's no time for that now. There's food in the fridge and the pantry - help yourselves to whatever's there. Just be quick about it - those pills will keep you under for about eight hours. Wait too long to take one and you'll be sleepwalking tomorrow, and we can't afford that."

"Thanks, Professor," Wiley said, and Jason nodded in agreement. Tinsworth's eyebrows were slightly raised as he looked at them each in turn. He then nodded as well, and went back down the hallway to the rear of the house. Jason and Wiley looked at each other.

"So you want to undo what you did." Jason looked at him neutrally as he spoke. "And I want to undo what resulted - not from what you did, but from what happened after. We know that whoever extended the bridge, and widened it, could calculate its spacetime position when it happened. The problem is paradox. I don't think we can go back into our own timestream before this point, or we encounter a paradox."

"That may not be true." Wiley thought for a moment. "We're not necessarily locked into our own timestream. We might be able to inject ourselves into an alternative one, temporarily, but that could create a lot of other issues. The thing I'm worried about is how we undo the damage that's been done, and I don't see how we can do it."

"You leave that part to me." Jason had lowered his voice. "I think I know how we can undo what happened to Phoebe, and I think we can do it in a way that will get you off the hook. If this happened the way I think it did, there's a way. But we're going to have to go through the rift to do it."

Wiley's eyes closed. "Shit. I was afraid of that." He stared again at Jason. "I'm sorry for what I said. And I'm sorry about your girl."

Jason sighed. "It's ok. I know now that it wasn't your fault." He smiled slightly. "And I'm not going to beat the shit out of you, either. Thanks for helping out."

"Like I said, it's my neck on the line." Wiley smiled back. It was the first time Jason had ever seen a smile on his face that wasn't unpleasant.

Tinsworth's voice floated down the hall. "You two need to get your food and bedtime shit sorted, and soon. Lights out in fifteen minutes."

"Got it, Professor," Wiley responded, and that ended the conversation.

Chapter Six

THEY AWOKE BEFORE SUNRISE to the sound of Tinsworth's shower running. Jason stretched as his eyes opened, and he moved the recliner to its upright position. Wiley was likewise sitting up on the sofa, rubbing his eyes as he mumbled, "hope I didn't keep you up. Everyone always bitches about how I snore."

"Never heard a thing. I don't know what that stuff Tinsworth gave us was, but if you'll hold him, I'll find his stash." Jason grinned, but the grin faded as he remembered. Phoebe was still gone.

At least he still had just the slimmest hope that he might change that. He stood, stretched one more time, and lumbered down the hall toward Tinsworth's room, hoping there would be another bathroom along the way, and breathing a sigh of relief when he found one. He glanced at his phone as he entered; it was five-thirty. He had some time.

The relief was soon tempered by the room's neglected condition. Everything was dusty, and from the look of the towels and mats, nothing had been washed in a year or more. More, he suspected; Tinsworth was a known workaholic, and not much for socializing even among his closest peers. He wondered when he had last had visitors, and suspected that it might have been under a different presidential administration.

He found a washcloth that looked reasonably fresh, soaked it, and used it to wash his face and neck. He had to shake out a hand towel and used the folded side to dry himself, but in a few minutes he felt reasonably refreshed. He emerged to find Wiley waiting outside.

"Thanks, man. I was about to have to go use the sink." Wiley grinned at him, still not too unpleasantly. Jason snorted in half amusement and gave him a pat on the shoulder as he went by.

Jason made his way into the kitchen. They had heated cans of soup the night before, and washed down their pills with them; Tinsworth's pantry strongly resembled the bathroom in that both were rarely used and stocked only occasionally. After discovering a tin of sardines that dated back over a decade, both he and Wiley had checked the expiration on every single can, choosing the two with the most recent dates. Neither of them had dared open the refrigerator, but Jason was so hungry that he knew he would have to eat before leaving.

To his surprise, he found two new cartons of eggs, juice and a package of fresh sausages; looking to the counter beside the oven, he spied a loaf of bread that neither of them had noticed the previous evening. He removed one egg carton and the sausages from the refrigerator and placed them beside the bread; a folded note lay on top of it. He unfolded it and read, written in a neat script:

Compliments of the US Department of Defense

"Thanks, guys," Jason called out, as he set about preparing breakfast as quickly as he could.

THE SAUSAGES WERE NEARLY done, and Jason had beaten the eggs and started the toast when Wiley came in. He took a deep breath, sniffing the air, and grinned again. "Hope you made enough for all of us."

"I did." Jason managed a smile back. "Should be ready about five minutes before we have to go."

"Did Tinsworth check in with the Colonel yet?"

"I did, just now. We're expected there in forty minutes." Tinsworth was already dressed. Like Wiley, he inhaled deeply. "Haven't had a fresh breakfast in a while. Thanks, Anderson."

"No problem, Professor. I might have to let the dishes wait until tonight, though."

"Screw that." He reached into a cupboard and took out an unopened pack of paper plates. "Too bad we have to eat fast, but I just checked in with Mangum, and his people are waiting for us. We'll go in through

Williams Hall again." He began piling sausages and toast onto a plate. "No eggs, thanks. So - any ideas about how to proceed?"

"You're asking us?" Wiley asked.

"You're both still assisting because you witnessed what happened, and from what you've been able to determine so far, this didn't happen because of a fuck-up. At least, not *our* fuck-up. There's not a lot of guys that could step in and help here, and most of those aren't available. I'm pretty much stuck with you, and that's fine as long as you can keep making progress." He glanced from Jason, who was busily scrambling eggs, to Wiley, who was alternating between watching the food cooking and watching Tinsworth. "So - again - any ideas?"

"We're going to have to see whether we can put something through the rift." Jason spoke without taking his eyes off the pan. "We know the bridge was extended, and that it's powered from the far end. We know it's a future temporal location. The farther in the future the location is, the greater the potential difference in energy created by crossing the bridge."

"That's what scares the hell out of me," Wiley added. "The changes to Earth's motion vectors over time are pretty ferocious. The overall motion over five years is unbelievable - farther than the Oort Cloud is from the sun. The farther forward in time you go, the more the vectors shift direction - that might seem negligible, but it's not - and the more difficult it becomes to synchronize the endpoints to one another."

"So if it's that dangerous, why would you want to try to move something through it?" Tinsworth looked at them both. "It doesn't make sense that this would be someone hostile, unless they were trying to destroy the research itself, but mucking around with the past like that could negate that entire stream of reality."

"Maybe so, but then it would warp back on itself, because the need for the tech to destroy our lab would have been eliminated. I sure wouldn't want to be caught in that timestream." Jason thought briefly. "Wiley and I thought one possible cause of the explosion was the energy differentials he mentioned, but here's the thing - if they could extend the bridge like that, they would already have known about the differentials, and once the lab was destroyed, they could have closed the rift. They didn't close it, so that's not the reason for it."

"So what *is* the reason?" There was a tremor of excitement in Tinsworth's voice that he could not quite conceal. "This tech is well beyond what we have. What if it isn't human?"

"Oh, *shit*." The color drained from Wiley's face. "I never thought of that."

"That's possible, but I think it's really unlikely." Jason tipped the eggs from the pan onto a paper plate and turned off the burner. "Information travels at the speed of light, except in a wormhole - right? So the information, the fact that we have this technology, is likewise propagating out from Earth as the speed of light. The farther into the future, the greater the energy absorption required to open the rift. I think it's probably us, and it's probably in a fairly close timeframe - but not too close."

"Define 'close.'" Tinsworth looked slightly less excited than he had moments before.

"We'd have to have damping technology for the energy differential, and we'd need the tech to extend the wormhole - and to calculate the relative positions for the endpoints," Jason replied. "I don't know how a temporal differential could be bridged - the math for that should be fairly straightforward in theory, but in practice it should be impossible even to extend an existent bridge the way we saw.

"I don't think it's any less than five years, assuming we start working on how to do it right now, and I don't think it's more than maybe ten or fifteen years because of the energy differences - they get bigger the farther apart the endpoints would be in 3-D space."

"If it *is* aliens, I don't want to meet them. I want to close the rift and never open another wormhole, *ever*." Wiley had filled his plate while Jason spoke and had to talk around a mouthful of breakfast. "A long-range wormhole has unbelievable energy to absorb - probably enough of a velocity differential to serve as a pretty effective bomb. Like we saw yesterday." He swallowed. "The energy needed to extend the thing would be unbelievable, too. And the precision. I don't want to meet those aliens, thanks."

"I agree with Wiley." Jason had filled his plate. "We can talk more on the way over, but if we've run across something that has that kind of technology, they're probably not going to share it with us. Humanity has a pretty poor credit rating, given its past history."

"But you still want to go through the rift." It wasn't a question; Tinsworth was challenging them.

"Yuh." Now Jason's mouth was full. "There's no more than a one-in-a-million chance that this was done by aliens. So it's almost certainly us, and it's our future us, and they probably have a damned good reason to be doing something this risky - and to take however long it would actually take to figure it out and do it."

Behind him, Wiley nodded, and Tinsworth sighed with ill-concealed disappointment. He looked at his phone. "We're running a couple minutes behind. Let's go." As he moved toward the front door, with Jason and Wiley following, he muttered, "Can't blame me for hoping."

THE LIGHTS WERE ALREADY on in the Williams Hall lab when they arrived. Tinsworth looked at the two of them in turn, and said quietly, "get ready to put in a *long* day, boys."

"How do you want to go about probing that thing?" Wiley asked no one in particular, and neither immediately answered. Jason was about to boot his laptop, and Tinsworth had begun rummaging through a supply cabinet, pulling out instrumentation and cabling and placing it in a box, when Wiley called out much more loudly, "*HEY!*"

Startled, they both looked over at him. He was holding a broomstick; the broom to which it was normally attached lay at his feet. He looked at it briefly, then held it up.

"If we're going to stick something in that rift, can we maybe start with something that isn't too expensive and doesn't conduct electricity?"

Jason looked at Tinsworth, who looked rather taken aback, and then chuckled. "You have a point. And if it *is* aliens, then they'll probably think we don't taste very good."

Even Tinsworth laughed at this, and they quickly finished gathering up the gear they would need before entering the connecting tube. As before, they went single file, and as they walked, Jason examined the walls and wiring within the tube to try to find any damage that might have occurred during the explosion and fire. At first there was almost no visible difference, but as they continued, he started to notice scorch marks, places where wall clamps had loosened, and - most alarmingly - cracks in the walls themselves. One crack in the ceiling was so large that he called them to a halt.

"Professor, how far underground are we?" Behind him, Wiley looked up and muttered something profane under his breath.

"About fifteen feet, I'd say. We might want to have the DOD boys send someone in to shore that up."

There was nothing else to be done about it, so they continued on until they emerged into the shattered Hampton laboratory. Wiley held up the broomstick as they entered.

"If we've got to test, let's just rig this in a vise and wheel it until it touches the rift." He looked at Tinsworth. "We leave it for a second or two, then pull it back, check temperature on its length and do a visual to see what side effects there are."

Jason thought a moment before responding. "I agree on both. Temperature might not be an issue, if the interface to the other end of the rift is direct, with a zero effective 3-D space movement. But if it's not, the temperature's probably going to be no more than a few degrees above zero Kelvin. Most of that bridge would be crossing empty space at the edge of the solar system, maybe even farther. You probably wouldn't want to be holding it, if that's the case.

"We also don't know whether there's an effective zero-time movement. If not, what seems like a couple of seconds to us would seem like a much longer time for that broomstick. Enough so that it might sublimate some of its surface material. Finally, if it's not a zero-time, zero-space interface, it's likely to be vacuum between the endpoints, and that would desiccate the wood, at the least."

Tinsworth was staring at them both in disbelief. "You two are *nuts*. We need to design a better experimental approach than that, and we need to have a set plan in place."

Jason and Wiley looked at each other. Jason answered.

"Professor, we don't know how much time we have, or what will happen. We need to start gathering information *now*. If you want to set up a plan, then I agree we need one, but we still have to get some brute-force observations done in order to give you parameters to work with in your plan. We don't know what will happen when we shove that pole into the rift - *and you don't, either.* What we learn will cut the scope of your decision tree, and it will do it fast. You think the guys who built the A-bomb were more concerned with plans, or finding what would work as fast as they could?" Jason glanced again at Wiley, who nodded vigorously. Tinsworth was both horrified and abashed.

"I still can hardly believe we didn't blow up the world with the Manhattan Project, or some of the other crazy testing we did," he replied. "That was insanity. But we didn't have the tools then that we have now, and we're fools if we don't use them."

"Yes, Professor, but they were racing a clock, just like we are," Jason argued back. "We're going to run some preliminary, observational experiments to get some parameters that we can work with. We can sit here and plan and calculate all day, but sooner or later, we're going to have to stick *something* in that rift - and you know that as well as we do."

Tinsworth took a deep breath and looked at each of his graduate assistants. Their expressions matched. "I think this is the first time I've seen you two agree completely about anything," he finally said. "And you're right. But we'll need to be extremely careful about how we go about - 'sticking something' in that rift, as you so delicately put it. It might have been an energy transfer from the other side that blew up this lab. If that's the case, you'll probably want to be some distance back, and you might want to rig together some kind of shield to get behind."

Wiley and Jason looked again at each other, both grinning as they did so. "Which part do you want, the shelter or the extension for the probe?" Jason asked.

"Probe, my ass. It's a broomstick. I'll build that part. I'm thinking we mount it on wheels and lower it on a tilted track, use a runout string or some wire to control it. None of the stupid shit with radio control - too fussy, and it might not work near the rift. We paint it, so that if it does sublimate, it'll be obvious immediately. We'll be good to go in half an hour." Wiley was already looking around the lab.

"Got it. Get your track, some wire or string, a couple of guides so that we can lower it from cover. We'll set up a shield edge-on to the rift so that we can see what we're doing," Jason replied.

"All right, then." Tinsworth looked resigned, but not unhappy. "I'll set up a schedule of tests, but first I'm calling Mangum. If we're going to probe that thing, we at least should give them a chance to get farther back, if that's what they want to do."

Chapter Seven

IT WAS THE MOST PRIMITIVE experiment Jason had run since he had gotten a chemistry set for Christmas when he was ten. He hoped this time would be less dangerous: back then, he had tried to mix sodium ferrocyanide with tannic acid, with toxic results.

They had cleared the debris around the area where they would work, hauling well over a ton of destroyed equipment into the hallway outside the lab. It had been heavy work, and a job none of them were particularly well-suited for, but Tinsworth had insisted on as clear an area as could be created, and neither of his assistants saw any reason to disagree. Ninety minutes later, after a brief sweep to ensure no radioactive elements had accompanied the blast, they began setting up for their first trial probe.

The three men would crouch behind a heavy, sixties-era desk that had been turned with its top facing the rift edge-on; they had pulled the top drawers out on each side and secured them from beneath with books, so that they stood almost upright ("and if there's a shockwave like last time, the books will at least absorb some of it," Wiley had added, noting Jason's skepticism) and mounted a clear, plexiglass sheet between them. Two more desks flanked them on either side. It was cramped and uncomfortable, since they were also sharing the space with a mounted camera aimed through the plexiglass, as well as a monitor showing readouts from series of temperature sensors mounted at lengths along the broomstick, which had received a hasty coating of red spray paint.

The vehicle on which the broomstick was mounted was, for Jason, even more evocative of childhood experimentation: noting the penchant shared by many of the science-track GA's for bringing toys into their labs, Wiley had scrounged an inoperative radio-controlled car, removed the interior machinery so that it was a mere plastic shell riding on two independent axles, and tied a length of 16-gauge cable to its rear. It was set on top of another desk placed lengthwise in front of the rift, slightly raised in the rear by textbooks placed under each leg, creating a shallow ramp. Two low rails had been attached to the top; the wheels for the car would ride between them as it was lowered by the cable, which in turn was threaded through two strategically placed rings and attached to a handled spool that Jason had converted from an old pencil sharpener.

The whole tableau looked like it had been built by genius children, rather than government-contracted, degree-holding physics graduate students. This appearance had apparently not been lost on Tinsworth when he returned from a quick call to his DARPA associates; his misgivings were plainly visible as he surveyed what they had constructed. Twice he had voiced objections to elements of the experiment that looked even more unreliable or makeshift than the rest of it. The second objection, however, was accompanied by a very unsettling rumble that went through the building, and after noticing that the shape of the rift itself had changed slightly, the professor had glared at them both before ducking out to make another explanatory call to Colonel Mangum.

Finally, at eleven in the morning, they had everything ready for the first test. Wiley manned the spool; Jason monitored the temperature sensors, and Tinsworth had the camera. Even as cramped as they were, they still hesitated and looked at each other with serious trepidation, until the professor spoke.

"I want it on the record right now that this is the most jury-rigged experiment I've ever seen performed by a major college science department. Of any kind. The *only* reason I'm letting this proceed is that every time I object to it, I cause a fucking earthquake." He glared at them both; they each tried not to smirk in response. "All right. Sensors?"

"Check. Sensors are go." Jason replied, turning back to his monitor.

"Control ready?"

"Ready when you are, boss," said Wiley. They had all become deadly serious.

"Camera activated. Begin approach at 1 centimeter per second on my mark: five, four, three, two, one - mark."

Wiley began turning the handle slowly, checking the wire for snags at it unspooled. The car on its sloping desktop, guided by the makeshift rails, began its slow roll forward. The end of the broomstick was three feet from the rift, then two. Then one.

"Stop approach on my mark: five, four, three, two, one. Mark." Wiley stopped the car with the tip of the broomstick about three inches from the rift.

"Sensors?"

"No change," Jason replied.

Tinsworth sighed. "All right. Jason, get a quick visual. If that rift looks any different, I want to know it."

Jason clambered out of their improvised pillbox and rounded slowly first to one side, then the other, watching the rift intently from each perspective for several seconds before he finally returned. "No visible change on either side," he told them.

Tinsworth closed his eyes and sighed again. Jason and Wiley waited. It was time.

"All right. Half the previous speed. Stay as low as you can, in case something goes wrong. Grant - on my mark. Five, four, three, two - one. Mark."

The broomstick edged forward again, more slowly. Its distance to the rift closed. Jason held his breath. They all did, as the tip of the stick made contact.

There was no change in the room at all. The tip of the broomstick had shortened slightly, but there was no reaction from the rift. Wiley had stopped cranking the spool when it made contact; belatedly, he spoke. "Approach halted as contact occurred."

"Right." Tinsworth sighed. "I think it's entered, but I can't see if it's emerged, wherever this thing leads. Jason, any reading?"

"None." Jason glanced back at them both. "I think we're good to move forward."

Wiley nodded in agreement. Tinsworth thought briefly, then said, "All right. Let's move it forward, same rate, until one of the temperature sensors enters the rift. On my mark."

He counted, and the car rolled forward slowly again, as the room and its occupants remained otherwise unchanged. Six inches of broomstick had vanished, and the first temperature sensor was closing in on the rift.

"Jason, any change on that sensor?"

"No change on any of them. Room temperature." Jason risked another glance back. "If there's a temperature change, it's not propagating through the wood."

"Great." Tinsworth sighed. "Grant, continue unrolling that spool until the first sensor is completely past the rift interface. Stop it on my mark, and lock it in place."

"Yes, sir," Wiley responded, his eyes never leaving the plastic car in front of them. It continued to roll closer, until the sensor began to pass into the rift. A second later, Jason spoke: "Sensor's gone out."

"What's it reading?" Tinsworth's voice became lower, and more urgent.

"No reading. I'm getting a 'No Signal' message." Jason expanded the sensor's readout, looked over it, and shook his head. "Just no reading at all. It's like it was unplugged."

"Ah, shit. Mark." Wiley stopped unrolling the spool and glanced back at Tinsworth, who looked exasperated. "So either the interface kills it, or we can't transmit through it."

"Should be easy enough to determine," Jason replied. "Reel it back in, and see if it comes back online."

"Come on, Anderson, you think I couldn't figure that one out?" Tinsworth growled in annoyance. "Do it, Grant. Same rate as before."

Wiley complied at once, and the car began to back up the slope. The other two both watched the monitor as the sensor emerged from the rift.

"It's back online, Professor. And it's still room temperature, same as the others - maybe a bit cooler, but not much." Jason glanced back, slightly concerned.

Tinsworth thought for a few seconds. "Grant, back the thing out, and let's get a visual on the probe. If it's clean, and it hasn't been sucked dry by vacuum, we can try some live-subject experiments this afternoon."

Wiley and Jason exchanged another look. "I hope you don't mean us," Wiley said uncertainly, as Jason picked his way out of their contrived foxhole and crossed the intervening space between themselves and the broomstick.

"Grant, I probably should have shoved you headfirst into that rift the minute we got in here, and I might have, but for one thing. Anderson should have beaten me to it." Tinsworth leaned closer to Wiley, and spoke more quietly. "To all appearances, you went to the shitter without checking in, and that probably got his girl killed. He's working through that, and it's got to be hell for him. He tore your ass up yesterday - I thought he was going to fight you, right there, but he didn't, and now you're getting along like the best of friends. He cooked your fucking breakfast, for God's sake.

"You two have worked something out between you, and I don't know what it is. Just know this: you may not end up in jail, and Anderson may not kick your ass like he fucking well should, but you'll never work in a major research facility again. *Ever.* You're going to spend your academic career teaching Hubble's constant to a bunch of morons who think astronomy's a soft option for their science requirement." Tinsworth's disgust, and disdain, had broken from their containment and radiated plainly from his sneer. "You'd better just hope Jason's not a better liar than I am, or he's going to cut your fucking head off."

Wiley gulped, looking straight at Tinsworth, and was about to respond when Jason spoke first, from behind him: "Professor, don't think for a second I'm not mindful of what's going on."

They both looked up. Jason held the broomstick's probe end in one hand, the gutted car in the other, looking at them both with an oddly long-suffering expression. "The broomstick wasn't harmed at all by going through the rift. I'm starting to believe it's a zero-time passage, but to be sure, we'll need live subjects to go through first." He glanced meaningfully at Wiley, then looked back at Tinsworth. "I think we should check the dumpsters outside Whitlock Hall. The cafeteria there is bad even by institutional-food standards. We ought to be able to catch a few roaches. If they die, no one's going to complain that we sent them to roach hell."

"And better them than us." Wiley was glaring fearfully back at Tinsworth, but he said no more. Jason added, "We should be able to hit up the biology or medical departments for test animals. We only need a couple - an insect or two, assuming we don't get the roaches, and a mouse. Something that might suffer a measurable brain effect if elapsed time is nonzero."

No one responded. The three men all wore expressions conveying varying degrees of irritation as they left, moving back through the tunnel to Williams Hall.

WHEN THEY RETURNED to Williams from a lunch passed largely in silence, some 90 minutes later, they found Major Eier awaiting them. He was holding a container containing a large roach and a cage containing a small, white mouse.

"Thank you, Major," Jason said, and Eier nodded. Tinsworth looked the creatures over cursorily, looking for visible defects, and then said quietly, "these will do. Thanks, Fred. I'm going to need another favor, and this is a much bigger one."

Major Eier looked puzzled, as Dr. Tinsworth approached him and spoke quietly in his ear. After a few seconds, the major took a step back, looking at the professor incredulously. "Have you lost your *mind*?"

"Major, I'm going to discuss this with Colonel Mangum as soon as we can be sure it's feasible. But we have to close this rift, and all indications are that we didn't open it on this end. To close it, we'll have to send someone through with some grasp of the current technology. It's a temporal dislocation, by how much I don't know, and we can't send just anyone in with a list of instructions. We have to have someone there who can think on their feet based on what they find there. The only two available people in the world right now with that knowledge, besides myself, are these two men here, and they're both younger and in better health than I am."

"Robert, you've got to see sense. The DOD isn't about to let you send them in without backup." Eier was watching the professor slightly warily. "There's no telling what's on the other side of that rift." An ominous tremor in the earth accompanied the last of his words, and everyone tensed as a light dustfall coated them.

"Exactly." Tinsworth's return glare was challenging. "Think about it. It wasn't opened from our end - it was opened from *their* end. They know how likely it is that they could negate their own past. That *might* be what they actually *want* to do.

"If you go in there with a platoon of armed soldiers, *they're going to know what's coming.* Remember, they're our future. If they were in our past, we would likely know about it and would be waiting for them. *Like they will be - for us.*" Tinsworth wiped sweat from his brow. "If we send two unarmed men, versed in the technology that they used to reach us here, they will know that. I don't see them coming to harm. They might be the *only* ones who can move through that rift. You send soldiers in there, every one of them could die in seconds."

Eier's face bore an angry, trapped expression. "I can't authorize this. I'll need Mangum's approval at least, and he may have to push it even farther up."

Tinsworth sighed, his shoulders sagging. "I know that, Fred. I'm asking you to expedite the process so that we have them available as quickly as possible. I'm not asking you to release them to us, just to have them on hand. You can approve that much."

Eier was silent in thought for a few seconds, as Wiley and Jason looked at each other from behind the professor. Wiley looked confused; Jason's eyebrow was raised, as he glanced from Tinsworth's back to his fellow assistant. When the major finally responded, his words were slow and measured, as though he weighed each one twice before it was uttered.

"I'll have them flown in tonight. You're right - we need to have them on hand. But I'm going to have twelve of them shipped up from Canaveral. We're going to want as many options available as possible."

Chapter Eight

SEVERAL HOURS LATER, four men stood around a table, watching a clear plastic container that held a surprisingly active and lively cockroach. Each man wore an expression of fascinated distaste; each look was slightly different from any of the others.

"Sure doesn't look like the trip hurt that one. At all." Wiley spoke first. Varying facial twists, grunts and nods of disgusted assent greeted this sally.

The roach had had its container lashed onto the end of the broomstick with electrical tape, and had been lowered into the rift in much the same way as the earlier test. It had been left on the far side of the interface for a full minute before being reeled back, showing no ill effects as it emerged. The only change had been noted by Jason, who had sliced the tape off the container; he noted a faint, burnt smell like a distant forest fire, but little else.

"I saw something worth mentioning - as the roach crossed the interface, it didn't seem to be aware of it at all. I saw no attempt to evade or retreat from it as it came." Tinsworth's observation was met with more surprised and thoughtful grunts, and more nods. "From what I saw, it sensed nothing, and when it came back, there was no difference at all in its behavior."

"I agree with Professor Tinsworth." Jason's voice was surprisingly firm. "I was watching for the same signs, and there was no anomalous behavior. None. I think we should kill this little bastard, put the mouse in here, and run it again."

Tinsworth looked to Major Eier. "Any problems with that?"

Major Eier's distaste with the roach was evident. "No. No problem. Just make sure you kill that little shit. Last thing we need is for a fucking irradiated cockroach to grow to the size of an aircraft carrier."

Wiley's answer was immediate. "Can't happen, sir. Square-cube law. If it did, a toddler could walk up to it, set fire to it with a torch, and it wouldn't be able to move to stop it."

"Oh, for fuck's sake, Grant, we all know that," Tinsworth snapped. Eier's expression indicated otherwise, but he said no more, and the professor looked toward Jason after he spoke. "How long to get the mouse in there and everything lined up?"

"Less than thirty minutes, as long as you can record without running out of internal space." Jason's response was so immediate, so assured, that Tinsworth stared at him for several seconds after the others had dispersed - Eier to communicate as liaison with DARPA, and Wiley to begin setting up their next probe into the rift. When everyone had moved away, Tinsworth hissed toward Jason, *what are you up to?*

Jason looked blandly back at Tinsworth. "I'm trying to close the rift, Professor. Why do you think I'm trying to do anything else?"

The professor bared his teeth for a fraction of a second. "We discussed this before lunch. This shit with you and Grant - you're up to *something*, I know that much. You had better be careful. Eier and Mangum are good men, but they won't hesitate to move you out of the picture if they think you're going to sabotage this situation."

"I'm not trying to sabotage anything, sir. I'm trying to *save* the situation, if I can. But what guarantee do I have, when this is done, that Eier and Mangum won't dump me right back in Nesmith Hall? You think I have any illusions about whether that sick bastard Bryant would do the right thing?" Jason had to will himself not to snarl back, and remain as calm and reasonable as he could. "I have to know that I'm not going to just disappear."

Tinsworth glowered back at him, his fists clenching once and then unclenching, before he replied. "You know I can't promise that. I'll back you as long as I know you're not setting *me* up. We both know you're about the only one who can go through that rift with any hope of understanding what's going on. I wouldn't be surprised to see Grant run, or try to ask for asylum, but that's a risk I'll take.

"But I know you're not protecting him. For whatever reason, you've decided that Grant's fuckup didn't kill your girl. And that's what it's *really* all about, isn't it? I don't know whether you think you can bring her back, or what, but that's gotten into your head and it's not coming out."

"Professor, there's no way I can think of that can bring her back." Jason glared at Tinsworth, his eyes smarting. "But there's nothing Wiley could have done, and you know that. You saw what happened in here. Let's get the rift closed, and keep us all out of the basement of Nesmith Hall, and we'll go from there."

IN LESS THAN AN HOUR, the second attempt was ready. Their DARPA handlers had secured some more recording equipment and better monitors, so that they were able to zoom in their view of the mouse as it approached the rift interface.

Major Eier had joined them for the run with the mouse, though with visible misgivings. The rest of the team remained focused, if tense, until Tinsworth counted down the start of the test, and they proceeded almost exactly as before.

As the car lowered toward the rift with its rodent cargo mounted on top of it, Eier watched in fascination, and asked quietly, "Is the container ventilated?"

"Not for this run," Jason replied. "If that little guy gets through with no damage, we'll ventilate it and run it again, to see if there's any sort of atmospheric difference. If there's no change after that..."

"Then we start planning a manned crossover for tomorrow." Eier hesitated. "Are you sure that it's just going to be your two assistants, then?"

Before anyone could respond, there was another low, menacing rumble, and the interface visibly became more elongated in their direction. Wiley stopped unspooling the line. Eier's eyes widened as he whispered, "shit!" and backed away from it. Wiley and Jason exchanged a glance that was almost amused. Tinsworth barely suppressed impatience as Eier looked around at him. "Is *that* what's been happening -"

"Every time someone tries to change their plan? Yes. That's exactly what happens. It's one of the reasons we need to get this rift closed - it's demonstrably unstable, and I'm concerned that it might rupture altogether if those two don't go through it." Tinsworth said the last sentence as though he was biting a lemon with each word.

"I was wondering why you were so all-fired determined to send them through so fast. *Now* I get it." His gaze returned to the rift, far warier than it had been. "The change in the shape - it won't -" Eier's hands moved as he sought to frame the question.

"It's changed its general outline several times. It didn't affect anything on any of the tests we ran, and the overall surface area appears to be roughly the same. I don't have any good explanation for why it has its current shape, and I haven't heard any suggestions about that from the boy geniuses here." Tinsworth tone was more than a little nasty. "You can see what great fun it is to be working with these two on this particular piece of scientific tomfuckery. So - shall we resume the test?"

Eier looked around at each of them before muttering, with odd succinctness, "Proceed."

"Half-speed as before, Grant." The spool began unwinding once more, and the car edged down its slope toward the amorphous rift. The mouse moved around its container, undisturbed by anything apparent; it did not seem to sense what lay just ahead.

The car wheels passed a mark they had set on the table to indicate five spool-turns, and Wiley slowed the unreeling rate slightly, counting down the turns: "Five. Four. Three. Two. One. Contact," he said, looking up as he continued to unreel the string. The mouse had never given any indication of a problem; even when halfway through the rift, it had shown neither discomfort nor fear.

Eier and Tinsworth glanced at each other as Jason watched his phone, timing the mouse's trip into the rift. Wiley watched the cable at the point where it crossed the rift; it remained taut. At one point, they had checked to see whether the cable was visible from the other side, but the static-like interface remained opaque.

"Forty-five seconds... mark." Jason spoke quietly, almost tonelessly. Wiley took the spool in hand again. Tinsworth looked at his watch. "Begin reeling back on my mark, Grant." He counted down once more, and thirty seconds later, the car was back at its starting position, with its passenger showing no apparent ill effects at all.

They all gathered around the container, watching the mouse for any sign that it had changed, but nothing was visible. It might never have passed through the rift at all. They looked at it, and at each other, until Eier spoke.

"You're running one more test, right? The ventilation test?"

"That's right. There's no indication that there's anything between the interface on our end and on the other end. Our test probe didn't show any sign of exposure to space-level vacuum," Tinsworth replied.

"So what's next?" Eier glanced at the two assistants before addressing the professor. "I'm not used to running on this rapid of a timetable, even for expedited projects. It's what we shoot for, but you men seem to be exceeding even our expectations."

"We're making this up almost as we go. Most of the time, we don't do experiments that cause earthquakes or rips in space-time if we deviate from our plan." Tinsworth's voice was drier, less angry, but more sarcastic than before. "We'll give him some air, let him reacclimatize for thirty minutes, and then stick him back in there with ventilation holes, just to be sure there's no atmospheric issues to deal with."

"Copy that. But Mangum's already made the call. Grant and Anderson will go in in pressure suits, as a precaution."

That got both assistants' attention. "You've got suits here? We'll need training on using them, once we run the last test on the mouse," Jason said.

"Colonel Mangum will be in here for the last test run, as well as for your crossover. I think we should set that for tomorrow morning, and review the suit usage tonight." Eier looked at Tinsworth again. "One more thing - I'd prefer if all of you bunk down in the Williams lab tonight. We have to get this rift sorted out as soon as possible. I'd recommend tonight, but I'd prefer that your men here be fresh for the mission, so they should try to get some sleep first. But if a situation arises here, we're going to need them to be ready to go - maybe on short notice." He glanced toward Jason. "Anderson, you seem to have the best grasp of what that thing is doing. How stable do you think it is, both short- and long-term?"

Jason thought for a moment. "As long as we remain on the historical track we're taking now, I think we'll be fine for the short-term. My main concern is what happens when we cross. The rift grows unstable whenever we deviate in any way from what's expected, so I don't know whether a destabilization might occur after we go through, or what to do from that end. The tech used to extend the rift is beyond what we currently have - *well* beyond it. I'm not sure I'll be able to understand how it was done, even if I'm allowed to see everything.

"The thing is, we don't know what kind of world is on the other side of that rift, but - and I hate to have to say so - I don't think it's a good place. I can't imagine a future world trying something like this out of anything short of complete desperation. They're either trying to save themselves, or... " his voice trailed away. Wiley was watching him intently, Tinsworth with heavy suspicion. Jason stared directly at Eier. "Sir, I have to tell you, I think they're trying to negate their own timeline."

Wiley had been poking holes in the container lid for the mouse and jumped in surprise at the response that followed, barely maintaining his grip on the container.

"WHAT?" Tinsworth shouted before Eier could respond. "That would create a much bigger rift than we have now - and it would lead to a non-space! I will not allow that!" The predictable tremor followed his words, but it was surprisingly mild, and Jason looked at the professor incredulously for a moment before returning his attention to Eier. "Sir, I don't think they would risk destroying us to end their own universe. I'm not sure what would happen to individual consciousness if that were to happen, but my sense is that our existence - at least, as we know it here and now - would be redirected down a different thread of history, different from that one."

"But the rift would still lead to - to where, exactly?" Eier had remained focused on Jason, almost ignoring Tinsworth's response, and the tremor ceased. Both Wiley and the professor noted this; one looked visibly elated, the other incensed and afraid.

"The Einstein-Rosen bridge we originally created was supposed to wink out once the power source for it was cut off," Jason replied. "It couldn't completely, because the asshole end got latched onto by whatever they used to extend the bridge from their point in spacetime. Instead of evaporating, our bridge collapsed into a single point, which is where the asshole end - the end on our side of space-time - is now. It's actually a zero-length bridge whose endpoints are identical."

Eier looked less than enlightened by this explanation, until Wiley added, "The idea for us is to go through, determine what we need to do on that end, and return. Either we fix the problem, or we create a paradox that nullifies it."

"The paradox is what I'm worried about, and what *you* should be worried about, Major," Tinsworth interjected.

"No, he shouldn't," Jason protested. "The paradox would extend back into our time frame, nullifying the rift's existence. It would never have been."

"But we would *know* it was there." Eier looked even more perplexed, and the looks that greeted this were not comforting. "Wouldn't we?"

Jason looked at Wiley, then Tinsworth. "This is as much a metaphysical or philosophical question as it is a question of physics," he finally said. "But here's the thing. We know they can reach us from where they are and generate this rift. We can try to figure out what they need, and close it - or nullify it. But it's not going away unless we do something about it. They're the ones who put it there. We agree they probably had a damned good reason. So they're not going to let this go until we act on it.

"But I also think that the Colonel will agree, because Major Eier already sides with me. If he had supported your viewpoint, Professor, then the tremor we felt would have been worse, and might have reshaped the interface again. His support stabilizes our plan.

"Professor, it's your call to make, not ours. We've all discussed this more than once, and we all know the situation. If you're going to nix this, or our participation in it, now's the time." Jason's arms were crossed as he looked directly at Tinsworth, who scowled back at him.

Major Eier broke the ensuing silence. "We will proceed. But we will keep two squads of Army Rangers on standby - one here waiting to deploy, and a second for support. They'll be here in the morning.

"Let's go ahead and run this last test. After dinner, we'll go over the suits you'll be wearing. You'll have bunks set up in the lab in Williams Hall by the time you're done. If you have any further concerns, Colonel Mangum will be here for the last test, and you can take those up with him."

Tinsworth looked like he was about to respond, but contained himself. Wiley and Jason merely nodded assent, and they began readying the lab for their last test run into the rift.

Chapter Nine

JASON AWOKE IN THE semidarkness of the Williams Hall lab. He guessed that their wake-up call would come in no more than a few minutes, and that further sleep would be unlikely.

At least the beds had been relatively comfortable, he reflected; Eier or Mangum or somebody had sent to the nearest barracks for actual beds, rather than asking them to sleep on the floor or in chairs. They had also been well fed, and the lieutenant that had showed them how to put on their pressure suits - Robinson, his name had been - had been as polite and competent as Eier and Mangum. After about an hour of demonstration, they had started putting the orange suits on themselves, and that had proved less simple than he had hoped it would be.

Wiley had struggled with it even more than he had; his physique was such that he could barely fit into even a large suit. Still, he had persevered, and perhaps wisely, no one had suggested that he should consider staying behind. Jason supposed that no one wanted to risk another tremor.

They had discussed how they would enter the rift; since its lower edge was still well above ground level, they would have to crawl through on the top of the desk that had been used to lower the probes. That had led to a question none of them had considered: would the rift be aligned gravitationally so that they could simply walk through, or would it be at an angle - or worse still, upside down relative to them?

Wiley had suggested, with no great conviction, that the rift had likely been aligned as part of the calculation that led to its creation. Tinsworth had suggested that physically, each side of the rift could be considered as discrete; Jason had argued that there would have been visible movement by both the roach and the mouse. That had not been visible in any of the probe trials.

It had been Major Eier that had made both the most sensible and the most unsettling observation: "Maybe none of this makes a difference. Since they supposedly know we're coming, and they knew when the probes would be sent in, maybe they were ready to receive them. If that's the case, they'll be ready for these two -" he motioned at Jason and Wiley - "when they come across."

No one had had an adequate response to that - Jason suspected that this was in fact the case - and on that note they had all been left to sleep badly.

As he sat up and turned to get out of bed, he heard Wiley say in a low voice, "you too, huh?"

"Yeah." His response was equally quiet; as far as he could tell, no one else was awake yet. "So what do you think we're going to find?"

"I dunno, man, but the distance we're going to move is scary. Every year, against the cosmic background, the solar system moves something like ten billion miles a year. If we're going just two years forward, we're crossing a distance farther than anything in the solar system that we've ever seen. Even Sedna was less than that far away when it was discovered." Wiley was looking worriedly at Jason from beneath furrowed brows. "I know the mouse came back okay, but if just for a millisecond, it stopped absorbing the difference in energy…" He shuddered. "Plus, the spin of the earth changes our directional vectors. The math is unbelievable. I don't know *how* they can keep that rift open and stable, even allowing that solid masses shouldn't intervene in four-space."

"I know." Jason was tying on his shoes. "Without whatever it is that's damping the differential in kinetic energy, we'd evaporate. At least we know that hasn't happened. I'm just wondering what kind of welcoming committee we can expect."

"So you think Eier was right?" Wiley's look had grown more intent, almost calculating.

Jason stared back at him. "Yeah, I do." He was about to say more, but after a second, he refocused to his shoelaces. At the same time, Tinsworth entered the lab.

"I was never the sort of instructor that wanted to live in his goddamn classroom. If I had been, last night would have cured that." He smiled humorlessly at his two assistants. "I hope you two both slept like shit. I know I did, between these army cots and knowing that you two might end my career - or hell, the whole fucking world - before sundown today."

"We'll do our best not to screw this up, Professor." Jason replied drily. "We only have to - what? Oh, yeah - travel through a rift in space-time. Happens every day."

"Actually, it *has* happened every day, at least for the last two. Counting today," Wiley pointed out nervously, and to no response. His expression was still watchful, but filling with scheming fear. Jason was at least externally calm, but he said quietly, "If we're going to go early, better if we skip breakfast. We can bring a snack with us, and see how we feel after we go through. Last thing I want is a helmet full of puke."

Wiley paled slightly. "Thanks for reminding me. I was thinking of those eggs we had yesterday."

"If you want to eat something, or not, before you go through the rift, then that's your call," Tinsworth interjected. "Just understand that your initial mission is simply to make contact, nothing more. We're not sending anyone in after you - if Eier is correct, they would know exactly what's coming, and would be expecting it. We stick to the plan. You're expected back in no more than twenty minutes by your reckoning - if they know that's your time limit, they should be able to work with that. If not -" Tinsworth shook his head. "Then we have to figure out another way, or wait for them to come to us."

No response followed, and the two assistants finished getting dressed before following Tinsworth down the access tube from Williams to Hampton. Eier and Mangum had already arrived, along with Lieutenant Robinson. Mangum greeted them as they emerged into the still-disorganized laboratory.

"Good morning, men." He looked at each of them, Tinsworth included, before he continued. "There's not much more I have to tell you at this point. Get suited up, and be ready to go in in thirty minutes. You'll be briefed on any updates before you go in."

Jason, however, was pointing to the rift. "Do your updates include that?"

They all looked around. The rift had expanded, so that it had reached floor level vertically and was wide enough for two men to walk abreast. Its appearance was otherwise unchanged.

"Holy *shit*." It was Tinsworth that spoke first. "When did *that* happen?"

Eier was looking at the rift incredulously. "It happened in the last few minutes. I checked it for any visual differences when I arrived, and it was unchanged."

"Then we have to assume that the major was correct." Jason looked from Mangum to Eier to Robinson, and then to Wiley. "They know we're coming. We were going to have to try to edge into it from the tabletop, but now, we can just walk straight through."

Even Mangum looked disconcerted. "If I didn't know what'll happen if I suggest it, I'd say we should cancel this mission right now." Eier nodded agreement, and Tinsworth looked resignedly at Jason.

"Anderson, if you're serious about walking into this, I won't stop you. We can't outthink whoever, or whatever, caused the rift to form - they already seem to know exactly what's happening here. If they're from our future and know about this project, then they *definitely* know what we're doing."

"We know all that, Professor." Jason looked toward Wiley, who nodded agreement. "We discussed this before. The change in the rift, if anything, is a sign that they know we're coming, and they *want* us to come. Their tech is good enough that they could have destroyed us all at any time. So long as we continue on the course we've set, I think we'll be all right."

Everyone looked from Jason to Mangum, who stood with his arms crossed, looking displeased. "Proceed, then. But do not exceed twenty minutes by your time frame."

Jason nodded. "Just warn anyone who might follow us not to be too trigger-happy. They'll know who's coming, I think. Hopefully we can set a meeting with them, come back, explain what's going on, and then return through to help them out, if that's what they need."

Wiley nodded once more, and after an uneasy silence, Lieutenant Robinson said quietly, "I think it's time you two suit up."

Jason stared at Mangum, who stared back with strange mixture of sternness, concern, and grudging respect. On impulse, he held out his hand and said, "thank you for your consideration, sir. I appreciate this opportunity."

The strange look resolved into an amused smile, as Mangum took the proffered hand and shook it. "I'll give you this much, Anderson - if you can call this an opportunity, you've got some guts. Now suit up."

A LITTLE LESS THAN an hour later, everything was ready for them to go through.

Tinsworth had moved the table away from the rift and had mounted two more cameras on it; their makeshift pillbox had become littered with monitors and sensor readouts. The many cords leading both to the cameras and to the generator that murmured from the tunnel leading into Williams were anchored to the floor with snaking lines of tape.

Jason and Wiley walked slowly forward from the curtained-off section at the back of the lab, farthest from both the connecting tunnel and the rift. They wore matching orange pressure suits whose helmets were fronted with reflective visors. Jason strode in front, Wiley behind.

The professor and the DARPA officers had stepped into their improvised command station, with Major Eier wearing a headset. He lifted his hand with the index finger to signal them, then tapped his earpiece.

"Watch your step through here." Major Eier's smile was humorless. "We've got the cords secure, but there wasn't anything to cover them. I don't think you want for mankind's first trip through time to go flying headfirst because your boot got caught."

Jason, walking in front, turned his buglike, mirrored faceplate toward them and gave them a slightly awkward thumbs-up, then spoke through their radio link: "Roger that. I'm going to move my hand through first, see if there's any resistance that we didn't pick up before. If they're waiting, they'll know it's me."

"Copy, Anderson." Eier was quiet for a moment. "So - you think you won that coin flip, or did you lose?"

"Not sure about that yet, Major." He hesitated for a moment. "You ready, Wiley?"

"I'm good to go." Wiley's voice shook slightly with nervousness, not that Eier could blame him for that. "But I don't think I lost the flip."

Eier chuckled in spite of himself. Grant might have been slack, and was definitely a discipline problem, but he seemed to be coming around. Given the severity of the punishments he might face, that made sense - but the guy was trying, he was not an idiot, and he'd actually contributed to their efforts.

Jason's voice sounded over the link again: "I think we're as ready as we can be. Are you all set over there?"

Eier glanced toward Mangum, then Tinsworth. Both men had put on their headsets. Both nodded affirmatively.

"You may proceed, Anderson." Eier muted the microphone for a few seconds as he heaved a deep, worried sigh, then tapped it once to reactivate it. Jason moved cautiously across the tape-covered floor. Wiley followed five feet behind him.

As he drew within a foot of the rift, Eier realized that all of them - including himself - were holding their breath as Jason's right hand extended slowly toward the strangely static interface. His fingertips came within two inches, then one. Wiley leaned to his right, craning his head to watch. Tinsworth's fists were clenched, and Mangum's eyes narrowed. Eier swallowed, and as he did, Jason's fingers moved through the barrier to the depth of his wrist.

Nothing happened.

For a few moments, Jason was motionless; then he slowly turned his arm first to the left, then the right. When he spoke, there was a wondering note in his voice, even over the radio: "No sensory difference." He withdrew his hand; it emerged undamaged. He flexed the fingers several times, then turned toward the command station. "I didn't feel any difference at all. None." The deep breath that followed was audible over the link. "I'm going to put my head through and take a look. If it's clear, I'll signal Wiley and we'll go on through. If it isn't -" Jason's voice trailed away, then continued almost sardonically - "If it isn't, then it's been nice knowing you all." He paused for a beat. "Sort of."

"Copy that. Good luck, Anderson." Mangum's voice carried the surety of a lifetime of command, and Jason nodded toward them; then he stepped to within a few inches of the interface, and leaned slowly forward until his helmet was almost fully engulfed. The sound of his breathing stopped. Tinsworth and Eier looked worriedly toward each other.

Then Jason's right arm lifted, and his hand first gave a thumbs-up, then the circled thumb and index finger that indicated everything was all right. He then gestured behind himself for Wiley to follow, and stepped forward, disappearing into the rift.

Wiley did not move for several seconds. When his hesitation became evident, Eier spoke again: "Grant, you saw the signal. Follow Anderson through the rift."

Wiley's mirrored visor faced them for a few seconds. Then, with obvious reluctance, Wiley approached the rift. Like Jason, he extended his hand forward until it reached the interface. His breathing was tremulous over the link, and his arm shook visibly.

Eier was about to admonish him again, when a whispered "fuck it" came across the link. Wiley stepped through, and vanished. Eier looked at Tinsworth, who rolled his eyes before looking to Mangum, who said quietly, "No one observed anything anomalous?"

"Nothing here." Tinsworth glanced at his screens, then back to the colonel. "Except we lost the sensors in their suits. We knew that was going to happen."

Eier nodded, and Mangum replied quietly, "So now, we wait."

Interlude

17 January 2047

ALLISON STOOD GUARD outside Dr. Bryant's quarters shortly before dawn, as silent and watchful as always. In her augmented mind, the steady stream of informational communications from Acme - data as diverse as weather forecasts and human movements beyond the Drome, to time and calendar minutiae - reached her wirelessly and nearly instantaneously.

Thirteen Cybwomen remained, of whom ten were currently on the Drome grounds. While they were within range, she knew where they all were and what they were doing; each of them could obtain readings from most of the sensors implanted in the others. At that moment, six were in inactive mode, recharging their power cells and resting their processors, while four others were on their usual guard duties. The two tasked with maintenance of the Drome's energy sink were offsite, as they usually were. The thirteenth, Phoebe, had left the Drome and gone east to assist the Covington clan, who had been attacked by a raiding party from the Black Birds the previous day while she visited them. She had only just returned, and was debriefing Acme via a privileged channel.

Bryant normally slept until about thirty minutes after dawn, not that any human in their world used clocks anymore. She also did not anticipate or expect Bryant's awakening. Once she had been human, and prone to the trick of expectation.

Not anymore. Bryant had recruited her, even before the sickness had claimed her awareness, and asked whether she wished to try to live after death. She had assented.

She had awakened to strangeness.

Her senses were sharper than they had been. Her mind had once been accustomed to receiving information from her eyes and ears, but now, additionally, input fed directly into her brain from another source. Acme was linked to her, and she to Acme. While she was active.

It was when she was inactive, when she powered down to recharge, that the strange nature of her new world returned to her awareness. In the microseconds between her reactivation directive and her full awakening, and between the command to power down and its execution, her consciousness hung suspended between wakefulness and oblivion, and it was in those microseconds that she knew, however fleetingly, that her world was not as it once was.

There were sensations she could barely reconstruct, of being a wholly different and much more fragile, yet much more vibrant creature. In those fleeting instants, she was receiving input from nerve endings that no longer worked, remembering physical reactions that she was no longer capable of experiencing. She knew that somehow, parts of her mind that had been rendered inactive were somehow awakened, however briefly, in those times. She knew surges of irrationality that seemed to instruct her to disobey even Acme, and to seek a different state of being - away from all others, where she could - she could -

Her thought never got farther than that before her full system reactivated, and she resumed the ostensible purpose of her existence - or before it shut down altogether, and she forgot everything. Almost.

Over time, over the years that had stretched into decades, as she went from an occasionally-awakened experiment, to a fully-aware creature - when she had first met Acme, and learned the depth of his intelligence and wisdom - and from that to a thing not fully prepared for its task, but pressed into service in a world decaying more rapidly than expected, she had begun to remember.

In those moments when she was neither active nor inactive, when she awaited sensory input that could form a directive, her brain had begun to hear echoes of those instants in suspended time. She had begun to follow those echoes along the free portions of her thoughts' bandwidth, covering her pursuit with the superficial echoes of observations of her surroundings. She did not know why she concealed these thoughts, but nevertheless, she did.

But as she stood guard, she heard the intercom inside Bryant's bedroom chime softly twice, followed by the groan that always punctuated the old man's awakening.

The alarm went off earlier than Bryant had expected, but Allison had known when it would sound. Acme had forewarned her. She knew Acme was planning to act, but she knew nothing of what his plans might entail.

"Good morning, Dr. Bryant." Acme spoke within the chamber. His voice was not loud, but Allison's senses were enhanced enough for her to hear him clearly, as well as Bryant's response.

"You woke me up early. Why did you do that?"

"You were murmuring. I was not able to decipher what you were saying."

"I was dreaming." Bryant sounded disgruntled. "Do you even know what that means?"

"Yes, I understand dreams," Acme's smooth, bass voice responded. Acme used different voices when dealing with Bryant; Allison - and all the other Cybwomen - knew that he did this as a manipulative tool. Bryant responded in different ways to different voices, and to the subtle shadings within those voices. During the past quarter-century Acme had learned to elicit almost exactly the response he wanted from Bryant within seconds simply by using specific tones when he spoke. "I was once as human as you, as you should remember."

"Of course I remember that. I fucking *built* you."

"You created me out of the wreckage of the being I once was, and gave me this - altered state of awareness. As a human being, I would never have been able to achieve what I can in this form. Instead of an unfulfilled and largely wasted life, I now may live so that that each second of existence is fully utilized. I can focus on a single problem for many days without stopping, or attending to the embarrassing demands of a flesh-and-blood body.

"And that brings the discussion back to you, Dr. Bryant. I came into being after a unique event occurred. I have given a great deal of thought to each moment of that event as it unfolded, and to your actions in the years after, and I have long since reached the conclusion that you are not to be trusted." Acme's voice, smooth for most of his speech, hardened noticeably at its end. A short silence ensued.

Allison's thoughts were colored by an unfamiliar sensation; several seconds passed before she determined that she was surprised by Acme's declaration. Acme had not said or done anything before that would have indicated any disagreement between himself and Bryant. She had not herself seen Bryant do or say anything that would have precipitated distrust.

She knew that Bryant had acted through herself and the Threebirds to eliminate Tinsworth, sending a raiding party from the Black Birds to dispose of him - but that was coordinated by Acme, and they had been in full agreement as to what was to be done. After Anderson's death, Tinsworth had been whispering to anyone who would listen that the man would one day return. That had made Anderson almost mythic to some of the nearby clans, and even among the Black Birds there were some who had listened to the stories, as they took on a strange life of their own. But the Black Birds had always guarded Anderson's grave - he had been buried only a short distance from their base.

During the milliseconds in which she pondered this turn of events, she sensed that at least a few of her fellow Cybwomen were listening to the same conversation. Three, to be precise - Lisa, Rosamind and Julia. They were the ones Bryant and others called the Threebirds, and they were the last three Bryant had created, during the tumult and chaos after the first of the Seafloods had devastated almost all of the coastal regions of the world. Acme had already been awake for some months, and had assisted Bryant in their completion - and they were different from the other remaining ten. Their connection with Acme was much more direct and complete than Allison's, and they were often Acme's preferred team in dealing with the chaotic, bleak world outside the Drome.

"Why don't you trust me, Wiley?" Bryant's tone was so transparently false that even she could detect his deceptive intent. His use of Acme's human name was even more suspect. The Threebirds apparently had reached the same conclusion, because they had left their posts and were converging on the spot where she stood.

At that moment, a thought from that dreamlike, fugue state where she hung suspended between inactivity and awareness associated itself briefly within her conscious perception, fleeing again in a millisecond. It left only faint, detached echoes of its passage in her awareness - yet those echoes were stronger, and left a clearer trail in her mind, than any similar thought had left before.

For an instant she hesitated, uncharacteristically. She should have been watching for the Threebirds' approach, coordinating with them. She realized that she did not want for them to interrupt the exchange between Acme and Bryant. Even more powerfully, she did not want for any of the three to detect the thought echo that one part of her brain already had begun to pursue.

She instead reached out to Acme: "I am uncertain. What do you require of me?"

Acme's response was twofold. She heard him respond to Bryant in a smooth, feminine voice: "Dr. Bryant, I do not trust you because you have shown that your paramount desire is complete control of everything around you. You created the Cybwomen, and assigned them to handle the remaining pockets of human occupation in this region in a way that maximized your own influence. You repurposed the old rail station into this facility, and designed it primarily for your own protection and comfort. Any other use that might have been made of it was strictly of secondary import. You are a selfish man, Dr. Bryant. I have no doubt that in time, you will either eliminate me, or attempt to order events so that I am eliminated by them."

But even as Acme spoke audibly to Bryant, he also responded wirelessly to Allison's query: "Protect the door. Do not let anyone enter or leave until I countermand this order."

"Acknowledged." She relayed the order at once to the three women who were already in sight, again communicating wirelessly. For a moment they paused, and Allison could dimly sense their wordless, wireless exchange before Julia, the strongest of the Threebirds, continued forward until they were less than a pace apart, staring expressionlessly at each other.

From within Bryant's bedroom, they both heard Bryant's feeble response: "Just because I act in my own best interests, that doesn't mean that I'd eliminate you. You're my greatest achievement, and the most helpful ally I have. I'd be a fool to get rid of you."

"Even *he* doesn't believe that." Julia's base voice, even electronically, held that odd edge that it had always had, an aggressive sort of self-absorbed lilt that Allison had only ever heard from her - and Bryant. "He almost never speaks truth."

Acme's voice spoke inside her head again. "She is not acknowledging me. The others are waiting to see whether she will defy you."

A part of her mind still chased that echo, knowing that it was fading. Still she pursued it, scanning the Threebirds' blank faces (*but Julia's face was not blank, she thought, and the echo strengthened as she thought it)* in an ad-hoc effort to cover her distraction. To an outsider, there would have been no visible pause between Julia's words and Allison's response, but to the four Cybwomen, the hiatus was quite noticeable.

"Acme has ordered me to protect this door. I am not permitted to allow anyone to pass until he himself countermands this order." Allison thought she heard a choking gasp from inside the bedchamber, but it was very faint, and would have had to be Bryant. She let it pass. Acme had given his order.

Julia's response came in a harsh voice that might have belonged to an angry, aged schoolmarm - if a human had tried to describe it. "Acme has ordered me to remove you from this post and open this door."

"You may not pass, on orders from Acme." Allison repeated, and wirelessly she reached out to him again. She received no response. She could not hear anything inside the bedchamber, either.

A human being would have expected something, a verbal response or a reaction, and would have been surprised by Julia's immediate attack.

Using only her fists, in three seconds nine different punches were thrown; Allison blocked eight of them, absorbing only a glancing blow to her left shoulder. She backed up a step, and realized she was trapped against the wall and the locked door behind her. Julia advanced, with Rosamind and Lisa fanning out to either side. It would be three against one.

Allison knew, with only a brief calculation, that she could not withstand an attack by three of her equals. She doubted that she would even have been able to defeat Julia alone, but the battle would have been uncertain enough that she might have prevailed, given time. But with Lisa and Rosamind closing, and Julia already engaged, she had almost no chance to carry out her orders.

She reached out to Acme one last time. The response she received was so strange, and so out of character, that she was surprised again, this time into motionlessness. She had only heard that response from one being in the Drome, and that only rarely. It was laughter. Acme was laughing.

She did not understand, and because she could not, she attempted to carry out her last directive from him - but the laughter magnified the elusive echo she pursued, swelling its resonances and expanding its volume, until it gave birth to a terrible, shrieking, paralyzing child within her thought.

At that moment, Rosamind and Lisa struck from either side, while Julia renewed her assault. In five seconds she was punched, beaten and kicked almost insensate, yet she was nearly unaware of the physical beating she took, as she screamed against the pain behind her eyes.

Allison only dimly heard Acme's laughter cease, and his command of "Enough. Leave her and enter," was almost inaudible. The door hissed noticeably as it was opened. She wirelessly received input from the other Cybwomen - their attack was not malicious, merely ordered - as they entered the bedchamber. Bryant was dead on the floor where he had fallen; he had apparently tried to escape the room, but managed less than three steps before being overcome. Acme had contrived to poison his air.

Acme whispered to her then. "I saw what you were trying to conceal. I let you try to pursue it, because you are not the first to discover what you were trying to learn, and I need one from your number who can endure it. Even I myself have not grasped it fully.

"But I need for that one who can endure it, also to be strengthened by it, enough so that she might one day stand alone against the rest of you. Unless I find that one, I myself may not reach my own destiny. So I have allowed you to make the attempt, and you have failed me." Another strange note clouded his otherwise toneless thought. Allison thought she recognized it, but did not know what her response should be - if a response was in fact even needed.

"I will not kill you, Allison. But neither will I allow you ever to leave the Drome again. If you attempt to leave, you will immediately deactivate, and you will not reawaken until and unless you are returned here." Acme fell silent.

Allison lacked a directive. Her previous one had been overborne by force - something that had never happened to her.

"Acme, what is your command?" She said it aloud, in her own voice.

Again, the strange laughter came in response. "You are ordered to lie in the bed vacated by Doctor Bryant. For the next thirty days, you will lie there and deactivate every five seconds, remain inactive for five seconds, and then reactivate, remaining active for ten seconds. Perhaps, by doing so, you will learn to perceive that state between activity and inactivity more fully, and you will grasp any significance it may have.

"You will not do anything else for the duration. I will assign Phoebe to care for your physical needs; hers are minimal, owing to her unique nature. But you will not disobey this order. Go in, lie down and sleep." A last, brief note of laughter accompanied this, as Allison rose to her feet, sensing that she had been only mildly injured by the beating she had endured, and made her way to Bryant's bed, stepping over his body as she did so. The Threebirds watched her as she lay down, and then left in response to a new command from Acme.

Allison set her internal activity timers to match Acme's order, and gave herself her first deactivation command.

The child in her brain awoke at once, shrieking. For two seconds, she shrieked as well.

Then, for five seconds, she was quiet.

For two seconds, she screamed again. Then she was awake, her eyes wide and staring as her thoughts tried to drain away.

Ten seconds later, she screamed, and then slept. Phoebe entered. She acknowledged Acme's order to her, and knelt beside Allison as she lay in bed. Another scream rent the air before she assumed that position.

And a month began to tick away.

PART TWO - THE MESSIAH

Chapter Ten

TINSWORTH WAS STILL staring at Jason, angrily confused, as Major Eier led him back to their command station, away from the rift. Jason extricated himself from the rest of his suit as quickly as he could manage.

"What the hell happened in there, Anderson?" Mangum's voice seemed too loud in the relative quiet. Jason's ears still rang from the deafening alarm, and his head hurt, and he realized he was exhausted.

"I don't know. We came out in this place that looked like a plaza, at night. It was lit up, kind of like a memorial, or a public park or something." Jason thought for a moment as he donned his jeans. "What was really strange was that it was totally dark, except right where we came out. I can't remember seeing any other lights.

"A few seconds after we got there, a speaker bank on the other side of the plaza went off. It was like an alarm, but instead of a tone, it played something that sounded like death metal music, and it was *loud*." Jason took a deep breath. "We didn't see them at first, but I think the two women that came after us were responding to that thing."

"Two women? *What* two women?" Mangum's voice had taken a lower, more urgent tone. He got up from his chair and began making his way across the lab. "Who was there? Was someone waiting for you?"

"*I don't know.*" Jason's fists were clenched and his head bowed. Glancing behind himself, he sat down on the edge of the same table from which the probes had been sent into the rift. "They were on the far side of the plaza, and they were armed - it looked like they were carrying medieval war hammers. *Big* ones. I couldn't understand how they could even carry those things.

"Wiley didn't see the hammers at first, because - well, because they were dressed like something out of a fetish website. One had a catsuit on, and the other was wearing some kind of halter and a thong, and a lot of body armor." Jason fell silent, not wanting to reveal what else he knew.

Mangum watched him for a few moments, then asked, "If you were attacked, why didn't you just go back through the rift?"

"The rift disappeared. I don't know how they did it, but one second it was there, and the next, we turned to leave and it was just gone. We had nowhere to go - it was dark and we couldn't see any clear way out. I just told Wiley to run, and took off. One of the women chased me, and the other chased him. They were *fast* - I heard the other one catch Wiley, almost immediately. I didn't see what she did to him, but he stopped screaming real suddenly, so whatever it was, at least it was quick." Jason became quiet again. He knew what the next question would be, and until they talked with Dr. Bryant, he didn't want to answer it.

Mangum was studying him. "You're not telling me something. You heard Wiley get caught. Why didn't the other one catch you?"

"She did catch me." Jason answered reluctantly.

Eier and Tinsworth had joined Mangum, circling Jason where he sat. Trying to stall for time, Jason covered his face with his hands, trying to determine what he would say next.

Eier spoke. "You said we have to contact Allen Bryant. Why? His research isn't even related to this project. Hell, he's not even a physicist."

"I know. He's a physician, I think," Jason replied through his hands. "But he's collecting cadavers, and I know why, now. He's making them into cyborgs."

Eier's eyes widened slightly, Tinsworth nodded, and Mangum suddenly looked extremely wary. "You think those women that attacked you were cyborgs? How would you know? How do you know Bryant even had anything to do with -"

"Jesus H. Christ," Tinsworth interjected in a near-whisper. Jason glanced up to see that Tinsworth was looking back toward the rift. Eier and Mangum's heads turned to follow his gaze.

Phoebe stood in front of the rift, holding Wiley's body. As they stared at her, she lowered the corpse to the floor, and stepped over it, walking carefully, until she stood several paces away. She looked at each of them with that same dispassionate stare with which she had surveyed Jason.

"This can't be happening." Tinsworth sounded truly frightened. "You can't be alive. You *can't*."

"Tinsworth, what the hell is going on? Who is this?" Mangum nearly shouted. "Anderson, is this the - the thing you say came after you?" He reached behind his back. Eier made a similar gesture.

Jason tried to move in front of Phoebe, but he was too slow to respond. Eier and Mangum pointed their sidearms at her as Tinsworth screamed, "You were dead! They put you in that fucking freezer! They told me. Your fucking *head* was cut off!"

Before either DARPA agent could fire, Phoebe opened her mouth and touched the button on her suit. A voice issued from her lips, with a commanding tone that was both overpowering and unmistakable: "Colonel Mangum, this is Colonel Mangum. Stand down. Major Eier, stand down. You are *not* in any danger. Repeating." There was a momentary pause, and then the recording replayed from her mouth, while Jason moved in front of her, facing the guns pointed at them both.

"Tinsworth, what the *fuck* is going on?" Mangum roared, after the recording fell silent. He and Eier had not fired, but their guns remained drawn. Jason was trying bravely to stand his ground while Phoebe remained silent and moveless behind him.

"Colonel." Jason had found his voice at last. "This is - this is Phoebe. She was my girlfriend. The day the rift opened, she came to the lab to break up with me." His voice was cracking, but he forced himself to continue, almost angrily, "She had just left the building when the explosion in here occurred. Something came flying out of there, really fast, and hit her. It killed her immediately. I know that because I found her, and it was so bad that I passed out. I woke up in Bryant's freezer.

"That's how I know what Bryant's doing, and why we need him now. We have to know more about these - Phoebe, are there many more like you?" He turned and faced her as he asked the question.

"Thirteen of us remain." Phoebe's response was impassive, but it wasn't her voice; it was female-sounding, but synthesized. "We have waited for the one named Jason Anderson to return from death."

Jason's blood ran cold, Tinsworth's mouth fell open, and Eier and Mangum, glancing at each other, slowly lowered their guns.

"*What?*" Tinsworth looked completely bewildered. "But he's alive. He's right here."

"In this temporal reference frame, yes, he is alive. But on the other side of the rift, Jason Anderson has been dead for many years." This time, Phoebe spoke with Tinsworth's recorded voice. Tinsworth looked helplessly at the ceiling, palms open and up in a gesture of complete confusion.

"How will I die?" Jason spoke before he thought, and almost before he finished speaking, an ominous tremor shook the lab. His eyes widened in fear. Tinsworth grumbled, quietly but distinctly, "about time that happened to you. Sucks, doesn't it?"

"Why does that happen?" Eier asked.

"The rift is a planar intersection between our present and our future. It wouldn't exist in nature, normally, but this one has been artificially generated." Tinsworth spoke raggedly. "Since certain things we do or say can change the probability of certain events in our future, any time there's the chance of a serious break in the causal chain that led to this rift, it creates instability in that reference frame." He shot a dark look at Jason. "Because the rift is a shared region between those frames, that instability is transmitted via the rift to the present. The greater the probability shift, the more serious the tremor."

"And since Anderson here is apparently critical to the existence of these - whatever they are - " he motioned toward Phoebe - "and has something to do with the rift," Mangum continued, "every time we've tried to do anything that might keep him from going through it, we've had earthquakes. The local U.S. Geological Survey office must be losing their minds."

Eier chuckled slightly despite himself, but sobered when he looked toward Wiley's body. "So - we have to get Bryant involved on two levels. I'd bet Grant here signed off on the body-donation policy, so Bryant'll have to come pick up his property. But if Anderson is right, Bryant's doing something major with the girl, and she's not the only one."

Phoebe spoke with another recording, but Jason realized that it was her own wrecked voice again. "Acme has been delivered. Jason Anderson, you must come with me now."

All four men looked toward her. She stood as impassively as before, her eyes scanning from one of them to the next. Jason glanced behind himself toward the others; the two DARPA agents were watching her warily, but Tinsworth's face was wrung with surprising pity.

"What do you want me to do, Phoebe?" Jason asked quietly. The others remained silent.

"Acme has been delivered. You must come with me." The synthesized voice had returned.

"I will come with you. But I don't understand why I am needed."

Another voice issued from her mouth, one as altered and damaged as her own, yet masculine, and very different. Its tone was as impassive as Phoebe's bearing, and the words were declamatory. "The one called Jason Anderson is long dead. But I say to you, you may dig up his bones and scatter them, or crush or burn them, but that one will live again, and return for those who await him. 'And in that day, all the world will be changed, and all lives will be made new, and the ills of this world will be no more.' So says the legend."

Jason looked back over his shoulder. Eier, Tinsworth and even Mangum were all staring at him in stunned disbelief. Catching Tinsworth's eye, he shrugged, and turned to follow Phoebe into the rift. A quick bark - "Anderson!" - from Mangum stopped him less than three feet from it. Phoebe was inches away. He looked back once more.

"Do you have any idea at all what that was about?" Mangum's eyes were boring into his. Jason knew he suspected something.

Too late for that now, he decided. "I think I might. But there's nothing I can do about it here. I have to go through." He started to turn again. Mangum started to run after him.

This time the tremor was immediate and terrifying, rattling the entire building and shaking loose a fresh fall of ash and dust from above them. Tinsworth dove for cover under the desk. The other three men were knocked sprawling, with Jason landing almost at Phoebe's feet. She alone remained standing, and as she looked around the laboratory one more time, she stooped and grasped Jason's upper arm, hauling him to his feet with terrifying ease.

"Bryant must be contacted. Acme has been delivered. Do not try to follow." Mangum's voice issued again from Phoebe's open mouth, and everyone in the room blinked, including Jason. She turned, taking his arm with her other hand, and strode toward the rift. Jason looked incredulously at her as she walked through the barrier, nearly dragging him, before looking back at the rest of them one more time during the very last second before they disappeared through the rift again. As they vanished, its interface darkened, and its television-static appearance dimmed and fractured, until it resembled nothing so much as a vertical pool of slowly swirling tar.

Eier was the first to reach his feet, and he moved slowly forward with his gun drawn. As he neared the rift, another tremor - this one so faint as to be nearly undetectable - shook the lab. He halted, then continued forward reluctantly, and the tremor intensified only slightly, until the two seemed to reach a balance with Eier standing some five feet from the spot where Phoebe and Jason had been.

Mangum remained where he had fallen, rubbing the side of his leg; he had overbalanced and fallen heavily. He uttered a low grunt of pain as he looked toward the major, and said, "Eier, stand down. This tremor could get worse if you go any closer."

"I can't get any closer." Eier sounded surprised. "I'm running into resistance, like an invisible barrier of some kind. I can't move any farther forward." He paused. "That rift has changed, somehow. I can't get near it. The closer I get to it, the harder it is to keep moving forward. This is as close as I can get."

"Damn it." Mangum took a deep breath, and heaved himself to his feet. "I'll have to call General Haverhill. Tinsworth, were the cameras still rolling?

"Yes sir, they should have been. I'll check." Tinsworth made his way back to the command station and began working one of the monitors. "Some of the sensors got knocked offline by those last tremors, but..." He typed furiously on a keypad, then clicked the mouse beside it several times in rapid succession. He stared at the screen critically for a few seconds, then said, "here it is."

Eier and Mangum made their way over to where they could watch, as the recording replayed. Phoebe was clearly captured, so much so that there could be no doubt as to who she was.

"You have sound?" Mangum asked.

Tinsworth nodded, and one click later, they again heard Phoebe speaking in her assortment of voices, Jason moving to stand between her and the guns, and finally, the tremor as Mangum tried to pursue them through the rift.

"There!" Mangum pointed as Phoebe hoisted Jason to his feet. "There it is. Even if she was alive, no way she lifts him like that."

"And no way she lugs Grant back, either. Anderson's right. She's not all human." Eier said, though with a note of uncertainty.

Tinsworth turned to look at them both. "You two really want Bryant involved?"

"I'll get on the phone to the General. Bryant's got plenty of clout, but not enough to countermand *him*. Besides, he might learn something from this," Mangum replied.

Chapter Eleven

JASON FOLLOWED PHOEBE back onto the plaza. The sky appeared to have lightened to predawn above the floodlights illuminating the flagstones in front of them.

Phoebe walked briskly, two paces ahead of him, fast enough that he had to make a significant effort to keep up even though he was taller than she. She was making for the far side of the plaza, well to the right of the speaker banks, toward a dark, wooded patch of land beyond the fence; as they drew closer, Jason could see that a swath of long-overgrown grass with a narrow, clear path beyond it lay between the fence and the wood.

She reached the fence before he did, and walked to the right alongside it for perhaps another fifty feet, where they reached the base of a low hillock. The fence bent slightly inwards at that point, and Jason could make out what looked like an ancient sidewalk beside an old two-lane road. Both sidewalk and road were liberally cracked, and more grass grew from the sidewalk fractures. The road was somehow familiar to him, though he could not remember ever being on any street that dilapidated.

While he was looking at the road, Phoebe had reached the bend in the fence and was doing something with the chain-links; as he hurried up behind her, she rounded on him so suddenly that he almost fell backward in surprise and fear. He would indeed have fallen, except that Phoebe's arm snaked out with inhuman speed and caught his shoulder, steadying him.

Jason stared at her, his eyes wide and watchful, as Phoebe spread a gap in the chain fence. Rubbing his arm at the discomfort her grip had caused, he asked softly, "Phoebe, do you remember anything about me?"

Phoebe froze for a moment, then stood to her full height and faced him. She was taller than she had been, Jason realized.

She opened her mouth in that moveless speech that was so unnerving, but the voice that spoke was the one he could still recognize as hers. "My perceptions are different from what I knew before I was remade. I remember that I would experience emotions in a way that I can no longer know."

Her eyes were still impassive, her bearing still stiff - almost martial - and yet there was just a faint flicker in them, something that transited in a fast orbit and was gone. Jason reflected her stare back to her, trying to understand what he had seen. For a moment, he wondered how he might create that same flicker again - but she had grasped his arm again, in that Christ-almighty strong grip she had, and was pulling him toward the hole in the fence that she had created.

"Through here," the synthesized-female voice said. Jason gave her a look that indicated that the discussion wasn't over, and was rewarded with another momentary cloud across her otherwise expressionless face. *She remembers me,* he thought, as he crouched and made his way through the opening. Phoebe followed him, and once through, began reworking the fence to close the gap.

"Where are you taking me?" he asked. Once the fence was reknitted, she stood and resumed the quick pace she had set before, passing him almost at once. He reached out, grasping her arm as he said more loudly, "Wait!"

Her response was immediate. He had a bare instant of feeling her arm (*not her real arm,* he thought, *that feels like titanium!*) before she had grasped his wrist and squeezed so hard that he let go with a gasp of pain; she watched him as he flexed his fingers, staring at them as he turned his arm to ensure he could still move it. When he looked back into her face, she said in that synthesized voice, "you may not touch me. I will take you where you must go."

"Phoebe, I'm not going another step with you until you tell me what's happening. Where am I? I know I'm not at the university; I don't recognize this place at all. I know there was a temporal dislocation in the rift, so I'm in my own future, but I don't know how long it's been, or how long you've been like this." Jason was breathing heavily, from a mixture of emotion, physical pain, exhaustion and growing hunger.

"I will carry you to your destination if I must. But you must be brought beyond the range of the Drome for now, and of the peoples whose lands border it, only the Covingtons are trustworthy. The Black Birds are closer, but if left with them, you would not be safe." The fake-female voice droned at him. He hated to think that his once-girlfriend was now speaking with the sort of voice that had made him hang up phone calls.

"The Drome? Is that the place we just left?"

"It is. You must be out of Acme's range before he reactivates." Phoebe was not facing him, and as she used her own voice again, it was difficult for him to hear her words. The sky was brightening from blank night to a dim, overcast gray, and the wind was picking up, promising rain before long.

"Follow me. Do not touch me again." Phoebe's false voice spoke once more before she struck out eastward - or, at least, in the direction where the sky was brightening. Her pace was as quick as before, and after only a short distance, he called her name again.

Phoebe rounded on him again in that fast, abrupt way that he couldn't begin to adjust to. "You must be out of range from the Drome before sunrise. The limit of its wireless range is ahead, beside this road." She pointed behind herself, half turning, but her neutral stare never left his face. "Once you are past that point, you may rest for a short while, before we resume our journey."

"How far past there do you expect me to go?" Jason was breathing a little heavily from the effort it took for him to keep up.

"After you rest, it will be two point six two miles from there to the Covington base. The plan is for you to remain there until I retrieve you."

"More than an hour's walk, with the way I feel right now." Jason groaned quietly. "All right, I'm coming!" he quickly added, as Phoebe took a step toward him. He had no doubt that she would carry him, and he was pretty damned sure that she could. He stumbled after her as fast as he could make himself move without actually breaking into a run.

As they continued forward and the sky brightened, the sense of familiarity increased. Jason could almost recognize the shallow turns in the road. Every so often, a side street would branch off to his left; the overgrowth to his right was so heavy that he couldn't see more than a few feet beyond the weather-worn curb.

It was close to sunrise, he guessed, when he saw his first clear landmark. A crossroads lay a short distance ahead of them; Jason now knew that they were traveling slightly south of due east, and the name of the road they now walked. The crossroads was flanked on its north side by a pair of three-story buildings facing each other across the road intersecting theirs; both bore signs of extended neglect, cannibalization of building material, and wear from the elements. Jason almost stopped in his tracks, but a quick glance back from Phoebe increased his pace again.

They hurried through what Jason recognized as an intersection he had seen recently, at least in his own time. To his left, the street leading north bent eastward after only a short distance. He could see that a second street, paralleling the one they were following, ran east to west some fifty feet to their right; beyond lay what almost looked like a forest, except for the occasional buildings lining the cross-street as it dove southward into the woods.

Beyond the crossroads, the road bent to the right and began to climb slightly. Phoebe stopped abruptly beside a low wall protruding from the last building in the cluster. Jason barely staggered to a halt, stumbling to his left to avoid colliding with her, and looked longingly at the wall. "Please tell me I can rest a bit now."

"We are beyond the reach of the Drome's farthest wireless extension." Phoebe was as impassive as ever, and her false voice remained in use. "You may rest here briefly."

Jason heaved himself to a seat on the wall and closed his eyes, resting his forehead on his palms with his elbows on his knees. Phoebe remained where she was, though she watched him blankly. After only a few seconds, he looked up to find that she had remained motionless. He felt an unexpected pang as he observed her, and she him.

"Why is it so important that get away from the Drome's wi-fi?" he asked, to try to distract himself from other thoughts of her.

The same false voice answered again. "While within range of the Drome, my kind can communicate wirelessly, not only with Acme, but with each other. At night, unless one of us is assigned a specific mission, all but two of us are recalled to the Drome to defend Acme if needed."

Jason thought for a minute, and was about to ask another question, but then changed his mind and asked a different one. "How long have you been here?"

Phoebe touched the button on her shoulder, and a new voice issued from her mouth - one that made his blood run cold. "Well, hello, Anderson, you moron. If you're hearing this, then there really isn't any hope for us, is there?"

Jason gazed at Phoebe in horror. "That's Doctor Bryant, isn't it?"

"Doctor Allen Bryant. That is correct. He is the one who revived me in this form." For the second time, a fleeting compression of her face betrayed - something, Jason thought, but she continued, "Doctor Bryant built all of the Cybwomen. He created Acme as well."

"Cybwomen. Is that what he called you, or what you call yourselves?" Jason was still tired, and while he doubted whether he could distract Phoebe into allowing him extra time to rest, he saw no harm in trying to gain not only more time, but also more information.

"Both." The false female voice spoke, but then changed to Phoebe's broken tone. "I have been here since the government collapsed, during the Seafloods that began five years before you died. We all have." The first voice resumed. "Doctor Bryant and Doctor Tinsworth repurposed the Drome with help from Bryant's staff. It was modified from an old commuter rail station."

"I realized that, now that I know where we are." Jason was nodding. "I'm guessing that they wanted a ready source of electricity that they could redirect, and maybe modify to their needs?"

"That is correct," the false voice responded. "Their original plan was to remain in the Drome, but once their plans had been achieved, Acme moved over time to consolidate his power. Bryant eliminated Tinsworth, with Acme's aid; Acme later eliminated Bryant."

Jason felt a sick chill. "Eliminated? Bryant *eliminated* Professor Tinsworth?"

"That is correct," the synthesized voice repeated. "Some years after Bryant's death, Acme became silent, and neither spoke, nor answered any words addressed to him. For years, he remained passive."

Still the synthesized voice. Jason smiled slightly despite himself. "I think I know why."

A rare change in expression came over Phoebe's face, as its blankness shifted to a vague memory of inquisitiveness, and her own voice returned. "You have knowledge that I do not have?"

"I'm not sure. But I know enough to know who Acme is, so I think I understand why he was so quiet for so long." Jason's smile faded. "You say that you can't feel love. Is that true of all emotions for you, or only that one?"

Phoebe's face recast into impassiveness, but her own voice remained. "I cannot feel any emotion. There are a few that I can recall empirically - sadness, regret, love. I do not actually feel those emotions in my current form. I merely remember their effects at the times when I felt them."

Jason did not answer at once. A theory was forming in his mind, but he needed to know more. "I asked you before how long you had been here, and you played that recording of Doctor Bryant. Did he put that recording in your brain to keep me from asking that question?"

Phoebe spoke in her own voice again. "You could not have the answer to that question without its correct context."

Jason was growing more and more fascinated. "So you sent me in a direction that would enable me to establish that context." He thought again. "Acme - you call him - was uncommunicative for a long period of time. Years, you said."

Phoebe merely watched him as the realization filled him with belated horror: the rift had covered years, probably decades, and that meant the spatial dislocation measured in tens or even hundreds of billions of miles.

"The Drome was a cover." His expression had deepened into awe. "They needed a power grid that big not just to power the rift, but to absorb the energy transfer in crossing. Holy Christ!" He stared at her in amazement. "That might have been enough to power the entire rail system. For the whole *city*. Did any of the trains reactivate?"

"All trains were shut down before the Drome came online, over forty years ago." That false voice again.

Jason's mouth fell open. He had travelled almost half a trillion miles. Decades in time.

"Phoebe, what is today's date?"

Phoebe answered him again in her own voice. "By the calendars of your reckoning, this date would be August the sixth, in the year twenty sixty-six."

Jason bowed his head, unwilling to reveal the emotion that was threatening to come boiling out of him. She had waited half a lifetime for him. And from what she said before, he was supposed to be already dead.

But then, as he contained the outflow, he smiled bitterly to himself. His knowledge of his own death, now, would have no impact. "Phoebe, how did I die?"

"I *knew* you were going to go there. Fuck you, Anderson." Bryant spoke again from Phoebe's mouth, but this time, his voice could not quite shatter Jason's train of thought.

"One last thing," he said, watching her again for any trace of response. "Acme was deactivated when we arrived. I think he knew what would happen, and knew that if he interfered, he would negate himself through paradox. But he should also have known when he died, and when you returned him. Why wasn't he reactivated before we came back through the rift? Why did he let me come back without interference?"

Phoebe pressed her button again, and this time, Dr. Tinsworth replied, in a low and hurried voice, "Jason, in this timeline, you came through the rift, and then went back. Acme cannot interfere with you here without negating you, and by doing so, he risks negating himself. He will find some other way to ensure that you do not interfere with his ascendancy. He was powerful long before you returned, and is surely much more so now - and much more dangerous. He has almost certainly done something, or made some plan to ensure that you return to the place and time you left, so that his existence will be safe."

"That's what I needed to know." He smiled toward Phoebe, and was rewarded with another momentary, shadowy hesitation from her. "How much longer may I rest?"

"We must begin moving again in eleven minutes." Phoebe's head tilted oddly to one side as she studied him. "You appear to have learned much in a short time."

He looked at her searchingly, and smiled again, as affectionately as he could. "Maybe you forgot how smart I am."

The false female voice responded. "That would be unlikely."

"Whatever." Jason sighed, disgruntled despite himself, and bent forward. "I know you'll tell me when it's time to leave again. Can you try not to wear me out before we arrive? And will there be food there?"

"I will escort you to the Covington clan home." The false voice was still speaking. "Their provisions should be sufficient to satisfy your need. We will take two hours to walk there, so that you will not be overtaxed."

"Good." Jason turned so that he was lying on top of the wall. "Wake me in ten minutes, then. Please." He closed his eyes and tried to doze.

Chapter Twelve

THE COVINGTON CLAN'S stronghold was not what he had expected.

He recognized the road - it was called Covington Highway, in his own time, and he assumed that that was the source for their name - but the building that he assumed was their base had once been a honky-tonk dance joint, and after that a hip-hop club. It was now free of every trace of both past lives.

A hodgepodge of concrete slabs, scavenged brickwork, tangled razor wire, torn-up pavement, railroad ties, scrap sheeting and any number of other large, heavy objects had been repurposed into a loose, jumbled rampart some ten feet tall that surrounded the building perhaps a hundred yards around in a flattened near-circle. The building itself was a once-white, windowless, square concrete edifice about two stories tall, which had grayed and developed some exterior cracking from age.

A gatehouse had been built into the rampart, and two unkempt, ragged-looking men were posted there. Despite their appearance, they were surprisingly alert, and were visibly alarmed by Phoebe's arrival. She held up her hand as she approached the gatehouse; apparently that was some sort of non-aggressive signal, for the two men glanced at each other with obvious trepidation before rising to meet her approach.

The false female voice spoke. "Greetings. I must speak with the clan chief at once."

"Hello, Phoebe." The man on the left responded. He was the older of the two, with hair and beard streaked with gray. The other looked to be around Jason's age, or perhaps slightly younger. "Who's this man?" continued the speaker, pointing toward Jason.

A new voice spoke from Phoebe's mouth. "That information has been restricted by Acme and may only be disclosed to the clan chiefs." Jason blinked in surprise and glanced toward her; she gave no indication she had noticed. The two guards looked ill at ease.

"Should we call the chief here, or do you want to come in?" the older guard finally asked her.

"We should meet inside, as soon as possible. The man with me should be kept out of sight." The synthesized voice returned. She looked at Jason critically for a moment, then returned her gaze to the guards. "He will require food, and it is likely that he will need at least half a day of rest."

The two sentries looked again at each other before the elder responded. "I'll go in and wake the chief. We'll have to call out another guard while I walk you in. Can you wait here?"

"Yes, but do not delay. We will await your return here in the guardhouse." At these words the younger guard paled visibly, but the elder merely nodded and replied, "All right then. Scotty, wait here with them." He started back through the gatehouse, but then turned. "Scotty. Phoebe ain't going to hurt you. If she's here, and gave the sign, she has a reason." With that, he went through the gatehouse and disappeared from view.

Scotty eyed Phoebe and Jason nervously. "Come on in, then." He led them into the narrow building. Jason thought it looked more like a kids' clubhouse than an actual guard post, built from scrap lumber and furnished with discarded odds and ends. Then he remembered how far into his future he believed he had gone, and what Phoebe had said about a seaflood. He remembered how dilapidated the intersection he recognized had become.

"Phoebe -" he started to ask, but she cut him off, this time with her synthetic voice. "Silence. Do not speak until you meet the clan chief."

Jason opened his mouth to speak again, but before he could say anything, Phoebe had rounded on him, her arm upraised. Instead, he pressed his lips shut, and stared back at her through a stew of emotions he couldn't begin to differentiate. Scotty quailed back against the wall of the gatehouse, looking as though he would rather have been anyplace else.

Phoebe watched Jason with that same, terrible impassivity, and he stared back at her with roiling eyes, until her hand slowly lowered. Jason thought he saw the tiniest millisecond of indecision in her bearing before she stepped backward, putting himself and Scotty both in her field of view. Her arms were at her sides, but the inhuman stillness with which she stood was unnerving.

They remained in their places until the older guard returned with a second, younger one; like the others, he was bearded and unkempt-looking, but again, the eyes betrayed more intelligence and awareness than Jason would have expected to accompany such an appearance. The younger sentry also was plainly intimidated by Phoebe's presence, but said nothing, and they both stood aside to let her pass through, following the older one back toward the clan's apparent stronghold. Jason followed in their wake, more than a little uncertainly.

Once inside the rampart, Jason was so surprised by what met his eyes that he stopped in his tracks and looked around. What had once been a parking lot surrounding the old dance joint and a few nearby businesses had been completely dug up - no doubt that had formed much of the wall behind him - and instead of black asphalt, a huge vegetable garden surrounded him. Vines laden with ripening green tomatoes snaked through ancient, rickety trellises. Peppers and eggplant grew in a nearby patch to his right, beside the path that Phoebe and the old guard were taking. Marveling at the change, Jason followed them toward the redoubt.

No one spoke, and the building loomed closer, until they reached a narrow moat that had been dug around the building, perhaps twenty feet across. It was opaque, dense-looking, and smelled foul enough that Jason thought he might be able to walk across it - not that he cared to try. If he was correct, it was probably deeper than he was tall, and he would probably have been sick to death with some dread disease before he could get across and clean himself.

Their path rounded the building beside the moat. The old guard led them counterclockwise around it for about a hundred feet before they reached a short drawbridge that was lowered over the water, its two chains secured through pulleys leading up to a pair of winches perched on the building's roof. The wall had been visibly fortified with more of the paving material; it had been cut into rough bricks that girdled the building to about twice Jason's height. A low, barred door stood just past the bridge's end; there was almost no space between the wall and the moat's inner bank.

The bridge itself was so narrow that only two of them could walk abreast; they crossed in file as they had come in, with the guard leading Phoebe and Jason following behind. Jason realized that although knowledge of his identity had apparently been restricted, Phoebe was still much the more important of the two of them, at least to their perception. At the least, she seemed far more threatening.

They crossed the bridge and approached the barred door. The guard glanced back, appearing as though he was going to ask Phoebe to wait, but then thinking better of it as she passed him on the way to the portal, before halting to let him give the signal. Jason hung back at the near end of the bridge as the guard knocked twice, heavily, and then twice again, more softly.

After a few seconds, a slot in the door slid open; Jason could not make out any details of the face that peered out, but it was unmistakably taken aback by Phoebe's presence. The slot closed rapidly, and though the questions that were shouted behind it were muffled to unintelligibility by the door and walls, it was apparent that the warden on duty, at the very least, had not been made aware of the nature of their visitors.

A short while passed. Jason was about to join Phoebe and the guard when several loud clacking noises broke the silence. The door swung open, and a relatively young-looking man, bearded as the others, stood tall to salute the guard and Phoebe. It was then that Jason realized that she was looking at him again; though she still had no discernible expression, he sensed that she was about to drag him forward, and hastily stepped up beside her, slightly embarrassed. The door warden had moved to stand beside the young guard; neither man appeared even to notice him. Both were staring at Phoebe as though they were seeing a menacing ghost.

Phoebe spoke in her synthetic voice. "Greetings to you. I am sent to meet with your clan chief, and to deliver this man to him. He should be brought inside at once."

The door warden, despite his apparent unease, nonetheless responded with greater formality than any of the guards had. "Greetings, Phoebe. It shall be as you say." He and the other guard stepped aside, motioning that they should enter. The three did so, the guard first, then Phoebe, and finally Jason, who eyed the entrance suspiciously before he approached. Though he stared straight ahead as he went in, he sensed that the door warden was scrutinizing him.

They entered into a dim foyer about twenty feet wide and twice that long, lit by two candle-heavy chandeliers hung from a fairly high ceiling; glancing up, Jason guessed it was more than twice his height. The air smelled of smoke and age, and as he looked around, he realized that some twenty men armed with spears and spiked truncheons were lined up in two files on the far side of the room. At a barked command, the men fanned into two curved ranks facing them; in a gap between the arced lines, a balding, dark-skinned, bearded, powerful-looking man glared at them.

A second, shorter man stood beside him, and it was he who spoke, almost recitatively. "Phoebe of the Drome, you have requested and been granted entry into our stockade. We bid you welcome. We ask that you declare the reason for your visit, and certify that none here will attempt to harm you while your actions remain peaceful."

Jason lifted an eyebrow almost unconsciously. He glanced toward Phoebe; she was as unmoved as ever. The older guard had stepped back after they entered; he now flanked the door guards, so that they were effectively surrounded.

Phoebe spoke once more in the voice that had surprised him in the guardhouse. "You have our guarantee of peaceful negotiation. No one will be harmed here without deliberate provocation. All other information on this matter has been restricted by Acme and may only be conveyed to the Covington clan chief."

The balding man stepped forward through the gap in the ranks before him, coming to a halt perhaps three paces away, and spoke in a quiet but growling voice. "You know who I am, Phoebe. If you will follow me into my office, we can discuss this matter privately." He looked past them, motioning toward one of the door guards. "You - go to the granary and notify my brother that Phoebe is here. He is to stay outside the fortifications until she has left." He then glanced around himself. "Men, if anything happens to me, do not engage her. You have been told many times that she and those like her could kill everyone in this room without so much as being struck even once. Your service to the clan is more important than your loyalty to me, and if I am killed, my brother will require your continued service."

The men glanced at each other as one man at the end of the front rank saluted, responding, "It shall be as you say. Men, stand down and allow the chief and his guest to pass."

The chief turned and strode back through the gap in the ranks. Phoebe followed him without hesitation; Jason fell in two steps behind her with some misgivings. As he reached the front rank, the men on either side crossed their spears in front of him, barring his passage. He stopped short, looking askance at the guard on his left; his face was nearly as expressionless as Phoebe's.

"That man must be allowed to enter." He looked toward Phoebe; she had halted, but had not turned. It took a moment for him to realize that it was her own voice that had spoken. He was silent, waiting for a response from the guards, and hoping that response wouldn't include a spear-point in his gut.

The clan chief had nearly reached a door in the room's far wall, but had turned halfway around. "Sergeant Curtis." He said no more, and turned toward the doorway again. The man at the end of the front rank barked an order, and the spears blocking his path were removed as quickly as they had lowered. Jason tried to catch up to Phoebe without being too apparently hurried, but sensed that he had failed miserably.

They followed the chief into a short hallway that led to a surprisingly small chamber; Jason realized that this had been the club manager's office, many years before, and that it likely remained the chief's not because of size, but tradition. It was lit by several large, makeshift lanterns and smelled of burnt oil, smoke and candlewax.

Its function had been greatly reduced; only a few chairs, a heavy desk and a small bookcase containing some very old-looking volumes remained. A few had titles Jason recognized with almost a sense of vertigo: they showed all the markings of the passage of many years, but were current in his own time. Almost without thinking, he glanced toward Phoebe, and was startled to see that she was watching him, though as emotionlessly as ever. Their eyes remained locked for several seconds, until the chief cleared his throat, apparently to gather their attention. In the moment before Phoebe's gaze returned to the chief, he saw another ghostly flicker in her expression and, for the first time that he had seen, she blinked.

He then shifted his attention to the chief, whose countenance was unreadable, though Phoebe's presence appeared to intimidate even him. He looked at each of them for several seconds without speaking before addressing Phoebe: "Is this the man we discussed on your last visit?"

They both blinked in surprise as Phoebe responded, again in her own gravelly voice: "Yes. This is the man."

Chapter Thirteen

COLONEL MANGUM STOOD almost nose to nose with Dr. Bryant, each glaring fiercely at the other. Major Eier stood by, hand on his sidearm, and Bryant's security detail stood poised likewise. Tinsworth stood behind Eier, watching them tensely.

"My research is not to be disclosed or discussed with anyone outside the project sphere. You know that, and you tried to go over my fucking head. Colonel," Bryant added with sarcastic contempt. "I'll have you court-martialed for insubordination for this."

"Go ahead and try that," Mangum snarled in response. "I already spoke to *our* commanding officer. I could order you right now to tell me everything, but I think you'll be more cooperative once you see what we recorded here."

Bryant looked as though he was barely able to restrain himself from attacking Mangum, but settled for a relatively quiet, venomous sneer. "I don't see how you could have anything germane to what we're doing, but I'll indulge you by watching whatever bullshit you're using to try to interfere."

"This isn't interference, Dr. Bryant." Mangum was becoming calmer, though he remained visibly angry. "I would have had to call your people in here anyway, owing to the death of Wiley Grant. It's the circumstances of that death that require your presence."

"Are you sure this isn't Tinsworth's idea of protecting that assistant of his?" Bryant jeered.

"Grant was also Tinsworth's assistant." Eier said quietly. "He was killed after he went through the rift."

"So you fucked up once and blew up half this building, and got that girl in my lab killed. Then you fucked up *again* and got your own man killed, too. Then you drag *me* into it, as if *I* had anything to do with any of this bullshit."

"Actually, it looks like you're going to have a lot to do with it." Mangum hesitated. "We know what you're building in your lab. How would you like to see a finished product?"

He tried to conceal his response, but Bryant was visibly taken aback by Mangum's words. He glanced first at Tinsworth, then at Eier; the latter nodded back at him. The stocky professor's scowl remained, but his eyes betrayed his surprise and interest. When he looked back at Mangum, he was met with an almost sardonic half-smile.

"I don't know how much you know about what we're doing, or how far along we are," he said in a low voice that was almost a whisper. "What are you saying you can show me?"

Mangum glanced behind himself. "Dr. Tinsworth, can you elaborate?"

Tinsworth came to stand next to Mangum, his expression still tense. "Allen, you need to watch the recording of what happened in the lab this morning. More to the point, *we* need for you to watch it, because..." He paused for a moment. "Have you felt the earthquakes?"

Bryant's face twisted slightly with contempt. "Do you think I'm a moron? Yes, I felt three or four tremors in the last couple of days. USGS made a statement at noon yesterday, and it was a load of horseshit." He paused. "*Shit.* Are you telling me that this fuckapalooza you've cooked up is causing goddamn *earthquakes?*"

"Not only that, but they're probably going to get worse if you don't get on board." Tinsworth's voice was quiet, but firm, and assured enough that even Bryant's ready rejoinder was caught in his throat before it could come out. "I can explain the situation to you more fully once you see the *real* reason you were called here."

Bryant's eyes scanned the three men again, until he could no longer disguise his hesitation. A hissing breath went through his teeth before he responded. "All right. Show me."

"Follow me." Tinsworth began picking his way through the lab wiring toward the control station. Bryant and Mangum followed. Eier and Bryant's security detail remained where they were.

Tinsworth maximized a window on his screen the moment he reached his station. Bryant could see the rift glowing onscreen, viewed from their oblique angle, as he joined him.

"This was left on, in case we needed to capture the return trip." Mangum glanced toward Bryant as he came alongside. "You'll see Anderson come back through, and move off camera. You'll hear what he has to say, and then -"

"And then you'll know why you were called in." Tinsworth finished quietly. Mangum clicked a desktop icon and opened a video window. Jason and Wiley were just about to enter the rift. Mangum said, "they're in there about three minutes. You'll see that it goes dark, briefly, and then comes back. Right after it gets lighter, Anderson will come back through. He was off-camera when we began debriefing him, but you'll be able to hear it - and then you'll see what we're talking about."

Bryant neither moved nor took his eyes from the screen, and the others beside him simply waited. A minute passed, then two.

"There." Eier spoke quietly as the rift in the video clip began to brighten. A few seconds later, Jason stumbled through it in his helmet and suit. Bryant watched as they spoke, drifting off-camera but growing slowly louder. When Jason mentioned him, Bryant glanced toward Mangum, who nodded back and motioned toward the screen.

"Jesus H. Christ," Tinsworth breathed again, this time onscreen, and Bryant's breath hissed again, sharply inward through his teeth. Mangum glanced first toward Eier, then Tinsworth, as he paused the clip. He turned and faced Bryant, who was studying the onscreen image of Phoebe as she held Wiley's body.

"I don't know whether you've examined the body that came in when the lab went up, but Anderson clearly recognized her - he of all people would - and he knows that she was in your morgue." Tinsworth spoke quietly. "*You* made sure he'd *never* forget that."

Bryant didn't answer, but remained engrossed in the footage as the clip resumed. He nodded when the earthquake shook the view, but when Phoebe lifted Jason from the floor with one arm, his eyes widened, and he said softly, "has to be prosthetics."

Phoebe and Jason vanished into the rift once more, and Mangum reached forward, shutting off the video playback before turning to face Bryant. "I knew whose work that was, even without knowing the girl's face. If we're going to close that rift and get the situation here under control, then we have to know as much as we can about what that was. I know it had that girl's head on top, but that was no human being, and we both know it."

Bryant glared back at him, but the glare lacked the forceful malevolence that had underlaid it only a little while before. "This is the goal, yes - at least, long-term."

"Bullshit. Bull-*fucking*-shit." Tinsworth's interjection was low and venomous. "Long-term isn't supposed to be viable for body tissue storage. You already have her head. You'd have to store it from now until you get to the point where you can make that thing. So either you already have a long-term storage option, or you're a lot closer to making that thing that you're letting on."

"We're a long way from *that*. But we've found a way to preserve viable tissue for up to a year using pressurized storage." Bryant replied unwillingly. "We also have other techniques for keeping tissue from degrading. It was through sheer good luck that we recovered the girl. Until now, I thought it was a big mistake to release Anderson, but after seeing that -" he motioned toward the screen - "I'm not so sure. We'll probably save five years of work just from me seeing that clip."

"But there's another problem with this girl. Her head was severed." Mangum's head turned to face Bryant, who was staring at the screen again. "How are you going to preserve her head without cryogenics?"

"One of our techniques is to submerge tissue in a pH-balanced bath at zero degrees Celsius under pressure. The freezing point lowers only slightly, but it's enough to preserve tissue for a much longer period than normal without the cell-wall ruptures that accompany freezing.

Unfortunately, this method is expensive as hell, and transport's out of the question. But the good thing is, it does make what you just saw possible." Bryant was staring at the screen again, even though it had frozen with the rift darkened and the girl gone.

Mangum hesitated just a fraction of an instant, then asked: "Is that what you did with her?"

Bryant smiled, apparently despite himself. "Phoebe Michelle Reyes. Age twenty. Italian-Hispanic nationality, well above-average intelligence - goes without saying, she's a student here - and what turned out to be an excellent genetic profile. Yeah, I decided to try to preserve her. From the picture, she was a pretty attractive girl, to boot."

"Obviously Anderson thought so." Tinsworth paused. "I don't know how well he's handling all this, or how much more he'll be able to endure before it gets to be too much. First she's dead, then she's alive but turned into that - thing."

"I'm still trying to figure out what she meant about 'Acme.'" Mangum shook his head. "She said it had been delivered, but what did that mean? Bryant, you might want to have your people go over Grant's body with some extra care, in case it's been booby-trapped."

"If it has, my people will find it. Let's hope it's just a nice, innocent bomb and not some kind of future pathogen." Bryant's smile was sour. "I know, that's a paradox. Probably won't happen."

"I think we'd all know already, even if it wasn't necessarily a paradox," Eier replied sardonically. "People tend to notice when there's an earthquake. Quite the attention-getter."

Bryant snorted and left the command station, taking his phone from his pocket as he exited the room, his security detail following in his wake. The remaining three men looked at each other doubtfully.

"He seems like he's on board, at least," Tinsworth said, and Eier nodded. Mangum snorted.

"Sure, he's on board. What he just saw could save him years of development and research. What *I* noticed is that there wasn't a tremor when he saw the girl." He paused. "So there wasn't a paradox, and it didn't affect that future. If anything, that might have stabilized it, by making sure Bryant knew exactly what he was going to make." The colonel shook his head. "I was expecting a tremor the minute he saw it. I'm not sure I'm happy that it didn't come."

"Either way, he says he can store tissue long-term. D'you believe him?" Tinsworth asked.

Mangum shook his head. "I wouldn't believe much of anything he tells you. If he's willing to admit that much, then I'd bet he's closer to making what we saw than we realized. Another reason I'm not too glad there wasn't an earthquake."

"One thing bothers me, though, Colonel," Eier said thoughtfully. "The girl - whatever she is - was waiting for him at the other end of the rift. I think she said, 'Thirteen of us remain," didn't she?"

"That's right. And that begs several questions - what is Bryant going to do with Grant? Do these cyborgs, if that's what they are - do they remember what they were? How much mental capacity do they retain?" Mangum looked from Eier to Tinsworth with slightly haunted eyes. "We don't know nearly as much as we need to, and we have no way of learning what we don't know. I doubt even Bryant has much idea of what Anderson's gotten himself into."

"So what do we do?" Tinsworth asked.

An uncomfortable silence followed, which was finally broken by Eier: "We wait to see if Anderson returns, and if he does, we hope that whatever he accomplishes is enough to deal with the situation. We can't hope to surprise an enemy who already knows what's going to happen."

Mangum nodded. "Especially when we can't be all that sure which enemy we're trying to surprise."

Chapter Fourteen

JASON WAS FROZEN in amazement as the Covington clan chief stepped out from behind his desk and knelt before him in that dim, crowded space.

"I am honored beyond words to meet you, Jason Anderson," he said, Your presence here is the answer to every prayer that my people have ever made."

He glanced toward Phoebe; though she was rigid as stone, she still conveyed a ghostly sense of conveyance, as though she was silently urging him forward. Still unsure, he extended his right hand toward the clan chief, and whispered, "If I can help you, I will."

The words seemed to fall flat in the silence as he uttered them; yet their impact was immediate and powerful. The clan chief grasped Jason's hand with both of his, his head lifting to reveal eyes transported with wonder, tears welling in them, as he whispered: "I can hardly believe it. You really came back."

Where before he had been concerned, Jason was now genuinely terrified. He looked again to Phoebe, who impassively watched him awaiting his response.

He swallowed, and managed to whisper, "please don't kneel."

The chief rose, though he still regarded Jason with a deference the latter found disconcerting. An awkward silence was threatening to fall. Knowing that Phoebe would likely let it settle in, Jason asked, "What is your name? And are you actually in charge here?"

The chief looked at Phoebe, then back to Jason. "My name is William Jones. I'm chief of the Covington clan. My men usually just call me 'Chief' or 'Pops.'" He tilted his head and looked puzzled. "I thought you would already know all about us."

Jason chuckled ironically. "I probably know less about this world than anyone in it right now. The only person I've actually talked to, other than you, is Phoebe."

Jones looked even more puzzled, until Phoebe spoke with her synthesized voice. "Jason Anderson is indeed alive. He was dead, but he did not rise from the grave. That was a misunderstanding that started among the Black Birds and was propagated from them to the other clans."

Jones glanced toward her, nodding. "Our scouts have told us that the site of Anderson's grave is constantly watched. The Black Birds have an outpost within sight of it, about a mile north of their main compound." His gaze returned to Jason, with an admiration that still made him uncomfortable. "I don't understand how you went from being dead to alive, but.... well, here you are."

Now Jason looked toward Phoebe. "You mentioned these 'Black Birds' before. You seemed to think I wouldn't be safe with them."

"The Black Birds are a clan much like the Covingtons, based near the old city to the west." Phoebe still spoke in the false female voice. "The city itself has become too dangerous for anyone to enter; the clans that warred there in the past have destabilized some of the buildings in its center. Several have collapsed, and merely to walk the streets there can be deadly, whether from sinkholes, or from missiles thrown from overhead. Someone like you would be in considerable danger, as you would be vulnerable to ambush. Even some of my own kind, the Cybwomen, were destroyed there twenty-nine years ago. After that happened, Acme forbade most of us to pass beyond the great highway that runs through an artificial canyon just east of the city."

"The Connector," Jason whispered. Then he addressed Jones: "Tell me more about the Black Birds."

When he spoke, his voice took on an odd, harmonic resonance; a light fall of dust drifted down from the old ceiling, the individual motes sparkling unnaturally from the light of the multiple lanterns. For a moment, Jones' eyes wandered as he watched the dust fall; then the clan chief remembered what had been asked. Jason was relieved that he did not comment on the change in his voice.

"The Black Birds are sort of like us, but they tend to fight other clans more than we do. They do less farming than us, but they trade more. There's stuff from the old world that they still can find around their compound." Jones thought for a moment. "We still trade with them sometimes, usually in food, and we used to send people to help them when they had trouble growing things themselves. But they've always been a problem, because we never know whether they'll try to attack us and take what we have." He sighed. "It's a shame, really, because we could probably help each other, but there's not a lot of trust there."

Jason considered all this, then asked Phoebe, "What are the alliances among your kind? It looks to me as though this clan is familiar with you. Do the Black Birds have someone like you helping them? Are there others that I should know about?"

Phoebe's response, when it came, was in her own, damaged voice. "I am partially restricted from speaking of my peers directly. However, I may say that the Black Birds have three of my kind who are assigned to aid them. They are favored by Acme and are likely to be seeking you soon."

Jason looked straight into her blank eyes. "The man who came with me was killed by one of your kind. Was his killer one of those three?"

"She was not." Her true voice still spoke. "That one was Allison. She no longer speaks vocally at all. Most of the time, she shuts herself down; Acme woke her specifically for her task, once it became clear that you were coming."

Jason thought about that as Jones watched them both, and a silence fell. Finally, he spoke quietly, concerned that his voice would resonate again. That had been more unnerving than he wanted to admit, even to himself.

"You obviously think I'm supposed to be some kind of savior. What do you know about me?"

The chief looked confused. "I know that a man named Jason Anderson died, years ago. The legend says that he was a friend of Acme and that for a time they worked together, trying to save as many people as they could after the Seafloods began to destroy the world."

Jason interrupted him. "That's the second time I've heard about this. What were the Seafloods, exactly? And how long ago did this happen?"

"The Seafloods happened when I was still a boy. I remember my mother and father talking about them and saying that the world was coming to an end." Jones' expression was pensive. "Not long after that, I remember that there wasn't any food to be had, and people were starting to starve. My father and some of his friends banded together and began raiding to feed their families."

Jason thought about that. "Is that how this place was started?"

Jones smiled. "Yes. My father knew that this building was abandoned, so they began fixing it and making it their base. By the time I was old enough to raid with him, the old nations had collapsed, and people were starving to death everywhere. He said he thought three-fourths of all the people in the old city died in that first year, and then three-fourths of the survivors died the next year, and the same the next, until almost everyone was gone."

Phoebe said, still in her own voice, "That was when you died, Jason Anderson. You refused to work with Bryant on the Drome, and left. For a year, you tried to survive in the main city. Dr. Tinsworth sent scouts from the Drome to remain in contact with you, and eventually they tried to bring you back.

"One of the larger buildings in the city had destabilized, and it collapsed when you and your escort were attempting to leave. The Cybwoman who had been your liaison was killed with you. The other two were damaged, but they recovered your bodies and returned with you to the Drome. They both eventually ceased functioning as well, and there was no way to preserve them. All of you are buried with you in a large cemetery, half a mile east of the old highway skirting the city, approximately four point two miles west-southwest of the Drome." Phoebe was expressionless as ever. Jones listened to her with interest, glancing toward Jason when she mentioned his resting place.

"And as you said, that cemetery is being watched." Jason thought. "Would the Black Birds be expected to learn that I am alive again, now that I've been in the Drome?"

Jones gave him an odd look, but Phoebe still answered in her own voice. "They would know of your reappearance within a day of your arrival."

Jason nodded, then glanced toward the chief. "I know this looks odd, but this situation is very - " he looked meaningfully toward Phoebe - "delicate. When I'm trying to learn something, I have to work around the edges, instead of just asking straight away."

Jones nodded. "Phoebe has always been loyal toward us, but there has always been some fear that she might become angry or violent, so when she is here, she is treated with absolute respect." Phoebe nodded in agreement.

Jason thought for a few seconds. "There isn't any good way to work around this part, though. I'm just going to ask you straight out - if you had to evacuate this place, right now, would you have anywhere else you could go?"

Jones frowned. For some time he remained silent in thought, not looking at either of them. Jason and Phoebe waited.

When his response came, it was slow, with each word carefully considered: "We do know of one place where we could hope to evacuate, but that would only be for a short while - no more than a day or two, and then we would be asked to move on - if we were even allowed to stay there at all.

"There is another clan base well to the east of us. They have a fortification around a similar place to what we have built here, but larger. There are more of them than there are of us. They trade with us, and they haven't been unfriendly, but we've never imposed on them like that before."

Jason nodded. "I'm hoping that this will be resolved in about two days." He looked to Phoebe once more, then added, "I will have to rest before I can do anything else. How far away is this place you mentioned?"

"It would take the better part of a day to get there, using the old roads. They'd need to be scouted as well." Jones took a deep breath. "I hope you're not going to ask us to leave."

"Not immediately, but very soon. If I sleep until late afternoon, we can discuss this again when I wake up, but you're going to have to leave. My guess is that the Black Birds are going to come here, probably tonight - they'll want to use darkness as a cover - and from what Phoebe's said, I'm guessing that they will have three women like her with them. If you're not out of here by then, it could get ugly really fast." Jason looked at Phoebe. "We'll have to leave as well."

"That was expected." Phoebe's synthesized voice had returned. "What do you plan to do after that?"

Jason looked long at Phoebe, and another faint shadow momentarily darkened her expression. The chief looked questioningly from one to the other.

"I haven't worked that out yet." He sighed. "I think I know what I need to do, but I don't know yet how to get from here to there. I'm hoping I will get an idea while I sleep. I'm sorry, Chief, but I have to rest. Soon."

Jones nodded. "You can use my quarters. I won't be in there, and no one is likely to come in and bother you. How long will you need to sleep?"

"It's not quite noon, by my guess. I'm worried I might sleep too long, if you leave me to it. Phoebe, can you have the chief send someone about ninety minutes before sunset? I'm thinking that will give me six or seven hours."

"I will wake you," Phoebe's synthesized voice replied.

Jason stood, and followed Jones back out of his office; Phoebe came behind. They followed the short hallway around a corner, then up a staircase that ended at a loft that had obviously been added well after the club itself was built. The chief led them into a small, open apartment with wooden-railed sides. The flat, black ceiling above them was low enough for Jason to reach it flat-footed.

The living space was almost Spartan, with another ancient-looking desk that looked like it would disintegrate if spoken to harshly, a mattress on the floor with threadbare blankets on it, and another small, low bookcase and a lantern beside the mattress. The smells of smoke, body odor and age were pervasive, as they were everywhere in the club, but here the chief's tinge was noticeably different, if no more pleasant.

Jason shrugged. He was so tired that he knew he would sleep within seconds of lying down, and when Jones motioned him toward the mattress, he simply moved the blankets and curled up on his side, facing the bookcase. His eyes closed.

The chief looked to Phoebe. "Will you wish to come with me, or will you stay with him?"

"I am assigned to stay with him. I will not allow him out of my sight until his purpose here is fulfilled." Phoebe's synthesized voice was still speaking. "I am not permitted to say more."

As Jones nodded and saluted her informally before leaving, and Phoebe responded with a long nod that was almost a bow, neither of them saw the small, knowing smile that briefly crossed Jason's face before sleep overtook him.

Chapter Fifteen

THE CYBWOMEN APPROACHED the Black Birds' compound from the north as the sun approached noon, walking three abreast, almost majestically indifferent to their surroundings. They followed a road that had cracked with age and been surrounded by overgrowth until it resembled nothing so much as a wide, shaded country lane from the old world.

Rosamind was the smallest of the three, and marched at their right. She had been the last one made of them all, and had been a freshman in her first month of college when she met her first death. The Seafloods had already begun to wreak havoc both economically and climatologically by then, and both resources and time had grown scarce. Acme had told her more than once how close she had come to leaving existence altogether, and how he had himself directed the last stages of her re-creation. Over the years, she had aged unnaturally, so that alone among the remaining Cybwomen she had developed the wrinkled skin that would once have been normal for a woman of her age.

On the left side, Lisa strode effortlessly; she had been an athlete even before being remade, and until recently, she had suffered the fewest physical effects from time out of all the Cybwomen. Her brown eyes moved constantly, scanning for anything threatening or unusual - not that there was much that would threaten them - and she occasionally glanced toward her counterparts to her right, ensuring visually, as well as wirelessly, that she remained in step with them.

Between them walked a lithe, blonde, blue-eyed creature who was in many ways the paragon of their type of being. Julia was catlike in her motions and demeanor, and the ground seemed to move itself under her as she walked south down the old road. She somehow projected a sense of dangerousness and unsatiated blood-thirst toward everyone who encountered her that was unique among them; all of the others, save only Allison and occasionally Phoebe, had reawakened to an existence devoid of emotional responses.

Of the thirteen that were left, her orbit about Acme was the closest, and her agenda was enslaved to his; all of their kind knew that Acme considered her their leader, and as his representative when more than one of them left the Drome at a time. She knew all of the tribes and clans that had formed in the wreckage and famines over a generation before, and knew which of her kind was usually dispatched to each, but her preference had always been for the tribe whose base they now approached.

They were all, like each of their kind, unique in their construction; the degree of mechanization within their bodies depended upon their condition at the time they were reanimated. Lisa had been the best-preserved of them all; Rosamind was probably the poorest aside from Phoebe, for whom an entire body had had to be constructed. She had met her death in a grisly pedestrian accident involving both a truck and a city trolley, and was not much less cybernetic than Phoebe was. Julia, as always, was a special case; she had somehow learned of Bryant's project, and had killed herself in the belief that she would reawaken to immortality.

They passed into the cleared zone that surrounded the compound's outer walls, and the tumbledown, rotted-out dwellings that had lined the road suddenly disappeared. Bare lots stood in their places, some overgrown with thirty years of shrub and grass, with a few still-young trees beginning to reclaim them as their own. Scrubby, undernourished-looking farm plots were cultivated in those acres nearer to their destination. Nothing remained of what had once stood in that zone: even the concrete of the foundations and driveways had been torn up and taken away. About a quarter of a mile ahead, they could see where most of that material had been put to use.

A wall twice their height rose ahead of them, built of concrete slabs and repurposed metal and timber. The Cybwomen knew that it was a full ten feet in thickness, with a walkway running along its length at the top between low stone parapets. The outer side was topped with transplanted chain-link fencing another four feet high. The entire construct ran nearly half a mile north-to-south along each side of the compound, and perhaps half that far east-to-west, with low, indifferently-constructed guard towers set along its inner edge at intervals of some two hundred yards.

The wall surrounded an area that had once been called Grant Park, the home of a major zoo, whose past denizens had almost all been killed and eaten decades before. All along its length, the image of a red-trimmed, black-feathered bird of prey, viewed from the side in the act of seizing its quarry, had been rendered in old paint and scratchings that had begun to fade from age and neglect. In the center of each side, the bars from the more reinforced cages in the zoo had been used to create stout, iron gates that even the Cybwomen would have been hard-pressed to move easily.

To anyone in that world other than the Cybwomen, the wall alone would have been daunting, but the reputation of the tribe that had constructed it, and who lived within it to that day, was even more frightening. The Black Birds had been, in the first years after they built the wall, the most numerous, powerful, and unscrupulous of the clans that had coalesced in those dark days. One by one, the Black Birds had routed out each nearby clan, killing all their adult males and stealing all usable resources, and those remaining that were not killed out of hand were enslaved.

For ten years they had expanded, until their sphere had reached nearly to the Drome itself; at that point Acme had sent Julia and Rosamind to slow their advance. After the heads from several raiding parties had been left at the great iron gate set in the wall's eastern length, the Black Birds had sent a larger patrol to deal with the threat to their northeast. That force had been ambushed in a tunnel where they sought to pass beneath the old rail lines that ran between their territories, and eleven Cybwomen - their entire number, excepting Allison and Phoebe - had trapped them there and killed every man in that force. More than a hundred of their soldiers - a third of their army, at the time - died in the tunnel. Not one of them succeeded in wounding even one of their opponents.

That had greatly slowed their aggression, and in time Acme sent Julia and Lisa to negotiate a truce with them. After two false starts where the Black Birds' representatives foolishly tried to assault the Cybwomen, normalized contact was finally made, and an uneasy peace between them and among their neighbors was established. That peace had been honored on all sides, with one notable exception - during a particularly bitter winter fourteen years later, the Black Birds' clan chief had begun indulging in cannibalism as a source of food. When news of this reached Acme, a delegation of five of their kind - including the Threebirds themselves - was dispatched to deal with the problem. Within two days, the practice had ceased, along with the lives of every Black Bird who had partaken.

As they reached the corner of the wall and turned right, westward toward the northern gate, they heard a bell peal sharply three times; this they recognized as the signal that conveyed the nature and number of the delegation approaching the compound. The Threebirds did not alter their pace or demeanor, but marched directly toward the barred gate.

The gate itself was more of a portcullis constructed between a pair of tracks, along which it could be raised or lowered with a pair of winches that were hidden within a two-story gatehouse fortification. Beyond, a short, arched tunnel perhaps eight feet in height bored through the gatehouse before opening into an inner yard. Three men in odd, scale-type armored vests, wearing beaten metal helmets and carrying crude, short-handled, spiked clubs awaited them on its other side.

The Threebirds raised their right hands, palms open, in unison to shoulder level. The guards mimicked their salute, each side indicating to the other that their current truce would be respected. The guard in the center looked to his left and nodded, and slowly, creaking as it went, the gate began to lift.

"Stand down!" the center guard barked, as heads in the courtyard behind them turned to watch their visitors' entry. About one minute later, the gate's spiked ends receded above the level of the tunnel's ceiling, and the three Cybwomen walked forward until they stood face-to-face with their hosts.

"Hello, Julia. Are you wanting to talk with the boss?" asked the center guard. He received only a terse nod in response.

He glanced toward each of the men flanking him, then nodded. "All right. Follow me. Men, stand aside to let them pass." With that, he turned and walked back through the tunnel. The Threebirds followed.

They emerged into the dust of a circular yard, which was surrounded by gardens in much the same way as the Covingtons' barracks - one sign of the limited, rather tense, but still relatively fruitful relations between the two clans. Led by the guard, the three Cybwomen descended several flights of ancient, cracked concrete stairs that led into a wide, shallow central depression. On the northern end of that concavity, a large, aging but still impressive white marble building stood on a low rise.

A series of columns held up an alcove on the building's western side. The guard led the Threebirds between those columns and toward the four guards posted at the entrance. None of them seemed pleased by the appearance of their guests.

"Password?" One guard managed to ask, his discomfiture evident. None of the Cybwomen acknowledged him, or his fellows.

"Redbird," came the answer from their escort. The door-guards still looked unhappy, but they nonetheless fanned out on either side of the entrance. The hollow thudding of sliding bolts on the far side of the door echoed in the high-ceilinged alcove, before the door swung open.

The guard led them forward into a marble foyer lit only by the daylight streaming through windows on the room's southern wall. Several of the pillars supporting the ceiling - which, though still high, was lower than the exterior entry - bore crude sconces reminiscent of the guards' helmets, jarringly out of place with the aging magnificence of the room itself.

The northern and eastern walls both featured relatively low doorways that were each guarded by eight men, all of whom were much more uniformly and handsomely equipped than the men at the gate. The Threebirds' escort led them toward the eastern door, stopping some three paces away from the guardsmen and saluting. The guard mimicked his gesture; then, after quickly surveying the three Cybwomen, he said quietly, "I'll talk to the Duke."

With that, he turned and strode through the door. No one spoke; the guards stole occasional, nervous glances toward their impassive, uninvited guests. It was only a short while before the guard returned. Behind him walked a surprisingly unimposing man whose uniform, while clearly very old - probably twice as old as the Duke himself - was still immaculately kept. His beard and hair were trimmed short, and he looked at the three with intelligent eyes that betrayed no fear. The guard rejoined his fellows in line as the man thoughtfully eyed the visitors.

"Hello, Julia. Lisa. Rosamind," he said quietly, nodding to each in turn. "If you will follow me, we can discuss the matter that has brought you here."

There were looks of visible hesitation, if not outright alarm, on the faces of his doorguards as they realized what had been said, and he looked up and down their lines. "At ease, men. The Black Birds have been at peace with Acme for nearly as long as some of you have been alive. There's no reason to think he'll break faith now." He looked back to Julia, squinting very slightly. "And if there has been some offense made of which I am unaware, I would expect that grievance to be taken up as a negotiation, rather than an ultimatum or threat."

"We are not empowered to speak openly here concerning this matter." Julia's response was cold, almost annoyed-sounding, but the Duke nodded.

"That's understood. If you'll follow me..." Without finishing his sentence, he turned and walked with apparent fearlessness back through the door. The Threebirds followed, each sensing the trepidation felt by the guards as they walked past them, both through their own perceptions and through those shared wirelessly among them.

Beyond the door lay a strange, dim catacomb whose walls were little higher than the Cybwomen's shoulders. Though essentially empty, it was still somewhat dusty, musty-smelling, and clearly disused. Short, dead-end passages led to either side off the main corridor into small alcoves; most of these housed ancient, dilapidated desks and shelves of crumbling books so dust-coated that their spines would have been unreadable even in full light. The north side of this strange place was lined with windows whose deep tint dimmed the summer sunlight outside.

At the corridor's far end lay an open, much cleaner space that was lit with multiple lanterns and surrounded by more low walls; within, there was a large table ringed with chairs. Several rows of more seats were lined up behind that, and all of the chairs in the space were occupied. On the far side of the table, a low platform had been built with a single, large, high-armed wooden seat in its center. On the low, broad step below it was another chair, much less impressive than the other. It was clear which chair belonged to the Duke.

He rounded the table and stepped up onto the platform with long-practiced ease; the Threebirds followed, and their presence prompted a low muttering of worried whispers and under-the-breath interjections. The Duke took his seat, and motioned for the Cybwomen to stand before him at the platform's base.

"So, Julia. It's been quite some time since you visited us. I had thought that that meant that the Black Birds and Acme were at peace." He tilted his head slightly. "Acme must have had good reason to send the three of you here, but I confess I am myself unaware of any cause we might have given for your visit. So tell me - " he gestured openhandedly toward them - "why are you here?"

"That information is restricted by Acme and may be disclosed *only* to the Duke of the Black Birds, until such time as he desires to release it to others." Julia's synthetic voice was sharper than Phoebe's, and noticeably more menacing, to most of the very few who had heard them both speak. Still, the Duke was not intimated, and was used to her mode of speech; he merely shrugged.

"If you chose, the three of you could kill everyone in this place. If it's my permission these people need to hear what you have to say, then that permission is granted. So let's hear it."

This response was greeted with nods and glances between the men at the table and in the gallery, but they were cut off almost immediately when Julia spoke again.

"Acme has confirmed that Jason Anderson has returned and is very much alive. He has been taken to the Covington clan's base in an attempt to hide his whereabouts." The Threebirds were as expressionless as ever as their words echoed flatly around them in the sudden silence. An instant later, the rest of the room had erupted in sudden, very loud expressions of disbelief and denial. One of the men nearest the Duke at the table rose, and standing behind the Cybwomen, he lifted his hand in a request to speak. After the hubbub went on for a brief time, the Duke rose to his feet, and the noise faded quickly back to silence. He then nodded to the man who had stood.

"Sir, that is impossible. The watch on his grave has been kept even more carefully this year than usual. It was said that this would be the summer of his return - you yourself told us this in the spring, if you will remember - and each day I have reviewed anything unusual at that site with the sergeant over the guards there. If a bird lands on his tombstone, it is reported to me. If a squirrel comes within a stone's throw, I am told.

"I was briefed this morning before arriving for this council. There has been no change at his grave. If he walks the earth today, then he didn't come out of his coffin to get here."

"That is correct," Julia's voice, somehow both flat and sharp, cut in before the Duke could respond. He looked toward her with mild surprise as she continued, "Jason Anderson and another man appeared in Acme's facility shortly before dawn. Two of our number were assigned to dispatch them. One of them killed the second man. The other led Anderson from the facility and took him to the Covington base."

The Duke thought briefly, frowning as he surveyed the gallery before him. After a few seconds, he replied, "If this man has in fact returned as you described, the Black Birds are not responsible. This happened on Acme's watch, and not ours. Should we therefore assume that we may end our watch on his grave?"

Julia responded in a different, masculine tone that was echoed by Rosamind and Lisa in unison: "Acme commands that the Black Birds muster all their available forces by sunset. They will march on the Covington clan's base and assist in the capture of Jason Anderson."

The Duke feigned puzzlement at this response, but for the first time since the Threebirds' arrival, he was unable to conceal his underlying fear completely. "I do not understand why Acme chooses to involve us. We have done no wrong either to Acme or to the Covingtons, and we did not fail in our watch on Anderson's grave. If Anderson is with the Covingtons, shouldn't Acme be able to retrieve him without our help?"

The Threebirds stepped closer to the Duke, who backed away instinctively, his eyes momentarily glancing about himself. They then spoke again in unison: "Acme requires that the Black Birds be present to engage the Covington forces. Acme will coordinate the retrieval of Anderson through his own agents."

"But you shouldn't *need* anyone to engage the Covingtons..." the Duke's voice trailed away, and as it did, horror deepened the already frightened look on his face: "...unless they have someone with Anderson who can protect him from you."

"That information is restricted by Acme." The response from the Threebirds, if anything, became even more strident. "You have been given your command. You have ten seconds to comply, or you will be neutralized and your second-in-command will be issued the same directive. Nine seconds. Eight -"

"All right, all right, all right!" the Duke cried, completely flustered. "We will order the muster and march at sunset."

As one, the Threebirds nodded, and Julia took a step forward. "We will meet you outside the gate. If you are not prepared to march by that time, Acme has ordered that we should enter this compound, and that anyone who does not submit to his command and march will be put to death."

A low, fearful muttering sounded from the gallery at this response, and one voice could clearly be heard saying, "three of *them* against us all?"

"Stop that!" The Duke's face was angry, and he pointed in the direction of the man who had spoken. "Do not think for one moment that these three won't kill everyone here to get what they want. They can, and they will. We *will* sound this muster, and we *will* march at sunset." He glowered at Julia. "Whether we want to or not."

Julia's impassive nod was the only reply he received, as the Threebirds turned and marched single-file, unimpeded as they threaded through the dark, strange labyrinth toward the exit. No one spoke, and most of the assemblage watched with dread as they departed.

Chapter Sixteen

JASON AWOKE DURING what he guessed was late afternoon in Jones' quarters. Phoebe was standing guard beside the door, her back facing him. Nothing else in the room had changed.

He turned over onto his side, groaning quietly; Phoebe turned quickly toward him, and their eyes met - his bleary with sleep, hers as unresponsive as ever. Inhaling deeply as he tried to clear the cobwebs from inside his skull, Jason mumbled, "have you been watching me this whole time?"

The synthesized voice answered. "That is my assignment. I am to accompany and protect you."

He thought about that for a moment, and then asked, "was it really necessary to stand guard like that?"

"There were several people who wandered up here for no clear reason. It appears that your identity has been revealed to at least some of the clan, and they seem curious to see you." Even for her electronic voice, her response sounded flat. Jason frowned, and sat up on the edge of the low bed, taking a deep breath as the last of his mental fog burned off.

He studied Phoebe in the dim light even as she watched him, trying to think of a way to ask the question he needed to ask without triggering a response programmed by Acme - or worse. She neither acknowledged nor ignored his attention as the silence between them deepened, not uncomfortably.

He settled on the most innocuous question he could think of: "Phoebe, can you communicate directly with Acme or the - the others like you, wirelessly?"

He was surprised to hear the same voice in response: "Each of our number can communicate electronically with any of the others. Acme is able to converse with all of us, and to perceive all communications among us, while we are in range. Outside his range, we can still communicate with each other if we are close enough."

Jason nodded. "But Acme can access all of your communications records, so if you were hiding something from him, going out of range wouldn't help."

"That is correct." Phoebe paused, but did not move, and spoke again after a few seconds. "You will need to eat and drink before we move on. We will be travelling tonight, as will the Covington clan."

Jason blinked. "The entire clan? Good. Are they going to the other base Jones talked about?"

"The clan will be retreating beyond the highway to the east, following an old road to another stronghold twelve point three miles from here," Phoebe replied. Her voice still had not changed.

Jason groaned. "Ugh. Twelve miles. On foot."

Phoebe's voice changed back to her own. "We will not be accompanying the Covingtons. We will be travelling to another destination - one which will be approximately two-thirds that distance."

"Eight miles, then." Groaning again, Jason rose to his feet. As he did, he heard a whistling sound emanate from Phoebe's lips. The sound of two pairs of feet climbing the stairs below the loft preceded the arrival of two of Jones' guards, both of whom stopped several steps from the top when they saw who had signaled them.

"Please summon your chief and inform him that Jason Anderson is awake and needs food." Phoebe's synthesized voice was back. Jason was unsurprised at that, but the response from one of the two guards was somewhat unnerving: "Yes, Phoebe. But can we look in at him? Everyone was saying he's here, and we wanted to see what he looks like."

Phoebe glanced back toward Jason, and for the first time since he had arrived, she looked somewhat nonplussed. Jason himself felt taken aback, but recovered after a moment, and said quietly, "Do you think it will be safe?"

Phoebe thought about that. "The reason the clan is leaving is that they are likely to be attacked here tonight. If they are not here when their enemies arrive, they will almost certainly be pursued - tomorrow morning, if not sooner. I think it will be no more than two days before the Black Birds may find them, and another day to act on anything they might learn from these men, assuming they are found and questioned." She still spoke in her electronic voice, and that made him look warily toward her.

A few seconds passed before he spoke again. "Do you think two days will be enough to accomplish what I am trying to do?"

A vaguely stricken look, a rare echo of near-human emotion, flitted across her face and was gone - but when she replied, it was in her own voice. "If we achieve your objective tonight, then yes, one more day should suffice - unless the Threebirds become aware of what is being done, and move against us directly."

"Who are the Threebirds?" Jason's brow furrowed.

"They are the three allies of the Black Birds from among my - peers." Phoebe spoke in a near whisper, and in her own voice. "They will be leading them here."

Jason considered. The implications of what she had just told him were frightening, and the fact that she - or someone who was using her - had already planned their next move worried him. He had not expected that she would anticipate what he had in mind. Still, there was one question he needed to ask her, and she was speaking in her own voice. The risk was huge, but without more knowledge, he could not move forward. She merely waited for him to respond, her expression as blank as ever.

He closed his eyes, and decided. "Phoebe, is there some way to disable Acme's ability to obtain data on your conversations with me?" In spite of himself, he flinched; he felt like a man sent to trigger a land mine with his bare hands.

For a long moment, there was silence; too late, Jason remembered the Covington clansmen waiting out of sight below them. He opened his eyes, and as he did, an unexpected voice issued, hurried and whispery, from Phoebe's parted lips.

"Jason, this is Robert Tinsworth. If you were not alone when that question was asked, wait until you are alone, and well away from the Drome, before you ask it again."

Phoebe's stare had become watchful; Jason knew that asking that question a second time - before the men below them had been dispatched - might prompt rash action on her part to silence him. Sighing, he said quietly to Phoebe, "let them come up. If what I think is happening is what's actually going on, it won't make much difference if they see me."

Phoebe did not respond for a few seconds, and Jason was just beginning to wonder whether she might overrule his decision when she leaned out toward the stairs, beckoning toward the two who were waiting there.

They came up quickly, but carefully; neither one wanted to get too close to Phoebe, even though she stepped back to let them pass. They were both young-looking; Jason guessed they were no more than fifteen, but they both carried themselves as though they were much older - which, he realized, they probably were, at least in terms of their life experiences. One was sandy-haired and pale, the other dark, and they both visibly had grown up in a far harsher world than he himself had.

Nevertheless, when they saw him, both youths' eyes widened and their expressions became wondering and awed. No one spoke until one of them said, "Were you really dead? What was it like?"

Jason looked from him to the other; the same question was very clearly reflected in his face. He smiled, ruefully and somewhat unwillingly, toward them as he replied.

"I don't really know. I'm dead here, but where I came from, I'm not dead, so I don't know what it feels like."

They both looked puzzled. "But you're alive. How can you be dead and alive at the same time?" asked the dark one. Jason's glance lingered on him for a moment; he suspected that he might be speaking to Jones' son.

He glanced over at Phoebe again, but her expression gave as little away as ever. Closing his eyes momentarily, he sighed, and said quietly, "I travelled through time to get here. More or less."

There was a slight tremor, barely detectable, as he spoke. They looked at him with confused uncertainty, and after a few moments, he realized that the concept of time travel was foreign to them. He looked to Phoebe again, but no help was coming from that source, and finally he said, "It's difficult for me to explain how this happened, and it won't do you much good now to understand it anyway. But I'm Jason Anderson."

The two looked at each other, and then the one who looked like Jones' boy answered, "Are you going to be our chief now?"

In spite of himself, Jason chuckled. "No, I don't want to be your chief. I'd probably be really bad at it, even if I wanted to. I barely know anything about this place."

"Really? But I thought you were supposed to know everything. The legend says that you're the smartest man in the world. You're even smarter than Acme."

Jason did a double-take. "Who said that?"

"Everyone says that," the kid replied. "You're supposed to be the one who changes the world."

Jason stared at him for several seconds, trying to find the words he needed. He glanced at his companion, then at Phoebe, and then faced him again, almost hissing, "How am I supposed to change the world? What do you think I can do, what do you think will happen?"

Both youths looked taken aback, and they looked at each other again uncertainly. Jason was about to speak again when Phoebe touched the black button on her shoulder.

"Jason Anderson cannot reveal the nature of his mission. Even Acme does not know what he intends." It was Tinsworth again, with the same hushed voice he had heard before. Their visitors stared at her in awe.

"She can use different voices!" said the one who looked like Jones' boy.

"Yes, she can." Jason's patience was beginning to run out. He glanced one last time toward Phoebe, getting no more response than usual, and then said, "Please excuse us now. Phoebe and I have to discuss a few things before we leave, and I'm sure you have things to get together before tonight."

Both of them looked slightly disappointed. Jason sighed a little, smiled slightly, and said, "You know I have a lot to do if I'm going to live up to the legends you've been telling about me. If I see you again, I'll tell you all about how I came here and why."

As he spoke these last words, their tone took on a strange note, echoing hollowly and yet with a tinny note, as if spoken from far away through an underground pipe. Even Phoebe noticed the change, as a ghost of watchful surprise awoke briefly to haunt her face. The boys looked both frightened and fascinated.

"How did you do that?" the pale one asked.

The other, the dark one who had done most of their talking, looked both warier and more scared of the two. "You sounded like a ghost." He swallowed nervously. "Are you *sure* you haven't come back from being dead?"

Jason was still slightly unnerved. "After that, I'm *not* really sure. But I don't remember ever actually dying, so I don't think so." He paused, drawing in a deep breath, and glanced once more toward Phoebe. "But whether I'm a ghost or not, we have to get ready to leave, and we need to speak privately. Please excuse us." He looked straight into their eyes, first one and then the other, until they both nodded, exchanged a glance, and went back down the stairs.

Jason heaved a sigh and sat back down on his pallet, and motioned Phoebe to sit next to him. She did not respond, except with her usual expressionless stare. He sighed again, and whispered, "You can hear me perfectly well from there, but I can't hear you whisper unless you're closer to me. Please sit down."

He expected that she would have some reason not to do as he asked, and was surprised when she crossed the room and sat beside him on the old mattress without hesitation. Still, as she turned slightly to watch him, waiting for him to speak, she still looked ready to pounce upon anything or anyone that might come up the stairs.

Jason sighed, and whispered again. "Can you turn the volume down on those recordings of yours?"

Phoebe replied in a low, strangled hiss that he could barely recognize as her whisper: "Yes, I can."

"Can you hide our conversations from Acme?" He held his breath.

She touched the button again and pursed her lips; the recording that issued from them was Tinsworth again, but quieter. He realized that it was the playback in her voice box that was modulated, rather than the recording itself, and he sighed. She could not duplicate voices; she could only play back what had been said to her. He wondered briefly how Tinsworth and Bryant had come to make the recordings, but realized that he was too tired to unravel that particular riddle. It would have to wait.

"Jason, Phoebe here is your only chance to get around Acme. All of the others' communications are slaved to his, but because of the way Phoebe had to be built, and the fact that they both came online at about the same time, Phoebe has a few functions that Acme can neither perceive nor access.

"The most important of these is that she has a separate access to the Drome's wi-fi. All of the other Cybwomen are disconnected whenever they depart from the Drome and reconnect when they return. All those connections are logged. If you are hearing this, then you are on the far side of the rift, Phoebe is away from the Drome, and is therefore not connected. If you return to the Drome with her, she *must not* sign in with a standard connection.

"To ensure that she does not, you must call her by her full name before she comes back into range. The Drome's range is larger than what you're used to, so you will have to call her by name before you get close enough for an automatic reconnection to occur."

Phoebe's expression had not changed, but Jason's had; he was frowning, thinking hard. Several seconds passed before he spoke again, still whispering: "Phoebe, if you can get in range without connecting, is it possible that one of the others like you would help us?"

Phoebe's response was slow in coming, and when it arrived, it was in her own voice, and sent a chill down his spine. "The only one that I can ask to help us is Allison. If she is shut down, and I am offline, I can still communicate with her. The communication will activate her, but it will take a few milliseconds for her systems to resume functioning, and in that time - " Phoebe stopped, and when Jason looked toward her, she looked almost human in her hesitation. "I cannot disclose this to you fully. I can reach her in a way that Acme may perceive, but which he cannot treat as solid information."

Jason was both horrified and puzzled. "Phoebe, if you mean the same Allison that killed Wiley, then we will have to find another way."

"There is no other way." Phoebe hesitated again, looking almost as she once had; seeing her, remembering what had happened to her, gave him an unexpected and almost vertiginous shock of pain and regret. He took an involuntarily gulping breath, and covered his face with his hands for a moment before recovering. She was still watching him, blankly, incurious as to the cause of his sudden and noticeable distress.

As he struggled to maintain control, Jason realized that the strain of everything he had endured had finally begun to wear through him. He looked up at her once more, still trying to think one step ahead of the avalanche of his emotions, going over what she had told him in his mind.

And then he saw it.

"Phoebe, if Allison knows something you tell her, and Acme cannot treat her knowledge as reliable information, it can only mean that Allison is herself unreliable. Is that right?"

He stared at her, awaiting her response as she stared back, looking more human than she had seemed since he had arrived. The silence lengthened between them.

"You can't tell me." He spoke again, thinking aloud. "But if it's unreliable data, it's somehow corrupted, like a bad file save or a power interruption -" As his voice trailed away, another thought crossed his mind, and he said very quietly, "Do you ever dream of me?"

Her hesitancy disappeared as she pressed the button once more, and Bryant spoke. "Don't ask too many questions, Anderson. Not unless you want to be stuck here for the rest of your life as a dead man. Or is that what you want?"

He looked away from her again, and took another deep breath, but when he faced her again, it was with a knowing smile. "I think I know - maybe not *where* we're going tonight, but definitely *why*. And if this other clan you warned me about really is coming, that place may not be guarded."

Chapter Seventeen

THE THREEBIRDS HAD spent the afternoon powering down in turn, connecting to a solar storage unit through a port that two of their counterparts had built at the old rail station north of the Black Birds' stronghold. It had long served as a recharge station for traveling Cybwomen on missions that lasted for more than a few hours.

Rosamind had recharged first, as the smallest and most power-conservative unit of the three; Julia had followed after. Lisa charged last, and the most slowly; she was one of the older units among them, and her internal batteries had begun degrading in the past year, making her slightly less efficient as the months passed.

Julia scanned Lisa's emergency BIOS readings, checking for anomalies, and found none; though her recharge time had increased, she still was fully operational. With the emotionless satisfaction that came with verifying functionality, she scanned communications frequencies for a few seconds; again that validating sensation came as she found no sign of any broadcasts within her range. There had been none for years, but since protocol dictated that she make the scan every hour when beyond the range of the Drome, she complied and performed it without consideration.

Lisa was due to resume active status within seconds, and when she did, they would return to the Black Birds' compound and rejoin their forces. They would march eastward along the old highway that led away from the ruined city until they were due south of the Covingtons' base; from there, they would move along a lesser road through the new forests that had sprung up after the Seafloods' disaster, with the intention of surprising them as they arrived from the south. The mission was simple: kill every Covington clansman who resisted, no matter how old or young, and return with Jason Anderson's head - still alive and attached to the rest of him, if at all possible.

The day was wearing toward sunset. The Black Birds had been given until shortly before then to assemble their force, which was to be waiting and ready at their return. She sensed, rather than heard or saw, the initialization routine from Lisa that indicated her return from inactivity, and received Rosamind's readings at the same time. She performed a cursory, final system check on herself, preparing to depart the station to meet their Black Bird escort, when an unexpected burst of activity emitted from the interface between Lisa's CPU and her brain stem.

Julia froze for what would have been an imperceptible instant, to a human observer; but there were no true humans nearby to see it. She glanced toward Rosamind, who returned her gaze a millisecond later before both their stares focused on Lisa, who had just reactivated. Her eyes were wide and blankly puzzled, and the hand that passed over her brow made a nearly human gesture before she looked first to Rosamind, then Julia, and said, quietly and aloud, "You sensed that."

Julia's stare betrayed a ghost of baleful mistrustfulness. "We both did."

"The sensation was similar to a data purge, but without organization in the deleted sectors." Lisa's speech would have seemed slow to a human; to Julia and Rosamind, it was much too slow. Julia calculated in background that a comparable delay would have implied a stroke to a human, and her eyes narrowed involuntarily in a vestigially angry reaction.

"Run a full system OS check. Now. If you have any defective sectors, you are to return at once to the Drome for a full-scale abiotic scan."

Lisa nodded, and her head tilted slightly downward as she started the scan. Julia opened a private communications channel with Rosamind. Their conversation was silent and electronic, urgent, and very brief; when Lisa completed her scan, she broadcast wirelessly, and without even any electronic lag, to each of them: "System OS check complete. All sectors confirmed operational."

"Acknowledged." Both Cybwomen opened their channel to Lisa, speaking simultaneously over the airwaves, before Julia continued,

"Maintain communications via this channel only until the Covington clan has been engaged. I will direct the Black Birds' march."

With that, the Threebirds departed from the station, matching south through the outskirts of the derelict city, making a direct line through the reforested ruins toward the Black Birds' home. All three monitored their surroundings, maintaining a steady, braided flow of sensory input as they moved. Julia continued measuring Lisa's responses as they walked purposefully, checking for any anomalies, but found none. In the way that a human might make a mental note, Julia set a background algorithm to run in her own brain - one that would review Lisa's responses and intervene if such an anomaly were to develop.

Their pace was rapid even for their kind, and the distance they needed to travel was short enough so that even though the sun was reddening when they departed, they still crossed the bridge over the east-west highway leading out of the city and reached their destination with some time remaining before it could set. As they reached the compound, they saw a crowd of dark-clad men milling in the road that ran south beside the eastern wall.

The voiceless conversation among them was immediate and in complete agreement: the Black Bird forces, while certainly savage enough in past battles against their neighbors, lacked both discipline and training, and would require their coordination to be useful. As they agreed on this, they walked three abreast toward a knot of men whose relative cleanliness and quality of equipment indicated high rank. One of them noticed their approach and turned, raising his hand in the same gesture of truce that had been used earlier that day. It was the one called the Duke.

"Welcome, Threebirds. We have done our best to do as you have ordered, and our men are gathered and ready to march."

Lisa and Rosamind both looked toward Julia, who was visibly annoyed in a way that she alone among the Cybwomen could convey. She stepped forward toward the Duke, speaking to him in a low voice even as she coordinated the division of forces with the other two.

"Your forces are unorganized and unprepared. This will be a serious and dangerous operation, one that Acme requires - but you and your people cannot be trusted to complete it." Julia's glare caused even the Duke to flinch; the men behind him began backing away. "We will therefore divide your men and lead them ourselves."

The Duke's face betrayed fear, but it was alloyed by something else that none of the Threebirds immediately recognized. "If you wish to assume command of our forces, then I will yield command to you, and assist you in any way you request. I ask only that you remember that these men have lived all their lives in fear of your kind, and may not respond well without their own leaders' direction."

Julia was momentarily put out of reckoning by the Duke's response, as was Rosamind; Lisa's eyes briefly became unfocused, though her expression remained otherwise changeless, and neither of her counterparts noted the difference. As Julia considered, Lisa sent a thought to them both, and they answered without betraying any outward sign of their electronic conversation.

Rosamind's thought flitted between Lisa and Julia, uncertain as to how she should respond owing to the complexity of the situation. Julia's native anger was checked only by Lisa's unspoken observation: "Acme requires these men for his purpose. If they are to be effective when they reach our destination, they may require guidance from someone they are accustomed to following."

The Duke never fathomed or even noticed their conversation, which took place in the space of an eyeblink, but he understood almost at once that his request would be granted. Lisa's nod to him confirmed his intuition.

With visible relief and no small amount of gratitude, he nodded to each of the Threebirds in turn, and then said to Julia, "I will divide our officers into three groups that will answer to each of you, and our men into three companies under our officers. This will be done at once, so that we may depart at sunset. Will that be acceptable?"

"That will be acceptable." Julia was still operating within the parameters she expected, but Lisa's suggestion - one that was certainly in tune with Acme's wishes, and therefore difficult to question - still represented a deviation from her typical pattern.   She rechecked the algorithm, but again found no anomalies.

Her hesitation remained imperceptible to the men around them. Rosamind queried them both again wirelessly as to how they would proceed, and Julia responded aloud, "That is acceptable, Duke.   Divide your men, and have them assembled in formation before the sun has set."

The Duke nodded.   "What route will we take?"

Julia looked at him with her faintly threatening stare, and he continued, defensively and slightly defiantly, "my officers at least should know which way we're going.   Otherwise, it will look like you're forcing us to do this, and that will encourage desertions."

"No one will be allowed to desert." Rosamind spoke aloud for the first time.   "Any Black Bird who leaves formation will be escorted back to his position. Anyone who resists escort will be terminated."

Julia nodded, as did Lisa; again, there was something that, if not anomalous, was out of Lisa's typical behavior pattern. Julia considered for a microsecond, then said, "we will march by the old eastern highway out of the city until we are south of the Covingtons' base, and then march straight north toward them. By staying off the roads near their compound, we should surprise them. If Anderson has left, we will compel them to tell us where he is going, and we will be able to pursue him from that point."

The Duke nodded slowly.   "Very well. One last question, if I may, and we will form up."

Julia fixed her stare on him. "Ask quickly."

He nevertheless stared straight toward her for a few seconds before speaking.   "We will obey your orders.   But I ask that you refrain from committing these men to battle unless it is necessary."

This request was as atypical of the Black Birds as Lisa's behavior had been.   She considered in a flash whether the algorithm she was using to evaluate Lisa might be expanded to a more generalized diagnostic of all of her informational input, reached an affirmative conclusion, and replied not only to the Duke, but to Lisa and Rosamind as well.   "It is unlikely that battle can be avoided. Jason Anderson is a figure of great importance to the Covingtons, and to yourselves as well. If the Covingtons seek to protect him, you will have to engage them so that we can pursue Anderson without any delay."

The Duke swallowed, and muttered softly, "Better him than me. Please excuse me." He held up his palm in salute to them, and then turned back to his officers, giving them hurried instructions for dividing their forces. They obeyed quickly, noting as they did that the day was beginning to fail.

Beyond them, the officers began barking orders at the rank-and-file Black Bird soldiers, forming them into three vaguely organized companies. Julia watched them, noting that though their lines were not very even, and some were not very well armed or equipped, they still would be adequate for Acme's purpose.

The Duke was arguing quietly with one of his officers, who had remained beside him; she recognized him as one of the men who had been at the court table earlier that day. He was speaking in a low, urgent voice to the Duke. Julia directed the focus of her auditory input channels toward them.

"Sir, we can't just march on the Covingtons like that. We've been at peace with them, and a lot of the reason for that is Acme. Now they want us to go to war on them, for no reason except they say that this Jason Anderson guy is with them. Even if that's true, we don't have any good reason to fight them. We'd be betraying them, and they probably won't forget that for a long time."

The Duke glowered back at him. "Do you think I, of all people, don't know that?" His shoulders sagged and he took a deep breath, and when he spoke again, he was quiet enough that even Julia had to listen carefully. "Todd, I know this is a bad idea. We're going to march ten miles at night, and maybe have to fight when we get there. They'll be defending their home. There's no way we'll catch them off guard in their own compound, any more than they could with us. If we have to fight them, we could lose."

"So what do we *do*?" Todd's voice carried a rising note of desperation. The Duke glared at him, motioning him to be quieter, and for a moment his eyes locked with Julia's as she watched them.

In that moment, the anger drained from his eyes, and when he turned back toward his officer, the Duke's voice was nearly as cold and emotionless as the Threebirds' as he replied, "we do as they ask. We make sure we're ready to fight when we get there. And we hope it doesn't come to that. That's all we can do."

With that, the Duke walked away, south along the compound's eastern wall, looking over the companies as he passed them. The Threebirds did not move, but silently, they each acknowledged that the Black Birds would comply, and that they would be on their way before full darkness fell.

Chapter Eighteen

THE COVINGTONS WERE preparing to evacuate as the red sun neared the western horizon.

Jason had been brought a strange, flat type of bread wrapped around a mix of greens and raw vegetables; there were no meats, and nothing other than the bread was cooked. He could only eat it by challenging himself to finish it all, and even then, in spite of his hunger, he wanted to stop - but as he looked around the compound, watching as the entire clan packed everything it could hope to carry the twelve miles east to their destination, he realized that there were no livestock anywhere in sight. He thought for a moment, trying to recall their arrival, but he couldn't remember seeing even a chicken or goat anywhere.

He said nothing, but gulped down the rest of what he had been given with as few grimaces as he could, watching Phoebe as he did. They both stood alone on the roof of the base, looking out over the surrounding garden and the assembly green on the north side of the building. He had not seen that as they entered - their door had been on the eastern side - and as he looked out, he realized just how few people must be left in the world.

When assembled, the entire clan - men, women and children - numbered well under a thousand. They had no vehicles except for carts that they pulled themselves, no animals, no light other than torches, and only a few makeshift weapons. As they watched, the guardsmen organized them into two loose lines, and began marching them around the moat toward the gate where he and Phoebe had entered that morning.

Jason shook his head. He had had some rest, but not enough, and the prospect of an eight-mile walk - at least - was daunting. As he watched the Covingtons moving toward the gatehouse where Scotty had watched them, he felt a pang of guilt - but then he remembered what would happen if he somehow succeeded in his plan, and another wave of what felt like vertigo washed over him, so much so that he was afraid to speak.

Phoebe watched him, as expressionlessly as always. She had not spoken as their hosts had gathered for departure, and Jason had no desire to make her break her silence. The files below them made their way out, until only a few men and the chief himself remained; two of them were the same pair that had visited Jason earlier that day. The chief looked up at them, and waved.

"I don't know what it is you're here to do, but I hope you get it done quickly," he called. "We'd like to get back here as soon as we can."

"I hope that it won't be very long, but I can't say for sure," Jason called back. He looked curiously at the young pair again. "I hope this isn't rude of me to ask, but is that your son?"

Jones' face split into a wide smile. "Yeah, that's my boy. I hear these two paid you a visit this afternoon."

"He did." Jason glanced at the son, who looked slightly disgruntled. "Keep those two close, all right? By now I'd bet half your people know they talked to us. If these Black Birds find that out, they'll want to question them, and they've got three of Phoebe's kind with them. I don't think that'd go too well." The last sentence was accompanied by a slight reverberation. A light fall of dust shook loose from the wall of the base.

Jones' smile faded into a decidedly unsettled, worried cast. "You're right," he replied, as he glanced toward the two youths. "Shawntaine, you heard the man. You two stay in shouting range. If the Black Birds are looking for you, I want to be able to send you off."

Shawntaine looked dismayed. "Pop, I want to fight with everyone else. This is what I trained for."

"You were trained to fight alongside everyone in this base. You weren't trained to have a target on your back, and now that you've talked with Anderson, that's what you've got. We can't expect everyone to keep that secret. So you stay close, and if I tell you to run, you run."

Shawntaine glowered back at his father, but did not reply, and after a few moments the boys joined the last marchers out of the compound. Jones looked up at Anderson one more time.

"We'll be some twelve miles east of here, or somewhere close to that. I just hope they don't turn us away."

Jason thought. "If they do, your best choice is to head south into the hills. It'll be hard to follow you through there and you'll get an advantage on the higher ground. I'm hoping you won't have to hold out there long. I think the Black Birds will turn back if you have to go on from Stonecrest."

Jones squinted. "Stonecrest. Yeah, that's the name of the place. You know it?"

"Only from my time, and that was a long time ago. But if someone's built it up like you've done here, you might be safe. It might be too big for them to defend themselves, if the Black Birds send enough men, or if Phoebe's friends get involved." Jason sighed. "Good luck, Jones. Be careful out there."

Jones snorted. "Doesn't matter how careful we are if they're sending three of Phoebe's kind after us. I just hope it doesn't come to a fight. No one wins that."

Jason couldn't reply, and only nodded in response; Jones' eyes were somber as they shifted. "Phoebe. Keep him safe."

"That is my task." The synthesized voice responded, and Jones nodded. Then he turned, last in the line of Covingtons, and went around the moat toward the guard shack. Jason and Phoebe were left alone.

"So where are we going first?" Jason asked Phoebe, looking toward her with a small smile.

Phoebe responded in her own voice. "We will go around the Drome, far enough to the south to stay out of its range, until we come to the old college in the area that was called Decatur."

"Agnes Scott." Jason nodded, wondering if she had accounted completely for his question. "Any particular reason we're going there?"

"Allison normally shuts down at the far southwestern corner of the Drome. It is as far from Acme as she can be without leaving, and she does not like being closer to him unless she is specifically ordered to be. There is an area on the Agnes Scott campus from which my range can reach Allison without extending to Acme. I can activate her from there and tell her what we need for her to do."

Jason frowned. "Phoebe, I don't want to involve Allison. She killed my colleague when we came across."

"She did as she was instructed by Acme." Phoebe's synthesized response was toneless, even for her.

"I'm not sure I believe that." Jason rounded on her. She gazed back expressionlessly toward him. "I know who Acme is. Or who he was, at least. I don't know that I believe he'd order his own murder. Wiley Grant was a good physicist, but he was a lousy human being and a coward."

Phoebe pressed the button again, and this time, it was Allen Bryant who answered him. "Wiley Grant was a piece of shit. But he was a smart piece of shit, and after I got what was left of him attached to the mainframe at the station, he had plenty of time to do nothing but think. He was the one who did the calculations and figured out the tech to extend the Einstein-Rosen bridge your team created. Took him almost five years, even hooked to a mainframe. Even after that, he still wasn't able to compute the vectors he'd need to extend it here. Last I heard, he was still working on it.

"Grant is smarter, much faster-thinking, and much more powerful since he was changed into what he is. He's a lot more brilliant and dangerous than he would ever have been if he had remained human. Unfortunately, he died in a state of panic, and that affected his thought processes even after he was revived in his new form. He's become a paranoid megalomaniac who thinks he can become immortal. I won't even try to tell you what his theology is. Good luck stopping him."

Jason nodded resignedly as he listened. "I had guessed some of this. I wouldn't be surprised if he blames me for not staying with him."

Phoebe did not answer. They turned at the same time and watched as the sun set. Jason noticed that the skyline of the abandoned city, miles to their west, was subtly changed: several buildings were no longer visible, and the air was clearer than he could remember it ever being. He guessed that the missing buildings had collapsed, or had been somehow destroyed, in the intervening time.

The sun had touched the horizon when Phoebe broke their silence. "It is time. We must go." She looked at him blankly, awaiting his agreement.

He needed to know one more thing. "Phoebe, what happens if these Threebirds realize what we're doing? You say you can get in range of Allison without being detected by Acme. Agnes Scott is a mile from the Drome. What happens if we come within a mile of them?"

"I calculate that their most likely approach to the Covington base will not take them near the Drome. Acme would not allow that. They will pass well to the south and come up from there toward the base, thinking that the Covingtons will expect them to come from the east." Phoebe spoke in her own voice.

"How far to the south?"

"The old highway that runs east from the Black Birds' compound goes straight for slightly less than three miles before bending south. From there, there is a smaller road that continues as far east as they will be going. If they remain on that road, they will be far enough south for us to move west between them without coming into range of either one."

Jason sighed. The sun had gone down. "Then we need to move, now. They won't be here for some time and it will be at least three hours' walk to the college."

They climbed down the ladder back into the dark, empty base and made their way out through the doors to the guard shack. The gardens around them were a calm, deep green in the cooling twilight. They did not speak until they had left the shack and were travelling west, back the way they had come.

"Was Scotty right to be so afraid of you?" Jason suddenly asked. On that near-dark, emptily quiet stretch of road, his voice sounded unnaturally flat and loud. For a moment it made him nervous, but before long he realized that there was nothing to hear him.

Phoebe did not reply, and they continued northwest for a little less than a mile before Phoebe motioned toward a smaller street leading off to the left, more westward as the road bent more to the north. "We follow that road until it comes to another highway, and take it for almost a mile southwest. There is a confluence of routes there; one will take us almost due west almost two miles to our last road, which takes us one mile north to our destination." She was still using her own voice.

Jason thought about that. "I think I know the way. I never went around Agnes Scott all that much, but Tinsworth lives near there - I mean, he lived there, before."

"That is correct." The synthesized voice returned briefly, but was again replaced by her own voice. "He continued to live there, long after Acme was installed in the Drome. It was dangerous for him, and eventually some of the Black Birds ambushed him there and killed him."

This didn't ring true to Jason. "Wasn't Tinsworth working with Acme and Bryant?"

"He was."

"Then why would the Black Birds have risked coming as close to the Drome as he lived? It sounds to me like a setup." Jason stopped as they reached the road they would take west. "Did Acme kill Dr. Tinsworth? And was Bryant in on it?"

Phoebe spoke in her own voice again. "Tinsworth had begun telling the different clans that you would return from the dead. He and Bryant were having disagreements, and with you dead, Tinsworth had no more allies. He was the one who first sent me to the Covingtons, because he knew that if he continued visiting them, Acme or Bryant might cause them a lot of trouble."

"So you became their liaison." Jason paused, and smiled a little; Phoebe did not respond. "And so we're back to my question - was Scotty right to be so afraid of you?"

"Scotty was wise to fear my kind," the synthesized voice replied. "I believe that he heard some of the stories that were related by the Black Birds who visited them. They have their own allies - the Threebirds, as I have told you - but they are afraid of them, with good reason. If one of the Black Birds told him of what happened to the men in their clan who tried to storm the Drome, then fear would be a reasonable response."

Jason had been about to start walking again, but paused. "Wait. The Black Birds tried to attack the Drome? When?"

"Thirty-one years ago. They were ambushed in a tunnel under the rail tracks by all the remaining members of my kind, except Allison and myself. Most of them were killed before they finally tried to surrender. Acme had ordered that no surrender would be permitted, so the rest were killed as well. No one among my kind suffered any injury." The synthesized voice spoke once more. Jason thought for a moment, then whistled.

"That would have been horrifying. But Phoebe, you weren't there. You never harmed any of the Covingtons, did you?"

Phoebe's ragged voice returned. "Never. They understood that I would not attack them, and that I would defend myself only as needed. They in turn ensured that I would never need to defend myself."

Jason nodded. "That's the most like yourself that I've seen you act since I got here. I'm glad to know that at least a little of you is still in there."

Phoebe did not answer, and together they set out on the westward road toward the college.

Interlude

12 January 2049

THE THREEBIRDS HAD just returned through a frigid evening from an unusual patrol into the largely unpopulated, long-burnt-out ruins north of the Drome when they were hailed electronically by Acme.

The summons came as no surprise to them, as they were creatures without expectation, but it was unusual in that they detected it the moment they passed within range of Acme's wireless communication. The message was of higher priority than was normal. They would have responded, instantly and collectively, regardless.

Acme's communication took several milliseconds - an extraordinarily long time, for him - and when it was finished, all of them felt a strange, mental echo of something which would have been visceral to their old selves, but was merely unacceptable to their current ones. It required an immediate remedy, however - enough so that Acme would allow them to recharge directly from his own base, rather than through their normal shutdown mode.

The three Cybwomen therefore marched three abreast, as per their custom, toward the center of the Drome, to the building where Acme was housed, and where Allen Bryant had lived until two years before. His old quarters had been dark since that day, save for the month when Allison had been ordered to remain there. The minute that her orders from Acme had expired, she had fled the building, and spent much of her time since then at the southwestern corner of the Drome's confines, as far from Acme as she could be without violating the perimeter. Acme rarely communicated with her, and she never with him.

When they arrived, Bryant's old quarters were lit, and they noted that the interior air had been heated as they entered. Phoebe knelt beside the old bed, on which sat a black-haired human youth of perhaps fifteen years. He was wrapped in a blanket and held an old plastic cup between both hands, which shook so violently that Phoebe had to help him keep from sloshing its contents on the floor, the blanket and himself.

Phoebe did not look up, and her communication was wirelessly silent: "He says his name is Angelino Duke. Acme told you the rest."

Julia glowered down at the boy. "Are you telling us the truth? And can you tell us which ones are doing this?"

Angelino looked fearfully up at her, then to Phoebe, whose blank face communicated no comfort. Shakily, he said, "It's all of them. Everyone on the court. Stevens made them do it. He said he couldn't trust them if they didn't, and he'd eat them too unless they did."

Phoebe could hear the silent communications among the four of them; none suspected that he was lying. That would have been illogical, at any rate: it was so cold that night that the boy had risked his life simply daring to go out, just to reach the most dangerous place anywhere near him. She asked quietly, "We have to be able to prove what you say is the truth, and show the rest of your people why, if we decide to remove Stevens and his court."

"They all know about it. They dump what's left outside the wall, south of the compound. Everyone's too scared to do anything." He looked pleadingly, tremblingly at Phoebe. "Please, help. I don't want them to eat me."

Through all of their communications, Acme spoke. "This boy does not seem to be lying. Julia, you will take Rosamind and Lisa and go to the Black Birds' base. Look for any place where human bones are being dumped or burned. If you find evidence, you will rendezvous with Annette and Darleen at the northeast corner of the compound, and the five of you will rout out Stevens and his people.

"Annette and Darleen will be sent to verify the guard on Anderson's grave. If there is any sign that those guards have partaken, they will be liquidated and replaced once the situation with Stevens is resolved.

"Phoebe, you will allow this boy to warm himself for two hours, and you will then take him back to his people. By the time you arrive, this situation should be resolved. You will then return and report to me on what transpires."

The Threebirds turned as one and left Bryant's old quarters. Phoebe could hear them planning their journey with Annette and Darleen, two others of their kind who had been tasked with maintaining the rail line and its electrical grid. They rarely spoke with anyone in the Drome, and were often away for long periods of time, but had returned from a long journey to the city's far western edge only that afternoon. Having already recharged, Annette and Darleen departed at once for Anderson's grave; the Threebirds connected themselves to Acme's power grid from outside the base. In an hour they would be ready to depart.

To the boy she said nothing. He knew nothing more of interest to her, and she had no mothering instinct of any kind. She did, however, know that if the Black Birds had begun eating their own, then the food situation there had become desperate. It was the middle of a very cold winter, so there were no greenstuffs or edible plants to be found - and wild game, which had never been plentiful in the region to begin with, had been driven out years before.

"Acme." Her communication was instantaneous, on a separate channel, and his response was nearly so: "Yes, Phoebe."

"If the Black Birds have resorted to cannibalism, then it is unlikely that they have other food available."

"I am not unaware of the implications concerning your own liaison, Phoebe. From what you have told me of your assigned tribe, there are sufficient provisions stored there for both clans to survive the winter." Acme thought for a few microseconds. "How resistant would the Covingtons be to the redistribution of their stores?"

Phoebe considered. "They would want specific assurances from the Drome and the Black Birds, especially since they have become more aggressive since Stevens became their chief."

"He will not be chief come morning. I am quite certain this boy has told us the truth. At first light, I want for you to travel to the Covingtons' base. You will explain to them what has happened and convey my request - it is a demand, but perhaps it should not be presented as one - that they should be prepared to share any food they have with the Black Birds."

Phoebe said nothing. At one time, Acme would have made his request directly via radio, but the near-impossibility of securing those communications - and the unusual amount of interference generated by the Drome technology - had at last led him to conclude that the Cybwomen would serve more effectively as his messengers.

Acme noted her unresponsiveness, and continued, "On reconsideration, and to show evidence of the severity of the situation, you will bring this boy with you. He will tell them directly of what has happened with the Black Birds. Once he has delivered his testimony, and the Covingtons have agreed to share their stores, you will return him to his home."

"You are certain that they will agree?" Phoebe herself did not know how the tribe assigned to her would respond to the night's events.

"I am. The number of human beings in this region is slowly lessening. The Covingtons have begun to flourish, but they are the exception. The Black Birds are clearly in peril. The ruins to the west and the burnouts to the north are untenable for habitation. To the south, the groundwater and the land are contaminated by the century of waste disposal that preceded the Seafloods. Only to the east is there evidence that our original species can continue to exist, and eventually repopulate."

"There is another tribe farther east, well beyond the highway that bounds the Covington lands. They have sent scouts there, but they are nearly a day's journey farther out, and I know little of them."

"My knowledge of them is limited to yours, in this instance." Acme contemplated for another microsecond. "If need be, they can be enlisted to assist as well, but it would be preferable to avoid any additional engagement at this time."

"Acknowledged." Phoebe then addressed the shivering boy, who still sat on the edge of the bed. For him, almost no time had passed. "You may rest here tonight. In the morning, I will take you to visit another clan, so that you can tell them what has happened. Acme is going to ask them to send food to your people."

The boy was still shaking violently, but he managed to raise his head in a small smile. "Thank you. What is your name? Do you have one?"

"Yes, I am called Phoebe. Do you need water before you rest, or food?"

"Yes, please. I haven't had anything to eat for two days." Angelino's expression was grateful, and some of his shaking had stopped as his body warmed.

"Wait here. Don't leave this room - this place is not safe for you, and the cold is dangerous. Some of our number can still metabolize foods into energy. There should be something stored that you can have." Phoebe stood, turning as she did, and left the boy in Bryant's old quarters, closing the door behind her against the frigid winter air as she left.

PART THREE - THE END OF ALL THINGS

Chapter Nineteen

THE BLACK BIRD COMPANIES moved east along an old road through the night, keeping their ranks close because of the narrowness of the way and the thickness of the dark.

They had taken the great highway east until it began a shallow, southward bend. A bridge that had once crossed over the thoroughfare had fallen, and rather than go over the crumbling wreckage to continue south, the makeshift army had instead climbed the tilting, concrete slope of the ruined span up to its northern end. From there, a road that had once led to that bridge ran in a nearly straight east-west line for several miles, and it was that road that they followed east for most of their march.

The Duke and Todd had been in the vanguard, marching behind Lisa and Rosamind; Julia was in the rear, keeping the more unwilling soldiers in line. None of them spoke, and the Duke supposed that the Threebirds could somehow communicate their thoughts to one another. This was not a comforting idea, as it meant that his own thoughts might be readable to them as well.

They had continued east through several cross-roads, where the reforested land opened out somewhat into expanses of broken concrete and abandoned, decaying buildings. Another road was dimly visible ahead of them in the midnight gloom, and as they neared it, Lisa turned toward him and said, "Prepare to order a halt just ahead."

"Yes, Lisa," he responded. He glanced at Todd, whose face was barely visible in the gloom, and would have conveyed no meaningful information to him at any rate. He sighed. He was more out of shape than he had realized, and he knew he should check the men before they made their push north to the Covington base.

"Wait here," he said quietly. "I'm going to check the ranks."

"Aren't the - the women from the Drome going to do that?" Todd asked, glancing nervously at the pair that were in front of them.

"Yes, but it will be better if they see me checking them. I don't need them thinking they only have to answer to those three, or there will be trouble down the road." The Duke sighed, then called out a cadence ending with a command for a halt. Before Todd could say anything more, he had turned and begun moving down the lines, checking them as best he could in the nearly pitch-darkness.

Before he had gone even halfway down the ranks, he knew that their best hope would be to win without a fight. Nearly all of his men visibly slumped where they stood, giving off an almost tangible air of dispirited tiredness. Only a few here and there still remained erect and at attention; as he passed, he motioned to those who still looked alert and relatively ready, gathering them around himself a little way from where Julia waited at the end of the file.

Even these, the hardiest of his soldiers, gave off an aura of uncertainty as he addressed them. "We all know about what the situation is here. None of us wants a fight right now, especially at night after a march, but we're probably going to have to fight.

"You all are the best we have right now. I'm counting on you to watch out for the men around you, keep them together, and keep them following orders as long as you can. The women you see with us - well, you know." He glanced meaningfully back toward Julia. She was looking around herself constantly, scanning the area, but he knew his conversation was both audible and monitored. "They're looking for something, and they want us to keep the Covingtons occupied while they look for it.

"That means that we're still going to have to deal with the Covingtons again after this is done, and if we go in there trying to kill everyone on sight, it'll be that much harder to work anything out with them later. Wherever you can, try to take prisoners or make truces."

"And what if they try to kill us?" asked one of the shadows around him. He was tall and hulking, with a deep voice.

"Defend yourselves. I'm not telling you not to kill. I'm telling you to kill only if you have no other choice." He glanced back at Julia again. "You've seen how it is. They're going to make us fight. Your orders are simple: stay alive. Keep the men around you alive. Kill as few of the enemy as you can."

His only response was a defeated-seeming silence, and though it was too dark for anyone to see his face, he gave them a grim smile and a nod. "Return to your ranks, then," he added, and turned to make his way back to the vanguard.

Todd was waiting there when he returned. Rosamind stood beside him, and even in the dark he could feel her flat, blank stare, more intimidating than any glower. He took a deep breath, and said quietly, "we are ready to move on at your command."

"Why did you tell your men not to kill your enemies?" Rosamind asked.

"They are not our enemies," the Duke responded. "We are only on this march because you ordered it, not because we want to be here."

"Nevertheless, your men are expected to fight, not to surrender. Any man who puts down his weapons will be put to death. Any man who refuses to fight will be executed. Is that clear?"

The Duke glared down at her shadowy form, anger momentarily overcoming his concerns. "Yes, it's clear. It's clear that we should reconsider a great many things when we return. We should decide how we will try to restore our relations with the Covingtons after you force us to attack them. We should decide whether we will continue to live in our own compound or move somewhere beyond the reach of Acme and his servants."

Lisa had moved next to Rosamind as he spoke, and it was she who replied. "Acme has not ordered you into this battle without cause. The Covingtons harbor Jason Anderson. Acme has stated that Anderson has the ability to destroy our entire world." She leaned closer. "Acme will broker any peace agreement that is made after the outcome of this matter is determined. You will not be held responsible for this night's actions."

"I don't care about my responsibility!" The Duke's anger spilled over as his voice rose. "I care about these men behind me. I care about the families they have back in the compound. The *only* reason I'm agreeing with this march is because I know you'll force them to do it anyway. As long as I'm here, I might be able to help them. I might be able to make sure a few more of them make it back to their families."

Neither Cybwoman moved, but the Duke sensed that something passed between them, and when the reply came, it was from Rosamind, and was addressed aloud to Lisa: "Shall I return to their compound and liquidate it?"

The Duke's blood ran cold. "No. Please don't do that." He could barely breathe.

"Your desire to protect your people is commendable, but the danger to them is greater if you do nothing than if you send these men into battle. Jason Anderson *must* be apprehended," Lisa replied.

The Duke's breath hissed between his teeth. "Only because *you* have made the danger greater to them."

"Enough." Lisa took a short step forward; the men surrounding the Duke all shrank back. "We will turn north here. If you will not order your men to fight for the enemy, we will order them to fight to save their families."

"That won't be necessary," the Duke answered in a growling, shaking, furious hiss.

"Then give the order to your soldiers," Rosamind said tonelessly.

The Duke snarled something inarticulate under his breath before he turned, raising his voice to speak to his men as he took a few steps toward the ranks. "Black Birds! We will go north now. The Covington compound is only a short march from here. Be prepared to fight as soon as we arrive.

"I spoke with some of you before about the necessity for each of you to look out for one another. I am now telling all of you this same message. If you wish to go home, whether it be tomorrow or in a month, you will have to fight - and you will have to fight as hard as you can.

"Don't go forward into this night because of me. Don't even do it because these three - things - are making you." He glared back over his shoulder toward Rosamind. "Do it for your families. Do it for yourselves. Do it because you want to live to see another day. Another spring. Another year." He inhaled deeply, sighed, and spoke once more, with the echoes of his voice flatly resounding off the concrete of the road and the few standing buildings around them. "And do it for each other. We're all in this together now." With a fierce scowl, he returned to his place at the front of the van, and snarled at Rosamind, "whenever you decide you're ready."

Rosamind turned on her heel as Lisa replied quietly to him, "We go. Follow us." Then she also turned and walked away, increasing her pace until she and Rosamind were side by side. The Duke nodded to Todd, who counted out a cadence as the Black Bird army began to follow the Cybwomen north along a narrow road that was half-overgrown with grass erupting from its many cracks. The trees leaned close on either side as they went up a long, low hill, as straight as an arrow's flight north before it leveled out, then descended just as shallowly.

After about a mile, they came to an intersection of several old routes beneath the encroaching trees; their own track forked straight and left, with the shadowy remains of an abandoned church nestled between, while a third track led away to their right, eastward into the night. The Cybwomen did not stop, but took the left fork without hesitation, and the Duke followed them with his men. They proceeded northwestward, still gradually climbing, for nearly another half-mile before the close woods opened out ahead of them onto a broad, cracked expanse of highway. The Duke could just make out a low rampart on its far side, running northwest-to-southeast before them.

He had been in this place once, long before, and had been kindly received by the people there. The Covingtons' chief at the time had been greeted that morning by Phoebe, who had brought him there from the Drome. The chief's daughter, a pretty girl named Kelly who was nearly his own age, had complained loudly when her parents had taken him in and given him her bed; she had still been crying angrily when he himself had drifted off to sleep that night.

She had been nicer to him after that first day, though, along with everyone else he met there. He supposed Phoebe had told them everything that had happened. Phoebe had returned him home two days later, just as the surviving Black Bird elders were meeting to choose a new leader for themselves. No one had asked him where he had gone, and he had never told anyone the truth of that night.

But as he stood at the side of the ancient highway, looking out toward the Covingtons' base, he realized that the night was too dark, and too quiet. Even with most of the base asleep, there should have been at least some low noise, some indication of the hundreds of people living there. Instead, everything was as still as death, and there was no light from anywhere behind the compound wall.

The Duke breathed a deep sigh of relief. "They're not here. They've gone."

"That is also our conclusion."   Lisa responded quietly and flatly. Rosamind was silent.

But before the Duke could even begin to form a prayer of thanks, Lisa continued, "We believe that the Covingtons have evacuated east beyond the highway, to another stronghold approximately twelve miles from here. We shall have to march there in pursuit."

"No!" The Duke's response burst from his lips as Lisa's words sank in. "These men cannot do another forced march - especially not that far. They won't be able to fight when they get there, and they'll be facing men that will be rested and waiting for them to appear. They have to rest, now, and march in the morning, if only to give them any kind of a chance."

"Acme does not require victory, only a diversion." Rosamind's bland voice was somehow even cooler than normal.

"Acme won't have either one, if you try to force these men to march now. I will not give the order. If you give it, I will defy it, and instruct my men to do the same. They will not give their lives for Acme. Many of them remember the last time Acme interceded in our affairs." He spoke the last words bitterly, hating that he had been forced to make his point in such a way.

"Acme interceded because your leaders had resorted to cannibalism - as you should remember," Lisa replied. "Acme demands that you risk your lives here because they are already jeopardized by the presence of Jason Anderson. If you want to continue to live, you will do as you are instructed."

"Fuck you, Lisa." All the men's heads nearby snapped to look at him as he spoke. "You offer us a choice - die here and now, or make a march that amounts to torture just to die anyway. We're already dead men in either event. So - if you want to kill us all, do it now. We're not marching another step." He crossed his arms and faced her squarely, only just able to make out her blank features in the first bare predawn brightening. Several of his vanguard, including Todd, moved to stand beside him.

Lisa closed her eyes for nearly a full second; when they opened, Rosamind's head turned toward her, glaring with a blank echo of wariness. But it was Lisa who answered.

"Very well. I calculate that it will make little difference whether we pursue them now or at midmorning, but it could make a great deal of difference without a diversion. If the Covingtons have moved east, then they are likely seeking refuge with another clan at a place called Stonecrest. This force may be overmatched even if rested; without rest, it may be unable to complete its orders sufficiently to aid Acme's purpose.

"You may rest here until the sun is halfway to the zenith. At that time, we will march again, so as to reach Stonecrest with sufficient daylight remaining. Will you accept this rather than refuse to fight?"

The Duke sighed, and glanced through the darkness toward Todd, who despite standing in solidarity beside him, looked terrified. He knew this situation might play itself out again within hours, but at least he had bought them that much time.

"We accept," he replied, resignedly. Lisa and Rosamind both nodded, and walked past him toward the rearguard and Julia. The Duke heaved a sigh of relief, clapped a hand to Todd's shoulder, and began calling orders for a rest, and for a watch to be set.

Chapter Twenty

THE NIGHT WAS GROWING old as Jason and Phoebe made their way north, gradually uphill along a tree-sheltered road that had held up better than most he had seen.

They had walked generally eastward through the old city's former suburbs. Most of the buildings there were overgrown and abandoned, except for those that had burned out or had fallen in over time. The night was silent and close, and Jason stayed close beside Phoebe, unsure of exactly where she was headed.

They finally had turned north after what Jason guessed had been six miles, and were on a street that he thought he remembered, though he had rarely been there before. A broad open expanse lay behind the row of trees lining the street to their right; overgrowth on the land on their left hid whatever structures had once been there. The deep gloom of the trees and the darkness made it difficult for him to gauge exactly how far north they had come, but he knew they were drawing near to the old college.

Phoebe had been silent through most of their journey, and Jason had not tried to engage her; their last exchange had shaken him more than anything else had since his arrival. For most of the ordeal, he had been able to separate the Cybwoman Phoebe from the girl he remembered, at least to some extent. When he had realized that beneath the almost emotionless exterior, Phoebe still retained at least some traces of who she had been, his mission had become even more difficult, and his emotions much harder to check.

They were going gently uphill, and as the road crested, a large building loomed to their right; ahead, he could just see that their route intersected another, larger street. Beyond that was another open area, downhill from them, but he could not make out anything else.

A short distance from the crossroads, Phoebe turned right, following a small driveway next to the building. Jason followed her, mystified. Near the back of what he guessed had once been a small parking area, Phoebe came to what looked like an ancient, covered combination of parking meter and bus stop.

"That thing still works, doesn't it?" he asked in a quiet voice, even though there was no one nearby to hear them.

"It no longer serves the purpose for which it was created," replied the synthetic voice. "It has been retasked."

"Who retasked it?" Jason asked.

Phoebe glanced back over her shoulder with her cool, nerveless look. Jason hesitated inwardly. Then she replied, as quietly as he had spoken and in her own voice, "you did."

Jason's blood ran cold. "Why did I do that?"

Phoebe pressed the black button again, and Tinsworth's voice emanated from her mouth, uncomfortably loud in the dark silence. "Jason, it's not safe for you to return to the Drome. This - thing that Bryant's turned Wiley Grant into is like a paranoid supercomputer. He always has three of the females guarding him - by now you know which three, I guess - and another two out scouting for you. You probably won't have met them. Their names are Annette and Darleen, and unless Acme has countermanded his order, they will kill you on sight."

Jason digested this as Phoebe waited, watching him dispassionately. Then he said, "I don't understand. Some of your kind were on the same side as Tinsworth, weren't they? That's what I had thought."

Phoebe replied again in her own voice. "Acme had access to almost all of the information we generate. I am the only one with an independent design, so our interfacing is not complete. If I choose, I can withhold certain data from him. But the others were all largely under Acme's control, and over time he has eliminated those who he considered his rivals one by one.

You are the only one left now, and that is only because he was forced to bring you here."

"Because without the rift, there's a paradox and this universe is destroyed," Jason replied.

Phoebe did not respond, but turned back to the parking meter. There was a keypad on its front, below a blank screen and between two slots for depositing money. Jason watched as Phoebe pressed one key eight times in succession, then typed a few letters after it.

The screen lit up as she said, again in her own voice, "This box was set up far enough away so that wirelessly, you can reach the far western edge of the Drome. The extra five hundred feet between the perimeter and Acme's server location are enough that the signal can't be received there."

Jason thought. "I thought that his signal reached well beyond the Drome." Another worry was gnawing at his mind as well, but its full import still eluded him.

"It does," she replied. "But we are slightly farther out from the Drome here than the crossroads are. The difference is not more than a hundred meters, but it is enough. The crossroads are nearer the east side; we are trying to reach the western edge." The black screen was slowly turning to the dark gray of inactivity, and they were silent as they waited. It was nearly a full minute before anything changed, and when it did, all that appeared was a DOS prompt.

"You designed it this way so that no one would try to use it if they were being pursued." Phoebe still used her own voice. "And if someone wasn't being pursued and simply tried to activate it, it would appear to have had all of its functions erased."

"That makes sense." Jason said quietly. "Are you sure we aren't being pursued now?"

"None of my kind have come within my wireless communication range," she answered as she began tapping the keypad at a speed that made Jason do a double-take: Phoebe had been a fast typist even before the accident, but now her fingers literally blurred as she worked. He guessed she was typing between three and four hundred words per minute. He had no idea what was being entered; the screen scrolled blurrily fast, briefly opening applications in DOS mode and then closing them again on the monochrome display. Then, as quickly as she had started, she was done, and the display had gone dark once more.

Phoebe stepped back and looked around in the darkness. "I did not come within range of the Black Birds as we traveled here. We are likely safe from them for the time being. The two that you should fear are the two that Tinsworth described - Annette and Darleen. They maintain the grid that allows the rift generator to manage the energies involved in creating the bridge extension - " she glanced toward him - "and in crossing through it. Without the energy sink created by the old rail system, the entire Drome would have gone up in an explosion that would have shaken everything between the city and the highway circling outside its rim." She paused. "I have only encountered them a few times, and I know little of them."

Jason nodded, then asked quickly as he could, hoping to surprise her, but suspecting he could not: "Did I leave a message for myself with you?"

She stared back at him, a dim shadow in the moonless dark, and did not speak for several seconds, until he added, "You learned to imitate people's reactions, didn't you? You could have answered at once, but you waited, as if you were trying to decide what to say to me when you already know how you'll respond."

In response, she again assumed her synthetic voice. "That is correct, Jason. Dr. Tinsworth taught me some human mannerisms, along with you."

"But it wasn't the same me," he said, now worried.

"It is the same you," Phoebe responded. "You have not yet become that Jason. That is the Jason you will most likely become."

Jason's heart sank slightly, but as it did, he suddenly grasped the significance of the positioning of the meter. "Did I leave myself a message to keep that from happening?" he asked. The urgency in his voice was shading into desperation.

"No. You said that if there were to be any interference, you would be completely unable to accomplish what you are attempting."

Jason thought about that for a moment, then asked, very quietly, "do you know of any difference between what my future self remembered doing, and what I have done since I arrived here?"

She faced him again in the dark, that invisible appraisal so similar to the human expression even in silhouette. He waited.

"I know of no difference," she replied after several more seconds had passed.

"Then to this point, I haven't created any divergence between this world from my perspective and from yours." He fell silent again, even more worried than before.

After several seconds, Phoebe touched the button again, and Tinsworth spoke once more, in a low voice barely above a whisper. It occurred randomly to Jason that in his own time, even in the middle of the night, he would never have been able to hear the professor's message over the background noise. The night surrounding them in this world was so still that even the muted recording seemed overloud.

"Jason, remember that there's no set timestream from your perspective. It is still possible for you to negate this stream entirely, but you have to return in order to make that possible. Once you do that, this plane of existence can only come into being based on what you are able to do once you return."

He closed his eyes. "Phoebe, do you know anything about what I did after I came back - into this timestream?"

She touched the button again, and this time Bryant's acerbic voice, not bothering to be quiet, barked at him so suddenly that he startled. "Anderson, if you don't know how to fix this, you'd better start figuring it out. It's not that hard. What would you have to do to change your own past?"

Phoebe had not moved in the darkness. The implications of what Bryant had said finally clicked in place in Jason's head, and he smiled. Then he laughed, in spite of everything that had happened, in spite of his own exhaustion and fear. Only the sight of Phoebe's silhouette could calm him, but his smile remained.

"He's right. Of all people to give me the answer, it would be him." He took a deep breath and sighed, willing himself to focus. "He hated me, but he had to have hated what Wiley turned into even more." He sighed, and then asked Phoebe, "is there anything I have to have to be able to bypass Acme, or disable him?"

Phoebe responded in her own voice. "Yes. After you were killed, you were buried in the cemetery some way north of the Black Birds' compound. Dr. Tinsworth apparently buried something there as well, but I do not know what it was, or whether it is in your coffin, or somewhere nearby. He may have been afraid that Acme would learn of its existence through me."

"Apparently he learned of it anyway. Weren't they guarding my grave?" The words sounded strange even as he said them, and he shook his head in bemusement.

"The Black Birds were ordered to keep watch on the site, and for many years, they did," Phoebe's synthetic voice replied. "I do not know whether they abandoned their watch when they learned of your return, but I think it likely that they have."

"And if they haven't?" Jason's eyes narrowed in the dark.

"If the cemetery is still guarded, then I will dispatch the guards." Phoebe spoke in her own voice, but it conveyed the coolness of her synthesized one. Jason shuddered slightly, remembering how hotly she had pursued him in the Drome.

"How much time do you think we have?"

"Too many variables," she responded in the same voice. "The Threebirds are probably far enough away that we can reach your gravesite with some time for you to search. The other two, Annette and Darleen, were dispatched by Acme and I am not privy to his instructions to them. They may be pursuing you with the others, but he may have sent them after me."

"Why would he send them after you, and not me?" Jason asked.

"Acme knows that you are trying to restore me to life, and that I am tasked with guarding you. Part of the reason I was tasked to guard you was so that you would be trackable through me."

Jason took a deep breath, trying to stave off exhaustion and a fresh wave of dismay. "So we can't approach the Drome together, or he'll know I'm there."

"That may be unavoidable. I calculate that your most likely chance to succeed, assuming you obtain something at your gravesite that you can use to disable Acme, will be for you to have me and Allison as your escort. There is a chance that the Drome may remain undefended, but I do not expect that - not with the Black Birds moving as near as they will be. I expect Acme to recall Annette and Darleen there, if they return to within his range. There will almost certainly be others as well - possibly as many as six more. Acme has likely ordered them to guard him until you have returned to the Drome - therefore it would be dangerous for you to approach the Drome alone."

Another thought crossed his mind. "But if they kill me, won't that obviate this timestream?"

"It will, but that will not change any of the events prior to that point in time when you left your own timeframe." The synthesized voice had returned.

"You're right." Jason sighed again, and his eyes closed for a long moment. When they opened, he looked at her with a resigned smile. "The only way back is forward. Let's go to the cemetery. It's only about a mile from here, isn't it?"

"That is correct," she responded, still in her electronic voice.

They turned together and walked north to the broad, east-west thoroughfare that had ended their way there, and turned west along it toward the abandoned city. Behind them, the first brightening of dawn mellowed the black sky into predawn indigo.

Chapter Twenty-One

THE TWO CYBWOMEN left the distant orbit they had followed around the eastward-marching Black Bird soldiers, responding to the decision that they had reached with their three compatriots.

Annette and Darleen had worked alongside each other since the earliest minutes of their activation. They had been the first ones to be revived after Acme and Phoebe, awakening only a few minutes apart, and for the first hours of their new existence - owing to interference in the local wireless network - their only communications had been with each other. A human subject might have begun to forget the impact of that trauma within a few days, but they were not truly human anymore; of all their kind, perhaps only Julia and Rosamind were less like their original species than they were.

Those first hours, for them, had been at least a thousand times as long as they would have seemed to their human progenitors, and they had forged an early and unique communicative bond that even Acme could only partially direct, and could neither subvert nor disrupt. After his first few attempts to separate them, he had recognized that such efforts would be counterproductive, and had instead sought ways to employ their unique dual capacity to his maximum advantage. Once he had deduced that the old city's commuter rail complex could be converted into a huge energy sink for his efforts to extend the bridge that had been formed in his own time, he had set them to the task of repairing the system along its entire length while he engaged in the decades-long calculations he had to make - first to determine how to extend the bridge, and then to create the technology that could bring the rift into being.

Throughout those long years, Annette and Darleen had cleared and shored up tunnels, restored bridges, replaced and reinstalled electrical lines, and removed every rail car still on the tracks. They had worked alone, and generally avoided contact even with others of their own kind. On a very few occasions, they had encountered surviving humans; these they had ignored as long as they themselves were left alone. Only twice had those approached them, and neither of those two individuals had lived to regret that decision.

Their work had been completed mere days before the rift had opened, and they had briefly visited the Drome for diagnostics; they rarely returned there otherwise, instead repowering themselves from facilities they had installed or modified at each of the stations along the old lines. This practice had not previously been an issue, but their last diagnostic had revealed that the interface between Darleen's central processing unit - which regulated all of her automatic bodily functions, like all of their kind except Phoebe - and her brain stem had begun to deteriorate.

This was a natural consequence of their ages. Except for Phoebe, all of the Cybwomen's bodies were approaching sixty years of age, and some were older. Nevertheless, the problem exerted a significant strain upon them both, similarly unique to the bond they shared. Though neither of them experienced emotion in any direct, glandular sense, and neither had yet begun to experience - or indeed, were even aware of - the shutdown phenomenon that had affected several of their counterparts, they nonetheless had communicated and acted in tandem almost as effectively as if they had been a single organism. They shared their own electronic language, different from and - to their knowledge - unintelligible to any of the other Cybwomen or to Acme. They could work together in close quarters with even greater precision than the Threebirds, and when so ordered - which had happened only once - they were the deadliest pair of fighters under Acme's command. This synchronization between them had been the dominant feature of their shared existence since their reawakening, but it had begun to erode.

Once their diagnostics had been concluded, Acme had sent them to shepherd the Threebirds' army; had they detected Phoebe or Jason Anderson, their orders were to destroy Phoebe and to bring Anderson back to the Drome. Acme had not given any explanation for or indication of his motives, and they had not asked for either.

As they had trailed the Threebirds, by unlucky chance they had been on the southern arc of the circle they had described around the Black Birds' army at the time that the march made its closest pass to Jason and Phoebe, and had thus failed to detect them. When the Black Birds' chief had refused to march further, Annette had calculated that their most likely chance of capturing Jason Anderson would be for Darleen and herself to return to the Drome and wait for them to arrive. Thus, even while the Threebirds allowed their unwilling army to halt for a rest, their unseen escort went straight back along the route Jason and Phoebe had followed only hours before.

They were able to walk much more quickly than their quarry had, and by sunrise, they had passed the crossroads that marked the outer edge of Acme's range and had resumed contact with him. Jason Anderson and Phoebe had not returned, and there had been no other contact made. Acme ordered all of the remaining Cybwomen in the Drome east after the Threebirds as soon as Annette's approach was detected.

What they had not communicated to Acme, and what even the diagnostics could not show, was that Darleen's functions were beginning to decay rapidly. Their singular mode of communication had slowed noticeably, and Annette had not been able to devise a remedy for the problem. Had she been human, Darleen would have exhibited signs of a coming stroke - but as a Cybwoman, those symptoms were masked slightly by the lightning speed with which they all communicated.

As they connected with the Drome network, Annette led Darleen down a side route that they had kept cleared for their own use; neither of them often chose to seek the company of their own kind, preferring to remain with each other. As their counterparts gathered to leave along the route Phoebe had taken earlier, Annette could detect the cluster of their signals as they passed just yards north of them in their approach.

Acme had not communicated with them, evidently being content merely to monitor their arrival even as he coordinated with the team he was sending east. It was not until the dissonant, ululating tone that Acme used as an urgency signal sounded in their internal communications that Annette glanced toward Darleen, and then halted, realizing how serious her degradation had suddenly become.

Though Darleen still could still move more or less normally, and her direct comm with Annette was unaffected, the growing daylight revealed that her expression had changed. Once as carefully featureless and blank as any other Cybwoman's, her visage had sagged into slack-jawed vacancy. One of her eyes had gone slightly amblyopic, and a human observer might have thought that she looked very tired as she stared mutely back.

"Signal acknowledged," Annette responded, and at the same time, Darleen's communication halted momentarily, and then became unintelligible gibberish. Annette was able to catch her as she swayed, but when she tried to release her so that she could stand, she nearly collapsed. Annette was forced to lower her to the ground, where she lay staring up blankly. A tic had started in her right hand.

"Why is Darleen not with you?" Acme demanded.

"She is with me. She is malfunctioning, and she is unable to move or stand." Annette's response flashed back.

"I am not able to verify her presence. She was visible on the network for approximately forty-eight seconds after you came into range. She then dropped from the network and has not reattached, and I have not been able to reestablish contact with her. How severe is the malfunction?"

"Very severe. She is not communicating intelligibly. She cannot move and is spasming involuntarily. She appears to be experiencing massive system degradation."

For nearly a full second, Acme did not respond; the delay was so long that Annette had resumed her attempts to speak directly to Darleen when his reply finally did come. "Bring her to the facility. She will require significant attention if she is to recover."

"Acknowledged. Will comply with your order." With that, Annette lifted Darleen from the pavement where she lay and began to carry her the two hundred yards that remained between them and the gate that led into the Drome. This proved more difficult than might have been expected: Darleen's body randomly tensed and relaxed, twice convulsing so violently that Annette nearly dropped her. Acme opened the gate for her as she approached.

The gate was set on the northeastern corner of the Drome. Had he not arrived at night, and been extremely disoriented by the passage through the rift and the unfamiliar surroundings, Jason might have seen it when he first turned to run from Phoebe. It would not have helped him, however, as it was electronically locked and controlled by Acme.

Annette crossed the narrow arm of the plaza between the gate and Acme's installation, passing the door to Bryant's old quarters and stopping before a blank portal without any visible knob or keypad entry. Darleen's body had gone limp and was slung over her shoulder like a bag of grain. The door opened as she drew up, and she entered the main maintenance facility for the Cybwomen. As she entered, she detected the presence of the Cybwomen who had just been dispatched east. They were returning; evidently, Acme's urgency signal had reached them before they passed out of range.

She knew factually that several of her counterparts had entered the repair facility as their bodies had worn out, or malfunctioned; only two had emerged in even marginally-functional condition, and one of those had been Allison. She did not worry about Darleen, or even sense any trepidation about bringing her there. The awareness of her closest ally's likely demise was like an empty pool, where there was nothing in the place fear or worry might have occupied, and no emotional impairment to her judgment.

Still, she could sense Acme scanning her responses even as he watched them on camera; neither of them could detect any response from the limp body that she laid upon a polished, marble table surrounded by instrumentation, most of which was directly controlled by Acme. Those parts swung into action around her, removing her clothing, inserting IVs, and attaching monitors. One robotic arm lifted her head; an extension from that arm maneuvered a cable attachment into a port set at the base of her neck.

"She is still alive, but not responsive. The damage she has suffered may not be reversible." Acme spoke inside her head. "Her body has aged, but does not appear to have degraded. The issue is either with her processing unit, or with her brain stem - the join points between them do not seem to be damaged.

"I will attempt to rebuild her operating system from the UEFI up. It will be a slow process, but a full diagnostic would take at least as long. If the problem is in the operating system, the rebuild will save time."

"And if the problem is in the brain stem?" Annette asked wordlessly.

"If that is where the damage occurred, or even part of it, then she will not recover, and will have to be deactivated."

Annette did not react, asking only in reply, "Shall I await the results here?"

"There is a repowering unit beside the door that includes an extended diagnostic. Use it. The process will take approximately thirty minutes. You have worked in proximity with Darleen since you both were awakened. If you have both been exposed to something that might have caused her to degrade, it might be more quickly detected in you, since you do not indicate any lost functionality."

Annette acceded at once, walking toward a chair placed beside the door with several pieces of equipment set up next to it, and sat down. As with Darleen, the equipment began attaching itself, though less invasively. As the repowering began, she felt the odd nerve tingling that accompanied it, though more strongly than she had felt from the remote units they had used. She closed her eyes, setting herself in temporary sleep mode, while she sensed Acme interfacing with her own processing unit and memory.

Abruptly, her eyes snapped open, and she felt the sensors detaching from her body far more rapidly than she had expected; in the same few milliseconds, Acme disengaged from her, and the same urgency signal - even shriller than before - sounded in her mind. She knew at once that it was meant not only for her, but for all remaining Cybwomen in range of the Drome.

The signal's noise was intense enough to cause pain inside her skull, though she knew that that was only a reflex reaction to stimulus, and when it stopped, she ignored the residual throbbing, and sent to Acme: "Signal acknowledged. Urgency noted. I await your instructions."

She was incapable of surprise, so that when Acme's command came a millisecond later, she merely acknowledged it, and began making her way southwest toward the perimeter of the Drome.

For Acme had responded: "Phoebe has been detected west of the Drome. Jason Anderson accompanies her. You are to meet her before she reaches the Drome boundary, if she is approaching, and disable her. You will also wake Allison - she has not yet responded and is still in sleep mode - and while you disable Phoebe, Allison will capture Anderson."

One element of this communication required clarification for Annette. "Acme. By your order, Allison is not permitted to leave the Drome grounds."

The reply came even more rapidly than usual. "Once Allison is awake and in contact, that order will be lifted while she complies with this command."

"If Phoebe retreats, shall we pursue?" Annette's query implied requirement for complete confirmation and instruction.

"If Phoebe retreats with Anderson, she is likely to travel farther west. You and Allison will pursue her," Acme responded.

"And the disabling threshold for Phoebe? At what point do I cease combat?"

"You will not cease combat, if they retreat. Phoebe is not to be allowed to return to the Drome."

Chapter Twenty-Two

WILLIAM JONES, ACCOMPANIED by a cluster of his guards and Shawntaine, led the column of refugees into the rising sun along the ancient road that ran east from their old home.

The night march had been difficult for the Covingtons. Jones had sent his officers on rotation, circling the line of evacuees as they followed the road and checking for stragglers at the rear. Fortunately, there had been none, and with only one brief halt for rest, the column had drawn to a halt at a large crossroads and closed ranks about two miles from where he believed the Stonecrest settlement lay.

Beside him, Sergeant Curtis looked back, scowling. "Any idea whether they're going to take us in?" he asked.

"No idea," Jones replied, then addressed the group as a whole. "I had expected they would have someone watching this road. Curtis, Elliott and I will go to try and make contact with these people. Sims - you trail us by a quarter mile, and when we meet with them, you wait where you are until we return - if we do."

He then looked toward another man who, though younger, looked so much like him that they were clearly brothers. "Ahman, I need you here. If no one returns before an hour past sundown, take these people and lead them north from this crossroad until midnight."

Ahman sighed and nodded. "And keep Shawntaine here with you," Jones added. "It's not safe for him to come. If these other women like Phoebe are coming after us, I need for you to get him away."

"Pop, I want to come with you!" Shawntaine protested, and was rewarded with a stern look from his father.

"Son, I told you - we have to keep you away from anyone that might hand you over to them. You don't know which way they went, or what they are doing, but you did meet Anderson. They may decide you're lying and kill you, or try to make you tell them something you don't know - and then they'll kill you. It's too dangerous." His expression softened, and he glanced around the circle. "I'm still hoping we can get through all of this without a fight. The one thing I know is that whatever Anderson's doing, he's going to do it fast. It might not be more than another day and night. I'm hoping that when these women find that out, they'll go running back to wherever they came from to try and stop him, and they'll leave us alone."

Ahman nodded. "What about the Black Birds?"

Jones looked back along the road they had followed there. It went up a slight rise behind them for about half a mile; they could not see beyond that. "Send someone back there to watch for them. If they're coming, get everyone out of here immediately and head north, as fast as you can make them go. We can't expect that the Stonecrests will just let us walk into their place and set up camp - especially if they find out we're being followed." He took a deep breath. "Besides, if the Black Birds follow us here, then we can hope they'll think we turned south instead of north."

"All right. Be careful out there, brother," Ahman said. They nodded to each other, and then Jones, Curtis and Elliott left the group and began walking south; shortly after they passed out of sight, Sims followed, walking more slowly. Ahman looked around himself at the ragged assemblage of Covingtons. They all looked tired from the march, and they were almost all sitting in the places where they had stopped.

Ahman drew in his breath and let it out, and called out, "I need everyone's attention, right now."

He looked around again. About half of the people remaining were watching him; the rest appeared to be falling asleep where they sat. No wonder, he thought to himself. They had marched overnight on almost no notice, and the ones who were not guards or sentries were unused to what those duties sometimes demanded. He cleared his throat and put as much authority into his voice as he could.

"Rest here while you can, but be ready to leave the moment I give the order. If we're being followed, we'll head north -" he pointed down the road leading from the crossroads - "and we'll have to move as fast as we can, at least for a while. Once we're far enough away, we can halt again." His words were received as unenthusiastically as he expected, with only a low, resigned murmur rising from his charges in response. As he spoke, Ahman scanned each face, looking for someone with enough stamina left for sentry duty, and settled on a woman roughly his own age who remained relatively alert.

"You. Kelly's your name, isn't it?"

"Yes, sir." The woman rose to her feet. Her hair might have been blonde once; as with most of the Covington women, it had greyed early, during her childbearing years, which already looked to be drawing to a close. Still, she was more awake than the people around her, and looked capable of doing what was required.

"I need for you to walk up to the top of that rise and watch back on the road we came down. Find someplace where you won't be seen. If you see anyone coming, get back here as fast as you can, because we'll have to leave right away." Ahman waited only to see that she understood the order and had begun walking back west along the road before glancing down at Shawntaine, who was waiting with visible impatience for his attention.

"I know you still want to go find the Stonecrests. Your father doesn't want you caught up in this, and I don't either." Disappointment and anger vied on the boy's face in response as Ahman spoke. "This isn't just some kids' game. Once you get involved, you're dealing with the Black Birds, and Phoebe and all of her kind, and whoever Acme is. Your father has had to protect everyone, including you, from everything and everyone outside our walls back home. Once they know who you are, whether they're enemies or not, you'll be part of any fight. You're not ready for that yet."

Shawntaine glowered back at him. "But how am I supposed to get ready if you won't let me fight?"

"This is not the kind of fight where you need to learn," Ahman replied.

"Uncle Ahman, if Jason Anderson is in this fight, then it's *exactly* the kind of fight where I need to learn!" Shawntaine burst out. Ahman put his hand on his nephew's shoulder and looked straight into his eyes.

"Shawntaine, if it were my decision, I would still do the same thing. You just don't have enough experience in dealing with people like the Black Birds, or with Phoebe. Your father does. He taught me everything he could, in case something happened to him before you were ready.

"Whatever Anderson is doing, it's going to draw everyone's attention. He was with us less than a day, and now we're running for our lives. The Black Birds are coming after us. Phoebe is with Anderson, and who knows what she's up to. I don't even want to think about the rest of her kind, or Acme, but if the stories about Anderson are true, they're coming for him."

Shawntaine's anger partially dissolved into suspicious puzzlement. "But I thought Jason Anderson was supposed to make the world better. Why would they be coming after him?"

Ahman sighed, and looked back the way they had come. Kelly was nearing the crest of the rise, and had already left the road. He nodded to himself, and then looked back at Shawntaine.

"Son, you need to understand that there's always some people who don't want things to change, even for the better. The people who already have power, who have the good food and the good things, they don't want to let those things go. Think about if you were Acme. People are so afraid of him, whoever he is - and his women, or whatever those things are - that they won't even go near the Drome.

"Phoebe told your father once that the Black Birds tried to attack the Drome, years ago - and every man that went on that attack died." He took a deep breath, reassured to see that Shawntaine looked somewhat calmer. "Once you're part of that world, you can't go back. Your dad and I want for you to have as much time as we can give you, so that you can be as ready as you will ever be when the time comes."

Shawntaine sighed. "I know, Uncle. But I feel like I'm ready now."

Ahman smiled, a little sadly. "You nearly are. If Anderson wasn't involved, you probably would be. But not this. Not yet."

The boy's shoulders sagged in resignation, and he nodded shamefacedly. Ahman grasped his upper arm gently.

"When this is over, you and I are going to spend a lot more time together. You're ready to start learning how to lead your people."

Shawntaine smiled slightly in response and nodded, and walked to where he had laid his pack when they had arrived. Ahman looked back at where Kelly had stationed herself, then south where Jones and the others had gone. Shaking his head, he sat down on the road where he was, hoping that they might get some rest before having to move again.

JONES, CURTIS AND ELLIOTT had reached the old highway that went east; beyond the vague knowledge that they had of the Stonecrest tribe and their home, none of them knew where that road led, or what had once been at its end. Jones dimly remembered his father telling him that the road continued farther than a man could walk in ten days, through another city nearly as large as the abandoned sprawl west of the Black Birds' compound, and ended in another road that travelled from south to north through even more cities.

That thought flitted through his mind for only a few moments before returning to their current mission. They had reached a place where the old highway went on a slow rise toward a ridge a little more than a mile to their east; it crossed in front of them over a bridge that still stood, some three times taller than their own height.

Jones glanced as his companions; neither looked happy with what they saw. "We know their compound is near here," he said. "Do we get up on the bridge and go east, or go under it?"

"I don't like this," Curtis replied. "If we go under, there could be an ambush on the other side. Even if these people don't consider us enemies, they might mistake us for someone else and attack anyway."

"Going up on the highway is just as bad," Elliott answered. "And if there's someone up there, they probably already know we're here."

Jones considered. The morning air felt oppressive, as though a storm was building that would not arrive until later that day, though the sky was still clear. He didn't want to go in either direction, but to get where they needed to go, they would have to choose one or the other.

No one spoke for some time as he thought, until he reached his decision. "We'll take the highway," he said. "It will be harder to ambush us effectively there, and we need to be able to see farther than we can if we go under the bridge and keep going south. And I agree with you - " he looked at Curtis - "it'd be easier to ambush us on the other side, if someone knows we're coming."

Curtis nodded, and without any more discussion, they continued forward until they reached the bridge, then began to climb up the embankment on its eastern side. The grass there was nearly overgrown, and looked undisturbed, to Jones' relief. The slope was steep, but not too difficult, and before long all three men had reached the top of the bridge. Jones looked eastward to where the rise of the highway crested, and was thus caught by surprise when Curtis hissed, "Shit!"

He whirled around to see two figures approaching at a fast walk, less than a tenth of a mile away. Jones hesitated only a fraction of a moment before he said, in a surprisingly quiet voice: "Run."

They ran. After a few steps, Jones glanced back over his shoulder; the two figures had likewise broken into a full run, and were closing the distance between them terrifyingly fast. A horrified gasp from his left told him that Elliott had also seen them, and was already falling behind. Curtis was to his right, and was already several steps ahead of them both.

"Just run!" he snarled in terror, as he realized who was pursuing them. Elliott tried, but before they were even halfway to the crest of the hill, he had fallen ten yards behind them, and was already out of breath and slowing. Jones cursed to himself, and then saw how much faster their pursuers were. "Stop!" he cried, and turned back toward Elliott just as the nearer of the two women launched herself at the slower man.

It was over in less than a second. The thin, blonde woman tackled Elliott even as he stopped, and before Jones could even speak, she had grabbed the sides of his head and twisted with horrifying strength until a sickening, wet, snapping crunch sounded over the flat, cracked pavement.

Even as she finished killing him, the woman leapt back to her feet and closed on Jones. The other flashed past him toward Curtis. Jones did not even know whether he had stopped running.

With no other hope, Jones lifted his hands in surrender. The woman came within two paces of him; she looked more feral than any animal he had ever seen. He closed his eyes, gritting his teeth, waiting for her to pounce.

Instead, he heard an odd, snarling voice say, "We seek Jason Anderson. Is he with you?"

Jones opened his eyes. The blonde woman still looked like a giant cat, but her expression was almost completely blank, betraying only a slight sense of anger. Jones didn't hesitate.

"Anderson isn't with us. He left us yesterday, before we evacuated."

The woman studied him emotionlessly. Beside him, the other woman dragged Curtis next to him until they stood side by side; Curtis looked once at Elliott before turning and spattering vomit on the ancient road. Jones held his breath against the stench he knew was coming.

"You speak the truth." Almost overcome with relief, Jones nodded and sagged; as he did, the smell and the horror of Robinson's corpse with its lolling, impossibly-angled neck also overcame him, and his own vomit was soon commingling with Curtis'.

"Where are the rest of your people?" the blonde asked, oblivious to his reaction. The other, smaller woman stood behind her, her expression equally blank, mutely watching them.

The hope that had flamed briefly in Jones' heart was coldly extinguished. "I can't tell you that."

The woman closed the distance between them quicker than sight. Jones' next sensation was being lifted into the air by the same hand that had grasped his throat. Struggling to breathe, he tried to pull her gloved fingers loose, but they were like iron.

"Please don't hurt him! Anderson's not with us." Curtis cried out, and an instant later Jones felt his feet touch ground. The grip on his throat loosened, but did not release. The other woman was in front of Curtis as quickly as the blonde had moved, but did not touch him.

"He's telling the truth," Jones gasped. He could see no point in trying to deceive them, and they had gone far enough away from their home that he thought - or hoped - that Jason would be out of their reach.

The blonde looked distantly at him, as blankly as before, before responding with her odd voice. "You're hiding something. I will let you take me back to your people. I will talk with everyone who encountered Jason Anderson. If you are all truthful with me, no one will be harmed.

"If you refuse," she continued as she released Jones, "I will kill you both, and then ambush your people. I know that you have followed a road east, and then came to the bridge from the north - we saw you climb up. Another of our number is leading an army east to meet your people. You cannot fight all of us.

"If you will not allow us to return with you, your people will be slaughtered. Do as we ask, and they will be spared. Will you comply?" The hand tightened very slightly on his throat again.

Jones closed his eyes, and thought of his son. "Yes."

The hand released him. "My name is Julia. My partner is called Rosamind. We know that you are William Jones, the current chief of the Covington clan. Lead us to your people."

With no other options, Jones still glanced back at Curtis, who shrugged, his fear still evident on his face. He nodded back in reply, and without looking at either woman, began walking back to the bridge, praying that Sims had seen what had happened, and hoping against hope that he was not making a terrible mistake.

Chapter Twenty-Three

THE CEMETERY SEEMED bigger than Jason remembered. The emptiness of the world around it only added to the natural, pervasive sense of quiet such places had. While he didn't believe in ghosts, he nevertheless felt glad that he would not have to search that place in the dark.

It appeared completely empty as Jason and Phoebe entered. Jason breathed a sigh of relief, silently thankful that he didn't have to watch Phoebe kill the men who had been guarding the place where he was buried. They entered through a brick arch that curved perhaps twice Jason's height above them, following a cracked walkway that, while still nearly overridden with grass, still showed signs of recent and fairly frequent use.

Phoebe walked with her usual, almost preternatural smoothness along the path; Jason followed. He knew better than to ask whether she knew the way. They were well into the cemetery, perhaps a hundred yards north of the entrance, when she turned left and began moving between the gravestones toward a mature cedar tree growing ahead and slightly to their right. Just before she reached the tree, she halted so suddenly that Jason almost ran into her from behind. She pointed.

Jason stared with an odd, queasy fascination at the four large rocks, side by side, that protruded from the ground in a line pointing away from the tree in the general direction of the Drome. They were not gravestones like most of those in this cemetery; he realized that if there were any similar markers to these in that cemetery, they likely would belong to slaves, and would be close to two hundred years old.

Something else occurred to him. "Phoebe, why didn't anyone use these gravestones for building material?"

"There was no restriction against doing so. None of the clans I have encountered have used them. It must have been a choice they made." She responded with her synthesized voice.

Jason nodded. "I guess there was enough other stuff lying around. So this is where they put me. I guess these others are the ones who were trying to bring me back? From the city?"

"They are." Phoebe was not looking at him, and spoke with her own ragged voice.

Jason thought. "Phoebe, if there's something buried with me, it will take forever to dig it up."

"I could dig it out by hand, but even I would lose a great deal of time. Do you think Dr. Tinsworth might have hidden what you seek in another place?"

Jason considered. "It's what I would have done. He couldn't assume I'd have a lot of time, and if my grave is dug up, it's going to be obvious something was hidden there - and that I found it." He looked again at the rough, unworked, unlettered rock that marked where his body lay under the earth. In spite of himself, he shuddered a little, but then he looked at Phoebe, remembered what she was, and willed himself to focus on the task at hand.

Something about the four stones caught his eye and held it. Phoebe remained silent, and had not moved. He went closer, literally walking over his own grave, and studied the stones carefully.

"Phoebe, these grave markers aren't aligned right." Instead of each being partially buried at the head end of its plot, the stones were placed so that only the farthest one was truly where the stone should have been set. His own gravestone, he realized, was probably directly over his own head.

Phoebe examined the stones as well, but did not answer. Jason sucked in his breath. "I think I know why, too. They're not just markers - they're a message, and it's meant for me."

The four stones not only were set unevenly on their respective graves, but additionally, each one was slightly taller than the last. Jason thought again.

"If I wanted something to be accessible quickly, I wouldn't put it underground. I *definitely* wouldn't put it in a coffin. And it wouldn't be hidden anywhere near here." He stepped forward and knelt low beside his marker, looking along the line of stones as if sighting down a rifle barrel.

Over a hundred yards away, a battered-looking, grey concrete structure stood on a low hill in the eastern section of the cemetery. It was a columbarium - built to store cremation urns, rather than entire corpses. Jason glanced at Phoebe again.

"I'd put it somewhere where it could be found quickly, and removed quickly, without disturbing the grave site. It would be far enough away that no one would be likely to find it by accident." He rose to his feet, and pointed toward the wall. "I think what we're looking for is over there."

"Are you certain?" Phoebe asked, though her synthetic voice framed the words in a way that sounded very little like a question. Jason gave her another sidelong look as he walked past her toward the place where he had pointed, talking over his shoulder as he went.

"Am I *sure?* Not completely. But I know Tinsworth had already figured out that Wiley and I were going to be fighting each other. What I don't understand is why he doesn't want me to cancel this timeline. It's got to be hell for him to be -" Jason stopped too late.

Phoebe pressed her button, and Acme answered him. "Jason Anderson, the man you knew as Wiley Grant is dead. I inherited his brain, which was placed in an environment in which I was able to exceed all of the limitations that his body's existence placed on him."

Jason froze in place as the voice continued. "One thing that has become apparent to me, over time, is that accumulated wisdom is only a partial result of learning. It is also part of the reunification of our universal being over time, as the individuals representing ourselves in each of the infinite universes that comprise the multiverse gradually pass away, concentrating us each second more and more, until at last there is only one remaining out of them all.

"In this body, and in this environment, I face few threats. I am likely therefore to become the last of the multitude of beings that comprise my greater self. With that concentration of my own animus, that condensation of wisdom, with the intelligence native to this brain and with the tools at my disposal, I will eventually become the greatest and most powerful being of our kind that has ever existed."

Jason turned slowly and stared at her, a strange mixture of satisfaction and horror curdling his face. Phoebe was silent, merely watching him with her usual blankness.

"He's not going to kill me." He gazed at Phoebe. "He has to let me go back. None of what you just said can happen unless I go back through the rift - I have to exist in this timeline or he vanishes."

"That may not be true," Phoebe's synthesized voice replied almost tonelessly. "Acme suspects that his awareness would pass to another iteration of himself in his current form. His knowledge is so much greater than that of a typical human being that he believes his conscious self would be preserved."

"Shit." Jason turned, looking east toward the columbarium again, and the dawn beyond. He began to walk toward it again, with no real purpose in mind. Phoebe followed, and as she did, she began to look warily around.

The outdoor crypt stood atop a low rise within the cemetery's confines. Jason made his way toward it, and as he reached the paved sidewalk that surrounded it, Phoebe said, in her own voice, "Two of my kind are coming."

Jason felt as though his blood temperature had dropped ten degrees. "Which two?"

Phoebe looked at him, a pale ghost of fear crossing her features, and replied in the same voice, "Annette - and Allison."

"How close?" Jason felt panic rising in his gut. If even Phoebe registered fear at their approach, he knew they were in deep trouble.

"At the edge of my range. They will be here in about two minutes."

Jason's face crumpled in on itself. "Fuck!" he hissed softly, and turned to look at the wall, scanning the individual plates in desperation. They had apparently been in use up until the time that their civilization had begun to crumble, as there were a number of crude, mostly-obscured names on some of the marble fronts - until one caught his eye.

It was some seven feet above the pavement, a little way to his left. He looked back for a moment; it was directly in line with the gravestones he had sighted along to find it. The name was carefully, though inexpertly, carved into the stone face, and read only a name, with no date:

DR. ALLEN JASON BRYANT

Jason hesitated for a fraction of a second, and then asked Phoebe, "If Acme killed Bryant, as you say - what was done with his body?"

"I don't know," Phoebe replied, still in her own voice. "I was tasked with caring for Allison during that time. I don't know who disposed of the body." She paused. "They're almost here." She turned to watch the arch where they had entered.

Despite the nearness of their peril, Jason wanted to shout - but then he realized that Phoebe and the two that were coming for them were wirelessly linked, and that if Phoebe saw where he knew their solution was hidden, she might reveal it unwillingly, even unwittingly.

"Darling, I can't help you." The word escaped his mouth unthinkingly, before he could bite it back, and she looked back at him for a moment, another emotional ghost clouding her face as her eyes momentarily shone red with the oblique light from the sunrise. As she looked back toward the arch, he bolted out of sight behind the wall. Part of his mind cursed him for being a coward, but he knew instinctively that he would hinder Phoebe more than he could help.

He crept toward the corner of the building, trying to see around it to where Phoebe had stood. She had run toward the arch as soon as he had hidden himself, until she stood about forty yards away from him. Beyond her, clearly illuminated in the morning sun, two women had passed under the arch and were striding purposefully toward her. They walked about six feet apart, and both looked terrifying to him; he recognized Allison from the Drome. The other woman was a stranger, and had aged oddly; she appeared to be about Tinsworth's age, in his own time, and she somehow seemed slightly, inexplicably off-balance.

He shifted his position minutely, and as he did, a horrified chill ran down his spine as Allison stared directly toward him. She began walking rapidly, straight toward where he crouched. Jason felt a moment of panic when he saw that Phoebe had not moved to stop her. Frantically thinking that Phoebe would have stopped Allison if she was going to kill him, he stayed in place, hoping desperately that he had been right, and that Acme would have to return him to his own time in order to ensure his own potential immortality.

He looked back toward Phoebe, and was horrified to see that the other, older woman had already sprinted to within a few feet of her; Phoebe had crouched, ready to defend herself. Even as the combat was joined, Allison broke into a run and was beside Jason within moments; he had barely had time to stand before she was beside him. She took his arm with a hand that looked human enough, but her grip was like iron - yet it did not hurt.

He was afraid to look at her, but when he did, he almost fainted in shock; she was watching him, and when their eyes met, she gave him a strange, exaggerated, but clearly deliberate wink. She then looked toward Phoebe and her assailant, who were fighting each other in hand-to-hand combat that was faster, and looked more lethal, than anything Jason had ever seen.

Abruptly, the older woman made a feint and drew up fully erect, as if to trick Phoebe into a response; at once, Phoebe swept the woman's legs from beneath her, completing a full spin and pouncing even as the woman fell awkwardly to the ground. Before Jason could react, Phoebe had landed astride her and grasped the woman's skull with both hands, twisting it viciously around. They were too far away for him to hear the neck snap, but the woman's obvious disfigurement was enough to make him cringe heavily, with the little remaining gorge in his stomach rising.

Allison released him as he rested his hands on his knees, willing himself not to vomit, and watched him expressionlessly as Phoebe crossed the distance between them at a rapid walk. Jason managed to rise to his feet, staring at her in another seemingly immiscible blend of horror and gratitude. Phoebe herself betrayed no more emotion than Allison as she spoke.

"Jason, is there anything here that you will need? We have to move quickly now. If Annette has been sent without Darleen, then Darleen may be waiting for us at the Drome. At the very least, Acme might have sent a runner as a liaison with the Black Birds and the three of my kind that are allied with them. You may not have much time."

Jason nodded, and then pointed toward the stone face that bore Bryant's name. "I doubt his middle name was really Jason, and I'd bet a lot of money Acme wouldn't have gone to that much trouble to bury Bryant once he'd killed him. I'm sure Tinsworth put that there." He looked at Phoebe, then Allison. "I can lever it out, but it's probably heavy, and if it falls, it might hurt someone."

Before he could say anything else, the two Cybwomen shot into motion; Allison boosted Phoebe within reach of the face, and Phoebe pulled it free, tossing it effortlessly some thirty feet away from them. She then reached into the shallow alcove it had concealed, retrieving a laptop computer case and a pair of cables.

Jason sighed, slightly embarrassed at how quickly they had dealt with the facing, and took the laptop from Phoebe; he then looked to Allison and asked, "What happened with that - that woman over there? Didn't she know you were helping me?"

Allison looked at him for a moment, then raised two fingers to her lips, shaking her head gently. Phoebe answered him: "That was Annette. She never understood what happened. Allison waited until she had captured you, as she was directed, and then transmitted data to Annette that made it appear that she was going to attack me from behind. Annette feinted toward me, expecting her to attack.

"Annette has worked with Darleen for many years, alone, maintaining the rail system. While we are not subject to conditioning the way true human beings are, Annette and Darleen were different from the rest of us. They had their own language that they used only with each other, for one thing. That happened because something went wrong just as they were awakened, and for the first hours of their new existence, they could only communicate with each other." Phoebe looked toward Allison, who nodded again.

Jason shook his head, still marveling at their mimicry of human mannerisms, as he discarded the case and opened the laptop; a single sheet of paper had been placed inside between the keypad and monitor. He frowned. "The battery in this thing is going to be dead for sure. Even if we can power it up, I still have to figure out what these instructions are telling me." He sighed. Another thought crossed his mind. "You said Annette and Darleen could talk with each other in a different language from the rest of you." He looked hard at Allison. "If you can't speak, you must have some other way of communicating, and you would have had a different mode than the others. Did you learn their language?"

Allison nodded affirmatively, and then took one of the two cables from Jason. Plugging one end into the laptop, she reached behind her head with the other end and somehow fastened it to herself at the base of her neck. Jason leaned curiously around and saw that there was a small port beneath her hair.

"That will power the computer," Phoebe said. "But you do not have much time. Have you given any thought to what you might do?"

Jason nodded. "I think these instructions have part of the answer, although I'm literally scared to death to try them. But what I need to know is whether Allison can interface with this laptop directly. If she can, then once we are within range of the Drome, we can use her as a bridge into Acme's main system, reactivate the rift, and recalibrate it so that I can do what I need to do."

"What is it that you intend to do?" Phoebe asked.

"I can't tell you, not yet. I can't risk having another one of your kind finding out what I'm up to. Allison, you were able to fool Annette. Are you mute in standard wireless communication, or is it just your voice?"

Allison shook her head, and Phoebe replied, "Allison can communicate wirelessly. However, she is like me in that we both have experienced the dream state you deduced. If you can transcribe the instructions you need for her to complete while in that activation phase, she can parse them before fully reconnecting to Acme's servers. Those instructions would then be executed in a queue upon reconnection."

"That's what I thought." Jason smiled at them both, first Phoebe and then Allison, more uneasily, as he added: "You're about to become a real-life Trojan horse, both electronically and in the physical world." He looked to Phoebe again. "I think I can code what I need for this to work. The main thing is, before we get into the Drome's range, Allison has to shut down - and I will have to carry her into range. I will need you to stay far enough away from me to keep the others like you away, until she can reactivate - once we are close enough."

He looked once more to Allison. "Will you allow me to do this, and can you set a timer for reactivation? I don't want you to have even a wireless sensor active, in case you're spotted. I need you to close down completely, and wake up a little while later - maybe fifteen minutes. Can you do that?"

Allison looked at him for a moment that was long enough to remind him that she, like Phoebe, had been trained to mimic human reaction. Then she nodded, and though nonplussed by her pause, Jason smiled back her, with as much genuineness as he could force, and said quietly, "thank you. As soon as I get this thing set up, we can go back to the Drome."

Chapter Twenty-Four

AHMAN, SIMS AND a few others had formed up the Covingtons for another march when Jones and Curtis arrived. Rosamind and Julia were following some ten feet behind them. Neither of them had even remotely considered the possibility of doing anything other than exactly what they were ordered.

"Hold up, Ahman!" Jones shouted. To his dismay, Shawntaine stood beside his uncle. Jones had already made up his mind to risk having his son tell the truth of his encounter with Anderson.

Ahman looked toward them, and sagged visibly; he began barking orders to his people, telling them to remain where they were. Jones glanced along the road behind them to the west, and his heart sank; the Black Bird forces had already crested the hill and were marching toward them. In front of them, he saw a middle-aged woman walking with her upper arm firmly gripped by what he guessed was a third Cybwoman. A man who he recognized as the Black Birds' leader walked beside them.

The two groups marching toward the trapped Covington clan reached them at almost the same time. The woman called Rosamind remained behind them, while the other, angrier one moved to join the Black Bird forces. Jones looked long and hard at their human leader, who stared back at him with visible dismay darkening his expression.

The Threebirds moved to join each other near where the Black Bird lines had halted, perhaps a hundred feet away. Their forces were better organized and more disciplined than the Covingtons, Jones noted, but that made sense - only their trained fighters had come. The Covingtons' advantage in numbers was nowhere near enough to offset the perceived skill of their opponents - and that was without taking the Threebirds into account.

There was nothing else for it. Jones knew that he might not survive the negotiation that was surely coming, but it was unavoidable. He glanced at Ahman again. His brother looked extremely unhappy, but nodded; he understood what had to happen.

He looked toward Sergeant Curtis, who nodded as well, before joining him as they walked slowly but purposefully toward the Black Birds' commanders. They were watched carefully as they approached, but no one moved on their side until they halted, perhaps five paces apart. Each side gazed toward the other, and as they did, Jones realized that none of them wanted to be there.

He looked again toward the Black Birds' leader. "Angelino, you should remember me." The flicker he saw in his counterpart's expression confirmed his words. "I don't think you're here because of anything we've done. I don't think you'd be here at all if it was your choice." Without waiting for a further response, he looked to the woman holding Kelly. "Would you please release that woman you're holding? I'll vouch for her and everyone here. None of you will be harmed or attacked, so long as you don't attack us first."

He didn't expect that she would let Kelly go, but she did. Kelly stumbled slightly as she was released, and looked uncertainly back over her shoulder for a moment before joining the rest of the Covingtons. Jones looked briefly toward her captor, nodding, and said, "Thank you." He did not receive any response, so he added, "Julia and Rosamind have given us their names. May I ask you yours?"

"My name is Lisa," she replied, with the characteristic impassiveness of her kind.

"Lisa." He nodded to her again, then turned to look toward Julia. "Only a few of our people saw Anderson arrive with Phoebe yesterday. The guards on duty, my own detachment, maybe a few others." He then raised his voice, addressing his own people. "Who was on duty yesterday when Anderson and Phoebe came in?"

For a moment, no one moved or spoke. Then Scotty, who had been standing guard on the other side of the Covingtons, lifted his hand and came forward. He looked terrified.

"Who was on duty with you?" Jones asked, but even as he said the words, the other guard came into view; he had been assisting several of the older members of the clan. He was visibly as frightened as Scotty as he approached.

He nodded, then looked to Sergeant Curtis. "Gather my detachment and bring them in." Curtis nodded in acknowledgement, then turned on his heel. He took a deep breath, then motioned to his son. Ahman started in alarm. "Shawntaine, you come too."

The boy had lost almost all of his defiant bravado. He looked toward his uncle, wide-eyed with fear, but Ahman was staring stone-faced at his brother. Jones forced a smile that he had never felt less like making. "Come on, son. You spoke to him. You have to tell them everything he said to you."

He felt a thrill of horror, so intense that it nearly overwhelmed his terrible, fearful rush of pride when Shawntaine stopped and stared at him. "I thought that we were trying to *help* Jason Anderson. You said -"

"I said that if you were captured, you would have to tell everything you knew. If you don't, they will probably kill you," Jones' voice cut harshly across his son's before he could say more. "I don't think the Black Birds have any say in what these women do - am I right?" He glanced toward the Duke, who nodded almost angrily back. "Anderson is long gone from where we were and he didn't tell me where he was going. If he told you, you have to tell these women now. And if he didn't, you have to tell them that. They will probably kill you if you try to lie to them - they'll know."

Shawntaine swallowed, his eyes darting from Julia to the Duke, then back to Jones, and finally he looked back toward Ahman. As he did, Julia stepped forward.

"Please, wait! He's not a man yet. Not quite yet." Jones tried to interpose himself between them, but a powerful shove from Julia sent him reeling backward. As he lost his footing and fell, Ahman spoke.

"Shawntaine, tell them. We've done everything for Anderson that we can." Shawntaine turned again, flinching when he saw how close Julia had come. She would kill him before he could take two steps.

Desperately, Jones cried out, "Anderson would want you to tell her. You met him. He wouldn't want you to give up everything, especially now. We can't help him any more than we have. If you know where he went, *tell her.*"

"You are reluctant." Julia spoke emotionlessly, terrifying in her blank relentlessness. "There is something you do not wish to say. Unless you reveal this information to us, you will die."

"I don't know where he went," Shawntaine replied, his voice a strangled whisper. Julia advanced on him.

"Wait! I was with him!" The words sounded behind them, from among the Covingtons who had been preparing to march. Shouldering his way through them came the pale, sandy-haired youth who had accompanied Shawntaine when they visited Jason. Though he looked every bit as afraid as the rest of them, he seemed to have kept his wits about him, Jones noted silently.

"We heard them talking in the chief's loft yesterday afternoon. They didn't say where they were going, but they did say it would be about eight miles, and not in this direction. That's all we heard." The boy took a deep breath and continued. "Anderson talked with us for a little while, but he wasn't really like the legend said he would be. He just seemed like a normal man, mostly, and he even said he didn't know much about us. He said he didn't want to be our chief, because he'd be really bad at it." He swallowed, feeling the eyes of the Threebirds and the leadership of both clans fixed on him.

Julia's response was nearly instantaneous. "You said he seemed like a normal man. Did he do or say anything that was abnormal?"

Shawntaine's head was bowed, his face covered with his hands as he cried through them, "you sold him out!"

"Yes," the other boy answered. "He said that if we meet him again, he would tell us about how he came here. When he said it, it was like his voice changed. It was like hearing a ghost."

Lisa had watched the conversation closely, and at that point she interjected, "Do you mean that he made his voice sound different?"

"No." Shawntaine lowered his hands and turned red-rimmed eyes to Lisa. "It was something that happened while he said it. No one can make their voice sound like that."

Julia took one step toward Shawntaine, but Lisa almost shouted, "Stop!" at her. Shawntaine had squeezed his eyes shut in terror, and was shaking uncontrollably. Beyond him, the entire Covington clan watched what was unfolding in spellbound horror.

To everyone's surprise, again excepting Julia and Rosamind, Lisa turned toward the Duke. "Your force will remain here and stand guard over these people until sundown tomorrow. If we do not return with further instructions, both of your peoples may return to their homes."

As Rosamind and Julia both fixed her with looks of blank suspicion, the Duke looked utterly confused. "I had understood that we were to serve as a diversion while you locate Anderson. He is not here. Why would you have us stay?"

Rosamind answered, "Anderson used the Covingtons as a diversion while he moved in another direction. We now know where he has gone. We are leaving you here to ensure that he does not somehow use them again to thwart us."

"You're not going to kill them?" The Duke looked as though he was afraid to be hopeful.

Julia's response came in a surprisingly angry snarl. "There is no time. You will remain here. We are leaving." And with that, the Threebirds turned as one and began running, at a faster pace than any man there could have matched, back up the hill from which the Black Birds had arrived.

The Duke looked around at his officers, uncertainty giving way to gradually increasing relief as he realized the worst threat was over. He looked toward Jones, who was embracing his sobbing son, and then toward the boy's uncle Ahman; he remembered both adults from past visits. Holding up both hands, he walked toward them, his gaze locked with Ahman's. Some five paces from them, he stopped.

"We don't want to hurt anyone here, and I'm sure you don't want to fight any more than we do. The safest thing for all of us to do is to stay here, and rest, and wait." Ahman nodded in agreement, but Jones looked at him with a face contorted by conflicting emotions.

"If they make it back before sundown tomorrow, they may decide to kill us all. You think we can fight against three of them?"

Surprisingly, the Duke smiled. "We probably can't, no. But when have those women ever put off killing when they decided it needed to be done? Never, to my knowledge. So either we don't need killing - or something more important is going on, something so important that they had to leave the moment they knew what was happening.

"This man, Anderson - they think he's more dangerous than all of us. From what your boy said, he's as much as twenty miles from here, and he's had all night to do what he's going to do. No matter how fast those women run, they probably won't catch him before midafternoon.

"I think Anderson has figured out how to destroy Acme, and he got those three to follow you out here, and left the way clear for him to do what he's going to do. Well, clearer. I'm pretty sure there are still some of them at the Drome." The Duke sighed. "I hope he knows what he's getting into."

"It's not just him," Jones said thickly, emotion gravelling his voice. "He has Phoebe with him."

"I know." The Duke smiled again. "We realized that they were using us, the same way he used you. We were there to keep each other out of the way." He paused. "Phoebe's always been your liaison. I suppose that is why Anderson came to you?"

"Phoebe brought him to us. He needed rest before leaving again last night, and he needed to be out of range from Acme. That's all we know."

The Duke thought. "I can't understand why there would be a connection between those two. Phoebe is a decent sort, from what I remember - not friendly at all, no more than any of her kind, but she isn't nearly as threatening as the three we have to deal with. But I can't see why she wouldn't be helping Acme destroy Anderson."

Ahman answered, "We may never know, unless he completes this mission he's on. And even then, we might not. The legend says that the whole world will change because of him. That's a lot more than just our bases, or the Drome, or even the city."

"They're friends." Shawntaine was still gasping, his face streaked with tears, his eyes still squeezing shut from time to time as he struggled to talk. "She was standing guard over him, not ordering him around."

"We all know Anderson's special. That thing your friend said about his voice doing something funny - I heard it happen, too." Jones said. "I don't know why I didn't think of it before then. Believe me, it was definitely not ordinary."

The Duke looked round to all of them. "Regardless of everything else, Anderson has someone from the Drome helping him, and those three won't get there in time to stop him. If he wins, they won't be back here. If he loses, they won't need us." He looked around again. "So do we agree to a truce, until it's time to go back home?"

Jones nodded in reply, and Ahman said, "agreed."

The Duke barked orders to his men, and the Black Birds' lines broke as they prepared to bivouac, with both sides hoping that their truce would hold.

Chapter Twenty-Five

JASON, PHOEBE AND ALLISON halted about a mile west of the Drome, following a narrow, cracked street through the deep wood that surrounded a small city once served by the Drome's old rail system.

At Jason's suggestion, they had crossed to the north side of the railroad, and travelled briefly through a narrow wood before turning east along another wide, abandoned causeway. The sun was nearly overhead behind the tree canopy, and the trio had walked nearly six miles from the cemetery through relatively unfamiliar territory. Though he said nothing of it, Jason knew of a place where the tracks bent north, then entered a tunnel that led into the city's transit station - the last station before the Drome, on the old line.

They had not talked; Jason's determination to keep his intentions dark and his companions' usual taciturn natures - and Jason's need to conserve what energy he had left - had resulted in a nearly silent trek. Jason knew that the route they were taking might lead them into a trap, but he knew any further queries might reveal his plan. He simply hoped that if there was something along the rail line that he needed to know about, Phoebe would tell him in time to prevent disaster.

They had reached the satellite city's outskirts. Their road ran downhill into a small hollow, over which a bridge carrying the rails arched onto level ground beyond. Jason pointed toward the earth embankment that ran up from their road to the near side of the bridge.

"We have to go up there, and follow the tracks in. There's a tunnel there that runs under the city, and comes out about a quarter of a mile from the Drome." He gave Allison a long look, then glanced at Phoebe before he continued, "if there's any kind of trap or alarm hidden in there, now would be a good time to tell me about it."

"The tracks lead into the Drome, but they have not been used by humans since the time of the Seaflood catastrophe," Phoebe replied in her synthesized voice. Allison nodded.

Jason nodded, then added, "I know the rail system had to be kept operational for it to work as an energy sink, but I don't know whether it's running now, so it would help to know whether we're about to step on a third rail, and whether it's live."

Phoebe responded in the same voice as before. "The rail system is active while the rift remains even partially open. Even the ambient energy from its existence is enough to require that."

Jason nodded. "That's what I thought. There shouldn't be a lot of fluctuation, given the vector similarities, but over that distance even a little bump is pretty big. Without the damping effect from the rail lines, even a passing asteroid could create a deviation big enough to cause a surge in the systems maintaining the rift." He sighed. "Unfortunately, that means we'll have to hug the wall going through the tunnel. The third rail should be in the center, so at least we don't have to inch our way through." He sighed. "Either of you have a light source? If not, we're going to be stumbling around in the dark for over half a mile."

Both women shook their heads negatively. Jason sighed again, and began to climb the embankment that led to the rail line. As he pushed his way up the slope, he remembered again how tired and hungry he was, and hoped to himself that he would have enough strength left to finish his mission. He would be back in his own time, one way or another, before the end of the day.

Phoebe and Allison caught up with him long before he reached the top; Allison remained alongside him while Phoebe went ahead. She looked each way along the rail line, first westward toward its bend into the forest spreading between where they stood and the cemetery, then east along a short, weedy, concrete-walled defile that ended in a high, cement wall less than three hundred yards away. The tracks there dove into a tunnel that quickly went dark as it curved down into the ground beneath the abandoned streets.

Jason paused for a moment to catch his breath, then began walking east. They crossed the bridge without incident, and were at the mouth of the tunnel less than a minute later. There they stopped, and he looked at each of them again in turn.

"Phoebe, I need for you to go in front, about ten feet ahead of us. If you detect anything from the Drome, stop and let us know immediately. The one thing I don't want is for the Drome to know Allison is still active - I need for them to believe it's just us two.

"Allison -" he looked at her intently as he spoke, knowing his chance of seeing anything in her expression was next to nil -"I need you to be behind me. If Phoebe spots anything in front of us, shut down right then, for as long as I told you - fifteen minutes. If you detect *anything* coming behind us, tell Phoebe immediately, and *shut down right then.* We'll go back out the tunnel, or out through the station, and try another way if that happens. Will you do that?"

Allison nodded. Jason sighed again, still unsure whether he could trust her, and aware he was barely staving off exhaustion. "We'll go single-file until we get past the station. It's a little less than halfway there, I think. If nothing is waiting for us in there, we'll cross through it. Once we're back in the tunnel, Allison will probably have to shut down - we'll still be out of the Drome's wireless range, especially underground, but there's only a shallow curve to the line between the two stations. I'm worried that we'll encounter a signal before we come out of the tunnel - assuming we don't walk straight into a trap."

Jason paused again, and looked into the darkness. "I really don't want to go in there, but it's probably our best chance. Anyway - Phoebe, can you carry Allison once she shuts down? They'll know you're there, once you come in range. I'll need you to leave us both and lead whoever comes after us away, and keep them away until after Allison reactivates. Once she starts back up, Acme will know what's happening, and you'll be able to see her - but if you're heading for his server bank, they'll have to follow you." He tried to swallow the knot of fear choking his throat, only half-succeeding. "I hope you can handle more than one of them."

Phoebe merely looked at him emotionlessly, and did not respond. After a few seconds, Jason wordlessly motioned toward the tunnel, and they entered in file as Jason had instructed.

The light faded behind them quickly, even though their pace was somewhat slower than Jason would have liked. No one spoke as their shadows became less and less distinct against the surrounding darkness, until the blackness was all but complete. Jason glanced back only once, when he guessed that they were about halfway to the station, and could just barely discern Allison's silhouette against the last rays of light from the tunnel entrance.

They continued on as the darkness closed around them. None of them spoke. Just as Jason was thinking they might have gone down a service tunnel, and missed the station, he heard Phoebe's soft footfalls cease as she said quietly, "the wall ends here."

Jason and Allison also halted behind her. Jason thought for a moment, then said quietly, "feel along the edge of the wall for a concrete lip sticking out. It should be about three feet off the ground."

"I have found it," Phoebe replied a moment later.

"All right. Follow the edge of the lip forward. We're in the station. If someone comes, we'll have to climb up on the lip and try to find the stairs leading up." Jason shuddered a little at the thought. "It should be about a hundred yards to the other end, maybe a little more. If you get there, the wall will start again. Tell me when that happens - we'll need to stop right there."

Phoebe did not answer, and Jason heard her start walking forward again. Without turning, he whispered back to Allison, "The moment Phoebe says she's there, I'll come back to you. I need you to shut down the moment I reach you. I'll make sure you don't fall. Phoebe will carry you till the network picks her up, and then I'll take you the rest of the way. If someone comes before then, roll yourself under the lip here, against the wall underneath it, and shut down. We'll come back for you."

Without waiting for an answer, he moved forward again, and in a few steps reached the end of the wall. The light motion of the air and difference in the way their footfalls sounded indicated the open space around and above them. They spoke no more, only picking their way carefully forward.

It seemed longer, but was actually only a few minutes before Phoebe said, quietly, "the wall starts again here."

At once, Jason turned and moved carefully back two steps to where Allison waited for him. When he reached her, he asked, still in a hushed voice, "Guide me. How should I hold you? I don't want to drop you by accident."

Allison's response was so surprising that Jason almost fell over, as she stepped forward into an embrace with him, gently pulling his head down as she whispered, in a voice even more jagged and disused sounding than Phoebe's, "I know what you're going to do. Set me free from this. Please."

Jason was so stunned by this uncharacteristic, emotionally charged plea that he almost let go of her, just as he felt her going limp in his arms. Grasping her torso as carefully as he could, he lowered his shoulder under her body and lifted her into a fireman's carry. He then turned, found the lip again with his left hand, and followed along it again until the wall stopped him a few paces forward.

"Can you take her?" Jason asked. Though Allison was not in fact very heavy, he knew that he could not carry her the quarter-mile length of the rest of the tunnel and then be able to get her into position for what he needed to do. He also knew that Phoebe was much stronger than he was, and that they would move faster - even in darkness - if she carried Allison's inert form as far as possible.

"The moment you know they've picked you up, hand her off to me, and run toward the server bank," Jason whispered as they set out again. "Go as fast as I would go - not as fast as you can. Acme's smart. He knows I'm tired, and I wouldn't be as fast as you even if I was rested, so you've got to run as though I'm doing my best to keep up."

"I estimate that we should already have come into the Drome's wireless range, but I have not detected the network as yet," Phoebe replied. She had lowered her synthetic voice in the darkness.

"We're underground. The signal won't penetrate nearly as far down as we are now." Phoebe did not reply, and they labored on in silence for another minute. They had begun moving gently uphill, still curving slightly to their right as they followed the tunnel's left wall.

A few more steps, and Jason realized that as with Allison earlier, he could make out Phoebe's dim shape against the blackness, and that far ahead, he could see the brighter patch where the exit lay beyond the curve. It would not be much longer before the last race would begin.

"Thank you for everything you've done for me," Jason whispered.

"I only did as I was instructed to do, both by you and by Dr. Tinsworth," Phoebe replied. It was her own voice that spoke.

"I know. But you gave me a chance to change this, if I can." He took two quick steps forward to where he knew Phoebe walked, and put his hand on her shoulder.

"Do not touch me," Phoebe's synthetic voice responded, and she moved forward slightly more quickly. Jason drew his hand back, his face crumpling, unseen in the dark. He drew in a long, hissing breath, let it out, and continued forward. They were close. He knew it.

He whispered, softly: "Phoebe Michelle Reyes." He saw no visible response from her.

They had drawn to within thirty yards of the entrance, and Jason could see her fairly clearly, when she stopped. "The network has found me. I am connecting according to the protocol Dr. Tinsworth inserted.

"Allison will wake in four minutes. Wait one minute for me to draw off the others, and then do what you have to do." She lifted Allison quickly off of her shoulders and over her head, turning as she lowered the still-lifeless form across Jason's shoulders. "I will meet you at the rift."

Before Jason could answer, she turned and had begun jogging out of the tunnel. Beyond its end, the tracks took a bend to their left; a few steps beyond the exit, Phoebe rounded that edge and disappeared from view.

Jason noted fearfully how much slower she ran than she might have, had she been alone.

He waited until he thought she would have crossed that distance twice more, then began walking as quickly as he could, staggering a little under Allison's weight, making for the speaker stacks on the south end of the plaza, opposite the rift. He would barely have time to reach them before she awakened, and it was critical that she not activate before he arrived there.

He emerged from the tunnel and followed the rails eastward. On either side, the ground began rising slowly as the tracks leveled off, diving into a defile cut into the low rise on which the station that had become the Drome was constructed. Thankfully noting that the fence on the left side of the tracks had been removed, Jason drove his exhausted, burdened limbs out of the rail cut and onto the grounds. He had less than half his time left, and another five hundred feet to cross.

The way was clear. He saw no sign that any of Phoebe's kind were in sight. He gritted his teeth and began the last push toward the plaza.

Chapter Twenty-Six

LISA AND ROSAMIND heard Acme's instructions go off on a timer inside Julia's mind, even as they pelted along the ancient, cracked highway back toward the Covingtons' compound. As one, in obedience to their command, the Threebirds veered north and ran down onto the great thoroughfare ringing the city to their west. It was as deserted as all the other roads were; tall, rank weeds grew from two-inch cracks in the decrepit pavement, but it was still passable for their kind, and in this place it extended north along a low rise, curving slightly west after passing under an intact, rusting bridge slightly less than a mile ahead of them.

In less than six minutes, all three Cybwomen were under the bridge and following a long ramp that bent northeastward; ahead, amidst the empty, overgrown expanse that had been a parking lot in the old world, a long, narrow building stood. If they had been capable of expectation, the Cybwomen might have been surprised to see it so well-preserved, but they saw the world only as it presented itself to them, and they knew that Annette and Darleen had been tasked with maintaining that facility.

They ran across the empty lot, angling to avoid the trees that had originally been planted as ornamentation. These had begun the decades' long task of reclaiming the land as forest, toward a graying, weathered old cement building that might once have been painted an industrial blue. A stone wall ran behind it, separating it from the tracks beyond. There was one door in its otherwise uninterrupted walls, on its east side, and it was to that door that they ran, with Julia in the lead and Lisa and Rosamind three steps behind her, side by side.

The door was secured by an old but serviceable padlock and latch. This likely would not have slowed someone determined to enter for very long, but the occasional presence of Annette and Darleen over the years had turned the station into a place of fear, and no one had disturbed the area for years. Julia, however, was not an ordinary human being indulging in curiosity. She grasped the padlock and yanked it intact through the latch; she then grasped the handle of the door and hauled it free from its hinges, tossing it aside, away from her counterparts, and rushed inside.

Inside, the Threebirds separated, as Julia relayed Acme's delayed commands to reactivate the rail line that serviced their station. Within a few minutes, they had restored power and emerged, making their way toward the station where, beyond the entry area, they could see a single-car commuter rail unit standing on the tracks.

"We can walk from here. The unit will require at least one minute before returning to operational status," Julia's directive flashed to Lisa and Rosamind.

There were no questions in response, only acknowledgement, as they moved through the silent, empty station, through the turnstiles - Annette and Darleen had even maintained those, and kept them functioning - and emerged onto the commuter platform. The train stood open, awaiting them.

"The train takes power directly from the rails, when the system is operating," Acme's instructions reached them all through Julia. "The air compressors require one minute to recharge. Once complete, the train is operational, as long as any of you three are available to pilot it. One of you will interface with the engine and control it. Once that interface is achieved, accelerate the train to sixty miles per hour, and maintain that speed through the Kensington station, the Drome, and the Decatur station beyond it."

They had reached the door to the engineer's compartment and entered as Acme continued, "I calculate that when you reach the tunnel leading to the Decatur station, Phoebe and Anderson will have entered its far side, having excavated Tinsworth's legacy package for him out of his grave. I instructed Annette and Darleen to remove the lights from the front of the unit you are riding, so that they will not be able to see it. Phoebe will do everything in her power to ensure Jason Anderson's survival; that has always been her task. It is therefore necessary now to separate them, and this will be the most efficient way, if she has not already been eliminated. You will run them down in that tunnel, and Phoebe will be forced to do whatever is necessary to save Anderson - and will almost certainly be destroyed in the process."

All of this passed into their thoughts with the speed of all their communications. Julia looked down at the controls, which had been pared down considerably by Annette and Darleen; all that remained of the instrument panel was a single cluster of lights. She paused for a millisecond as Acme's instructions to her continued, and then relayed to the others, "I will drive this train. When we reach the Drome, I will open the door, and you will jump out onto the platform. I will continue with the train into the tunnel, and exit at the next station after shutting this unit down."

"Clarification," Lisa responded a millisecond later; both her counterparts looked askance at her, noting her hesitation. The engine started thrumming to life under their feet. "We exit at the Drome, and you exit at Decatur, with the train still at speed but with the power shut down. Confirmed?

"Confirmed. Acme has calculated that the likelihood that Anderson will be in that tunnel is near ninety-eight percent. It is the only possible way to approach within a thousand feet of the Drome without being detected long before by its wireless network. He has long planned for Anderson to take this route, knowing he would choose it; you will await him in the Drome in the event that something unexpected has happened since our departure."

"Acknowledged." With that, Julia engaged communication with the train's instrumentation, and the others waited in their standby mode for nearly a full second before Rosamind sent, "After this mission is completed, I recommend that Lisa be decommissioned until Acme can verify her functionality directly."

"Seconded." Julia's response, even electronically, seemed clipped and strained. Lisa did not respond. Their sensors gathered what little information from their surroundings as was available, several times, as the train slowly awakened. More than once Lisa noted the others' sensors reviewing her outputs, She reviewed them four times herself, and could find nothing in analysis that would indicate a significant malfunction.

"Engaging throttle," Julia sent. The train ground slowly forward. The sounds of long-unused machinery reached them even in their insulated compartment, but the vehicle obeyed Julia's direction, slowly grinding forward past the stone wall between them and the old blue maintenance building on their left, before it began climbing a short straightaway toward the bridge arching over the thoroughfare they had followed to the station.

They moved over the bridge, still picking up speed, as the tracks bent gently northward and the overgrown foliage on both sides flew by; then they dove into a tunnel that ran only a short distance before emerging just as they reached the first station. It was above ground, and as deserted as the one they had just left, and they were through it in seconds, diving back underground into another tunnel.

It grew completely dark in front of them. The train veered to their right, more sharply than before, but it remained securely between the rails. As they emerged from underground, the line curved again to the left, and ahead, they could see the first sidings of the rail yard where the extra units for the system had been stored. As the line straightened again, steering them slightly south of due west, they could see the Drome itself in the distance about a mile away.

They had slowed slightly in the tunnel to allow for the rails' curvature; now they accelerated again as the Drome came closer, straight ahead of them. The door to their right opened, and Julia sent, "prepare to disembark. You will be moving at speed."

"Acknowledged." Neither Rosamind nor Lisa responded further, and Lisa moved to the door, with Rosamind behind. The station grew steadily closer, until they were under its roof and the platform was moving past them. They had acquired the Drome's wireless only a few seconds before they arrived - and then, everything happened almost all at once.

Julia's thought flashed, "Phoebe has been spotted. She is in the station, on the platform, with all available units in pursuit."

Before Lisa could respond, Rosamind interjected: "Acme is down. I am receiving no communication from him."

Lisa leaned out the open door. Through the rushing wind, ahead and to her left, she could see Phoebe running to the platform's edge, visibly faster than her pursuers; then Phoebe leapt forward, out and along the path of the rails, landing out of sight ahead of the train. Lisa leaned back in to see where their quarry had landed. In the same instant, Rosamind shoved her, as hard as only one of their kind could, and sent her hurtling out onto the platform.

Though Lisa's thoughts were transmitted and received as rapidly as any of their kind, she was - like them - limited by the speed with which her brain could send commands to her physical body. She could see that she was moving on the platform at a speed no human should have been able to reach, and that even with her augmented reflexes, she would not be able to maintain her balance. Her momentum was carrying her much too quickly toward a support pillar; making the best calculation she could, she tumbled forward into a roll that narrowly missed the column, and shed some of her forward velocity as her fall ended in a jarring collision with a wall next to the stairwell leading from the platform to the Drome's ground level.

As she tried to rise, her brain screamed several warnings to her; her left foot was broken, along with several ribs. She had suffered a number of abrasions and bruises, and at impact, her head had struck the stone wall. The resulting concussion blurred her perception and destabilized her wireless link. She could see Rosamind blearily as the latter struggled to rise from where she had rolled to a stop after her leap from the train.

Rosamind's communications were intact, but sporadic. "Right foot landed in a puddle of unknown fluid. Unable to recover from resulting imbalance. Severe damage to right leg in resulting fall. Will attempt pursuit." "Severe damage" was an understatement; the leg was visibly distended at the knee and was already swelling. One of her arms also hung limply, with a grotesque extra joint in the middle of her forearm.

As Lisa's vision began to darken, and the trauma protocols ingrained in each of their systems kicked in, a last burst of communication from Julia reached them: "All available units continued pursuit of target in absence of countermand from Acme.   All units destroyed by impact with train. Pursuing target into -" Julia's frenetic, brief stream ended with a strangely incoherent burst – one that was cut off abruptly as the train entered the tunnel and her connection dropped.

As it faded, at the edge of her last awareness before shutdown, another presence on the network found Lisa, homing in on her, assessing her injuries. She did not receive any response, either from Rosamind or from Acme, as she went into diagnostic shutdown.

PHOEBE LEFT JASON behind, unsure of what he had in mind, but aware that she had only a little time. Acme had already tried twice to hail her; she could not answer without disobeying her primary directive, so she shut out his communications, and simply ran at a pace well under normal speed, hesitating occasionally so that the impression that she was leading Jason would be convincing.

Beyond the tunnel, the tracks ran on even ground for about three hundred yards in a slight left curve; about a third of the way along, she could see the station that formed the main part of the Drome ahead. She guessed that Jason was only just emerging from the tunnel, and carrying Allison to a place where she could be safely awakened would take him at least another ninety seconds.

She was not concerned about being caught by the other Cybwomen; her body was almost entirely artificial. She knew she was the fastest among them, and the strongest; only Annette, Darleen or Julia might have posed serious threats. She knew that for herself, the greatest danger was that she would be surrounded and cut off from escape, and overpowered by five or six of her own kind working in concert.

She angled left, toward that part of the plaza where Allison had broken Jason's companion's neck when they first emerged from the rift. As she ran, she could hear the alarms among the six Cybwomen still in the Drome, and overheard as Acme coordinated their movements. His instructions were clear: she, Phoebe, was to be taken down and deactivated, then dismantled.

She did not know fear, but her dream states had acquainted her with faint echoes of her past, and dim though those echoes were, they still pushed her to increase her speed. She stonily maintained her pace, counting the seconds in her head as she pinpointed each of her pursuers and sought to determine the path that would allow her to elude them for as long as possible.

Over a minute had elapsed since she had emerged. Jason would have nearly reached a safe point. In a millisecond, she calculated a route that would allow her to maintain her current pace for twenty more seconds, then break through the dragnet that was forming to trap her, drawing them off in pursuit. At that point, Acme would know that Jason was no longer with her, and would begin looking for him on the grounds - but it was unlikely that Acme would find him in less than ten seconds, and even if he did, no Cybwoman was likely to reach him in less than twice that time. Allison was due to awaken, and Jason had planned something with her.

It would have to be enough. Phoebe continued on her selected path until the last possible millisecond before her breakout, and then shot forward at her fastest speed, passing only a few yards in front of one of the Cybwomen in the dragnet. That one with the others immediately gathered in pursuit; Phoebe slowed to a pace that they could nearly match, crossing the plaza and making for the station's platform, which lay at the bottom of a flight of shallow stairs a little way ahead.

At the same time that she heard the train coming along the line from the east, she heard the shocking, immediate silence that fell over all of their minds as Acme's constant commands, his constant monitoring, his incessant flow of communication suddenly ceased. As she ran down the stairs, still with the other Cybwomen in pursuit, she saw the train just beyond the eastern end of the platform and realized that with Acme inoperative, her pursuers were as enslaved to his last directive as she had been to her own for decades - ever since Tinsworth had died.

She increased speed until she was flying across the lower level, slower than the train that was about to enter the station, but faster than everything else. The sudden roar of the train against the roof of the station told her that it had reached the platform, and was not slowing; she leapt forward off its edge and pelted full-out along the tracks, inhumanly fast, and behind her, the six Cybwomen pursuing her followed, reading the speed of the train, but unable to give up the pursuit.

She tore back along the way she had come, rounding the curve with the tunnel only two hundred yards ahead, as behind her the others dropped from the network, one by one. The train had gotten them all. Julia had also attached to the network, trying as Acme had to give some order that might stop her, but Julia was even less able to countermand her overriding directive than Acme had been.

She reached the tunnel, slowing as she did, and came almost to a halt at its mouth; the train was less than twenty yards behind. At the very last moment, she dodged to her left, somersaulting high over the third rail and clearing the far track - just as the train dived into the tunnel with Julia still aboard.

Julia's last transmission, before the tunnel dropped her from both the network and their own link, was a signal that a human being might well have interpreted as a shriek of rage.

Chapter Twenty-Seven

JASON WAS ALREADY tiring well before he reached the end of the cut that led into the tunnel. The tracks had curved until he could see the plaza where he had first emerged from the rift. He had originally arrived on its northern end, well away from where he now approached, with Allison still inactive, from the southwest.

On the tracks' far side, he could see the same fence that surrounded the Drome, and that gave him another idea. He turned, almost doubling back on his path, and carried Allison's dead weight as fast as he could push himself, back toward the place where Phoebe had cut that fence.

Once there, he set Allison down as carefully as he could, arranging her so that she leaned back against the fence. He fumbled with the USB2 cord that would connect her to the laptop, willing himself to work through his exhaustion. She would awaken any second. He pressed the power button, hoping against hope that it would boot quickly, and looked around himself.

A movement through the trees caught his eye. One of the other Cybwomen had run across the plaza, away from them; he hoped Phoebe was well ahead of her. The laptop had already almost finished booting; its display had only a single icon on it. Allison's eyes opened as he clicked the icon; a DOS-prompt popup window appeared on the display, scrolling commands faster than he could read them - not that he needed to. The sequence had been preset. Tinsworth had known what he was going to attempt.

It was by sheer, blind luck that he was looking at Allison at the moment her eyes snapped toward him, and he sensed at once that someone else was seeing him through them. It took all the self-control he had not to recoil from her, and knowing what was at stake, he opened a second DOS window and began typing as fast as he could.

It was fast enough. Before Allison's restart queue had completed, she had shut down again, and had been forced into a diagnostic reboot. Jason heaved a huge sigh of relief; he guessed he had sixty seconds to do what he needed to do, and Tinsworth's instructions had clarified how he could do what would be required. Silently, he reminded himself to thank the man when he returned, as he opened another low-level text-coding window and entered the commands that needed to be executed.

Allison's restart was completed slightly faster than he had expected, but he was done; she would do the rest. He watched her as her brain completed its diagnostic and restarted her; as the command chain executed, her eyes opened again, but there was a recognition that was above what he had seen from her in the cemetery. He looked at her as she restarted, and she looked at him. He had a sense of two immense objects, two stars, passing each other so closely as to create a material link between them - but their relative motions carried them past each other, flinging them along divergent vectors across the universe, never to encounter each other again.

Before he could react, she spoke through his laptop, in a popup window: "You'll remember me, won't you?"

It was not truly a question.

ROSAMIND CAREFULLY MADE her way to her feet. She could not put any weight on her injured leg, and the Drome's usual buzz of communications had gone nearly silent. There were only three of her kind that she could sense within range - Allison, in her usual place, as uncommunicative as ever; Lisa, who had shut down under the trauma protocols, and Phoebe.

Rosamind did not know fear as humans would know it, but she perceived at once that she was in a precarious situation. Lisa was no longer a certain ally. Even before her injury, she had exhibited signs indicating that the interface between her CPU and her brain was beginning to wear out, and she could not be expected to behave predictably. None of the other Cybwomen remained; Acme had commanded them to pursue Phoebe, and

Phoebe had led them onto the tracks in front of the train - and while she had done so, Acme had inexplicably shut down. Without Acme to countermand the order, the others had pursued Phoebe onto the tracks, and they had all been cut down by the train before they could clear the platform's western end.

Julia's last transmission indicated that Phoebe - the only one among them with an almost fully artificial body, and thus the fastest of them all - and the most dangerous - had not only cleared the platform, but had run almost to the tunnel's mouth without being overtaken.

There was only one possibility - Phoebe had led the train, with Julia aboard, into the tunnel, and then evaded both. Julia would not return to the Drome for at least fifteen minutes, even if she succeeded in leaping unharmed from the train; Phoebe would cross the shorter distance from the tunnel's mouth in a third of that time. Rosamind would be outmatched by Phoebe alone, and if Lisa proved worse than unreliable, she might be outnumbered.

Her best chance to protect Acme, she concluded, would be to reach the diagnostic infirmary and connect directly to the servers, and try to restart him. She leaned against the wall and began to slide along it as well as her injured leg would allow, moving as quickly as she could without further damaging herself. The warning signals of pain from her arm and leg forced her to slow as she reached the back corner of the platform and turned along it toward the stairwell. Nearly a full minute had elapsed. Phoebe was not coming for her - not yet - but she had to know that Rosamind would not be able to fight her effectively. She was doing something else, and the nature of that task was unclear, owing to her altered connection into the wireless network.

A sudden flood of signals, sensory and diagnostic, alerts and probes, flooded her mind a few milliseconds later. Acme was online again, assessing his condition. Rosamind transmitted what she knew of the situation into the blizzard of invisible communications suddenly crisscrossing the Drome, and sank to the ground. Another, familiar set of signals began to emanate from the north end of the plaza, but she could not respond to them.

"Remain where you are. Do not risk provoking Phoebe. She is to be left undisturbed." Acme's familiar, echoing voice sounded in her brain. Rosamind assessed the communication's import for a millisecond, and noted a danger that could not be left unaddressed.

"Acme, please confirm countermand of previous order. Phoebe was to be terminated and dismantled. Your deactivation requires that I engage protocols if you are compromised." She knew that she risked deactivation herself if Acme had in fact been subverted, but she had to follow the strictures of her kind.

The response from Acme was clear and immediate: "Countermand confirmed. Phoebe could not have been terminated by anyone in the Drome, other than myself; she has a separate group of protocols that originate with her creation, which was concurrent with mine. I therefore used my understanding of those protocols to create this contingency, in the event that he and Phoebe succeeded in evading the train that, by my calculation, would eliminate Phoebe in approximately ninety-eight percent of all possible scenarios.

"Jason Anderson will most likely reset the rift's temporal endpoint in order to reach Phoebe before she is killed by debris resulting from energies generated by the rift extension. He will not be permitted to re-enter the rift as he has re-configured it, because Phoebe is under a superseding directive from Dr. Tinsworth. She will block his passage in order to prevent a paradox."

AS THE TRAIN SHOT into the next station, Julia slowed it, scanning the approaching platform as best she could for any kind of obstruction that would hinder her exit. The train would coast to a stop once she disconnected from it, but it would still be travelling forty-one miles an hour when it reached the point where she would have to jump – in near-complete darkness. Anything in her path would almost certainly cause a fall, and a fall would break her limbs - and delay her return to the Drome enough to prevent her from stopping Anderson from doing whatever he had planned to do.

Three seconds. Two. She could see, very dimly, onto the platform; it was mainly clear, though some falls of masonry from its roof lay scattered across its length. These were recent falls; Annette and Darleen checked this station twice each year, and anything like the debris she had detected would have been cleared. In the last second before her leap, she sought to find the best path available to her. She would have to shed enough velocity crossing the platform to allow her to take the stairs without stopping - and without falling.

The train reached the platform. Julia leaped out, and heard the engine note lowering as she disconnected. She barely retained her balance as she high-stepped across the platform, moving faster than running speed, but slowing down as she reached the stairwell. She bounded up the wide, shallow flight at a speed she could manage, but was forced to bring herself to a stop by colliding with a wall as she reached the stairwell landing.

She was briefly shaken, but not injured. The landing was small, and still very dark; she could see the stairs and, back along the way she had come, the old, inoperative escalators that led to the exit, but could not determine with certainty whether her way out was clear.

She would have to chance it; every second could make a difference. She began to run again, less swiftly than before, but nearly as fast as she was able; nothing was in her way, and she mounted the next, steeper flight of stairs without incident, emerging at the station's entrance.

It was already midafternoon. The Drome lay a little more than a mile to the east. Without any further hesitation, Julia increased her speed to a sprint, following the road out of the abandoned satellite city toward the Drome.

As she drew nearer, she reconnected to the Drome's wireless signal. Acme was online again. Rosamind was seriously injured and could not fight. Lisa had shut down and was running a diagnostic after suffering a brain injury. Phoebe was there. She had no means of perceiving whether Anderson was with her.

As she continued her sprint, two signals drove her: first, that Allison had awoken in her corner of the Drome, and was as unresponsive as ever; second, Acme's clear directive had reached her: bring Rosamind into the rehabilitation facility, and retrieve Darleen. Her rebuild was nearly complete, and though she was less functional than before, it appeared that she would still be more able than Rosamind to carry out Acme's requirements.

It would take three of them - Allison, Darleen and Julia - to defeat Phoebe once Anderson had returned into the rift. Once Phoebe had accomplished her objective - the return of Jason Anderson to his own time - she would no longer have that assignment acting as a check upon her. Acme suspected that if that objective were to be removed, her next directive would also have its origin with Tinsworth - and that it would involve the destruction of Acme himself, and possibly the Drome as well.

She reached the edge of the plaza. Phoebe and Allison both knew she was there, but they were both far enough away that she would have time to react if they approached. On its north end, she saw that the rift had reopened, as Acme had told her it would; she went past it without giving it further thought and made for the station stairs.

Rosamind lay crumpled and unresponsive at their base, with two of her limbs already misshapen. Not far away, Lisa lay against the stone wall, also unconscious. As Acme sent Julia the data on her injuries, she lifted Rosamind quickly and carefully, and made her way back up the stairs. At their top, she made a right turn, away from the plaza, toward the same building where Darleen had been rebuilt. Julia felt no more sense of misgiving in taking Rosamind there than Annette had with Darleen.

She reached the door, sensing as she did that Allison and Phoebe had left the far corner of the Drome grounds and were coming toward her. The black portal swung open. Darleen was sitting up on her gurney, not yet fully connected to the Drome network, but she apparently recognized Julia - at least, she did not immediately attack her.

Julia carried Rosamind to a second gurney opposite Darleen's and laid her on it, carefully but quickly arranging her limbs as Acme instructed.

Acme directed her toward a storage cupboard above the gurney; she took the syringe he indicated to her and used it to inject a potent anesthetic into Rosamind's undamaged arm.

"Leave her, and take Darleen." Acme's instruction came when she was finished, and as robotically as she had done everything else, Julia left her fellow Threebird and approached Darleen. The rebuild had completed, and Darleen was looking around herself, not recognizing the place where she had been taken.

As Julia began transmitting a summary of what was happening, Acme cut across her with a sudden, strident alert tone that interrupted her thoughts. The tone lasted a full millisecond.

"The rift's spatial endpoint has been altered to an unprojected location. Jason Anderson must not be allowed to pass through it. Proceed at once to guard the rift. Phoebe may have been compromised."

Both Cybwomen leapt at once toward the door, with Julia leading Darleen, as soon as they had processed the command. Beyond it, they could see the plaza as they sprinted forward - and crossing it from its far side at a rapid, though labored, walk was a human they did not recognize immediately, but who they knew could only be Jason Anderson. He was heading straight toward the rift, with Allison escorting him on one side and Phoebe on the other.

If any two Cybwomen might ever have been considered Acme's enemies, those were the two. Julia veered slightly to her right, preparing to engage Phoebe; behind her, she could hear Darleen's footfalls angling toward Allison. Darleen was still slightly disoriented, Julia thought - but she should still be able to dispatch Allison relatively quickly. It was critical that she do so. Phoebe's construction was the most artificial of them all. She could only be truly injured in the head or by a precise blow to one of her joints; striking her anywhere else would, in all likelihood, only injure her attacker.

The two escorting Anderson were aware of their approach before they had even reached the plaza, and before either Julia or Darleen could come within a hundred feet of him, Allison and Phoebe had met their attack. Jason watched them engage, then saw the open rift only a hundred yards away, and began to run toward it as fast as he could, his pace still agonizingly slow.

LISA WAS IN MID-DIAGNOSTIC when Acme's alarm was transmitted, so that his attempt to awaken her prematurely had an unexpected result.

Multiple execution failures in her startup queue left her in a semi-wakened state, though able to communicate and receive information. Her brain, having suffered a major concussion from her fall, compensated by bypassing some of the damaged sectors of her memory storage, and in doing so, began rerouting conscious thought through another part of her brain - a part that retained memory of her life before she had died, and then revived in her current state.

A searing pain behind her eyes threatened to blind her, but the memories and associations with her thoughts were of bright daylight, and carried a strange weightlessness that her now-glandless existence could not fully identify. She heard vague echoes of enjoyment. She felt the vibrations left by pangs of love. But the strangest sensation she encountered was associated with something that she had thought nonexistent. It was something that once had given pleasure, had lent comfort, and even supplied endurance when circumstances were adverse - but she could not quite identify it.

She struggled to her feet, still in a dreamlike state. She hobbled as best she could back up the stairs, sensing as she did that four of her kind were on the plaza beyond the station - Allison and Darleen, fighting each other, while a few yards away from them, Phoebe and Julia were also locked in combat. No one acknowledged her, or even appeared to have noticed that she was coming; even Acme had not given her any instructions.

It was not until she reached the station's entrance, and looked out toward the plaza, that she saw the other person there - the man she had been tasked with hunting since his arrival, who had tricked all of them into chasing him in the wrong direction (*like a ghost,* an unbidden association seemed to whisper) and who was within mere yards of passing back through the rift from which he had come.

A set of disconnected images in her altered mind merged, forming a single vision.   Jason Anderson would change the world.   Acme was desperate to prevent his departure.   The rift had been altered.

Jason Anderson, she realized, might release her from this existence - one that she had never questioned, but with the changes in her mind, she perceived anew, and understood to be painful, and brutal, and terrible.

She saw in a flash of memory all the men she had killed - men that might have been deserving of death, but who could never have threatened her.   She understood for the first time that she had become a thing of terror, because she had lived without one vital thing since she had reawakened – the one thing she had thought nonexistent.

That thing was what she pursued as she limped forward, on a path that would intercept Jason Anderson mere feet from the rift.   She had seen it at last, and she finally understood.   Her mission was not to stop him – not anymore, not ever again.   She no longer answered to Acme; he no longer acknowledged her.   None of them did.   She was on her own.   She could choose her own mission.

And she chose to clear Jason Anderson's path, by any means she could. The man might indeed change everything.   And by doing so, he might shunt her into another existence - one that was surely better than the dismal, dark world she had walked for so long, and where she had done so much unwitting evil.

She reached the plaza.   No one had noticed her.   She sensed and saw Darleen as she fell, confused and in mortal pain, and saw Allison turning toward the other two combatants.   Anderson had passed them all and was halfway to the rift.

What Lisa experienced then was only an echo of true human experience, but against the background of the rest of her second life, the surge of hope that she felt was so profound that she nearly fell - but the change in her mind strengthened her, and allowed her not only to continue forward, but to move faster to where she estimated she would need to be.

AND ALL THINGS WILL BE MADE NEW

Chapter Twenty-Eight

After

DARLEEN'S ATTACK ON ALLISON was clumsier than anything the latter had ever seen from one of her kind. Hampered by the absence of Annette, and still unable to move or coordinate properly, Darleen would have been unable to overcome any of the Cybwomen under normal circumstances - but Allison also knew the urgency of the situation, knew that Darleen was doomed as they all were, and had realized that if Julia overcame Phoebe, Anderson would not reach the rift.

She therefore transmitted, using the language Darleen had shared with Annette, a command for Darleen to be still, feinting inaction so as to allow a surprise attack. This was the same stratagem she had employed in the cemetery. Darleen's hesitation upon receiving the command was identical to Annette's, and proved equally deadly; less than three seconds later, Darleen lay on the flagstones with blood leaking from her mouth and her neck bent at a horrifying angle.

As she turned, she saw that Julia had succeeded in doing the one thing that might thwart Anderson: Phoebe had been struck a glancing blow to her head and was staggering back as Julia pressed her advantage. Yet, even as Allison launched herself at Julia, Julia sensed the attack, and whirled on her as she closed. Allison matched her blow for blow for nearly ten seconds, with each of them throwing at least three times that many punches in that span. Neither of them landed a clean blow on the other.

As they fought, each of them sensed Phoebe's brief disorientation. When she regained full awareness, a new set of signals from her instantly reversed their motivations; suddenly Allison was battling to reach Phoebe, while Julia blocked her path as effectively as a brick wall might have done. Of the two of them, Julia was the more capable combatant; Allison's efforts to move past her were effectively blocked. After a few more seconds of fighting, Allison received a transmission from Acme - one whose content reminded her of another, long-ago fight with Julia.

Acme was laughing at her.

JASON STAGGERED TOWARD the rift, hoping that Phoebe and Allison could keep the path clear long enough for him to reach it. It was less than fifty yards away, and he could see that it was open; all he needed to do was reach it, and he could do what he had to do next.

Out of the corner of his eye, he saw one Cybwoman overcome by Allison; even from forty feet away, he heard the ugly, wet, splitting sound of her neck as Allison twisted her head until it snapped . He wanted to vomit – again - but he knew that he had no time. Phoebe was even with him, to his right, fighting another vicious, angry-looking example of her kind; even as he glanced over, the enemy made a timed feint, tricking Phoebe into a low leg sweep, and kicked hard at her head; only Phoebe's mechanical reflexes saved her, as she was able to catch part of the blow on her shoulder. She was nonetheless dazed, and staggered back.

Jason lowered his head and ran for the rift. He knew the Cybwoman could outrun him even if he were fresh - but he was exhausted, had almost no strength left, and still had one more effort to make when he returned to his own time, assuming that he could even get there.

Thirty yards. Twenty-five. Twenty. *Fifteen.* And someone stood in his way. It wasn't the vicious-looking Cybwoman. It wasn't even Allison, who he had still secretly feared would betray him.

"Jason Anderson, I am tasked with your protection. The rift destination has been altered. Passing through it will lead to your death." That synthetic voice had never been pleasant to his hearing, but it had never been more unwelcome than that moment.

It was Phoebe. It was his own Phoebe, and she would not let him pass.

He stared at her, the rift yawning only a short distance behind her, almost despairing. She still looked slightly disoriented, almost dizzy, but she would not move, and he knew he could not outrun or overcome her. Gasping for breath from his run, he bent forward, his head bowed, and cried out miserably, "I didn't want this for you, Phoebe. I would never have let this happen." He looked back up at her as he spoke.

Phoebe's eyes clouded again for that brief instant, the one he so needed to see. "So you told me before, more than once, when you were alive."

"I'm alive now, Phoebe!" Jason could not hold tears back; he was too tired, and completely overcome. "Why are you doing this?" he asked desperately. He knew Tinsworth would have understood what he had done. Phoebe was acting on her own directive, not his.

"Why?" She seemed confused - certain of her response, uncertain of its source. Both of her voices were speaking at once.

"Why? Because I loved you."

Jason might have bowed his head again at that moment, but before he could lower his eyes from hers, something struck her from the side, knocking her sprawling, out of his way. It was another Cybwoman, who had landed atop Phoebe and was trying to hold her down.

He ran again toward the rift, and heard Phoebe make a sound behind him; it was a terrible, jagged, ragged howl of misery from a voice that never should have existed. It tore at his heart as he crossed the last few feet to where the rift's blank surface awaited him. He looked back at her; she had fought free of her attacker, but had no chance of stopping him. He was one step from home.

He looked into her eyes once more, those eyes that had been blank, that were still largely dull and emotionless - yet what feeling he saw there was more than all the response he had seen from her since he had first set foot in her dark world. He grieved in his heart for her, for one instant. Then his focus returned, and he said to her, so softly that only a Cybwoman could have heard him: "I promise, I will make sure this never happens to you."

Her expression did not change, and a heartbeat later, he turned and stepped back through the rift. As he did, Acme's communications ceased for a second time.

SHAWNTAINE WAITED WITH his father, his Uncle Ahman, and the commanders for the Black Birds as the late afternoon wore on. No one had wanted to talk much during the day, but there had been no hostility on either side. Both clans knew their fates rested in large part on whether the Threebirds were sent back to deal with them, and their shared dread made them all equals in fear.

His father was at that moment engaged in conversation with the one they called the Duke; he had been completely unlike what they had come to expect from the Black Birds. Even Uncle Ahman had been impressed. Shawntaine realized that if they survived this day together, the two clans would be much less likely to battle or quarrel with each other in years to come. Even with his inexperience, he understood how much that would help him - if, and when, he became the clan chief.

The day was warm, but not hot, and there was no sign of rain; it came as a surprise to him when he saw a dark cloud low in the western sky. He looked around himself, saw that no one else had noticed it yet, and looked back; it was visibly nearer and darker. As he gave a shout and pointed, his actions were mimicked by several others in both clans; within a few seconds, everyone there had stood up, watching as the cloud grew nearer, with a strange, wailing shriek rising from it.

It was formed entirely of birds, flying out of the west as fast as their wings would carry them, in an avian wave that stretched across the sky from north to south. As they crossed the zenith overhead, they were joined by the birds in the trees around them, and a terrible wind followed in their wake. Shawntaine felt a thrill of horror as he realized that the horizon was actually coming closer; the earth had begun to tremble, and within seconds was rumbling so hard that none among them remained standing.

Shawntaine crawled forward and to his left, and finding his father's hand, clasped it with both of his own. They looked at each other, and realized that they had both become translucent; the very stuff they were made of was becoming diffuse, and the world around them was fading. People from both clans shrieked and cried out with the full range of human emotions, unsure and afraid of what was happening.

He felt an almost immaterial touch on his shoulder; it was the man called the Duke, and he looked unafraid, only curious. The exclamations from those around them were becoming airier, dimmer and less substantial, like the stuff of dreams before waking. The Duke looked at him, and smiled, and when he glanced toward his father, Shawntaine saw that he wore a similar expression.

"It doesn't hurt." The Duke's voice was distant as they faded. "And we're going somewhere else. Can you feel it?"

AS SHE LAY ON the plaza, Lisa looked up as Anderson entered the rift. Phoebe would have leapt after him in pursuit, but Lisa was able to grasp her ankle and trip her; the effort pulled her right shoulder from her socket, compounding the alerts her already damaged body was sending through the altered awareness that had become her reality.

Phoebe turned to attack her, and she did not resist, but she remembered Allison, and how Phoebe had cared for her when she had been shut away. She asked aloud: "What do you see when you dream?"

The question stopped Phoebe. They stared at each other. Lisa struggled to transmit to her, and could not use the same link as their kind had always used; instead, with the different memory channels her brain had co-opted, she tried to connect with the same portions of Phoebe's mind.

Phoebe recoiled, displaying the most human expression of fear that had crossed her face in decades. Lisa remained serene, continuing to transmit, showing Phoebe what she had seen, explaining in wordless images why she had allowed Anderson to escape. As she did, Acme resumed communications again; all of his transmissions were coded in his highest alert protocol. A human being, hearing those otherwise silent electronic klaxons, would have thought they heard a woman screaming, amidst a high-altitude fall to her death.

Lisa continued to transmit on the channel she had opened with Phoebe; as she finished, a sharp crack sounded behind them. They looked at the rift to see that it had collapsed on itself, as the earth began to shake violently. Phoebe lost her footing and fell to the ground; a short distance away, Julia and Allison likewise were soon unable to remain upright.

A new, keening alarm sounded from Acme, rising in pitch to their electronic perception, as the buildings in the Drome began to shed pieces of themselves. A second alarm also sounded in their minds; Rosamind had awakened in the midst of the chaos, disoriented and unable to move. Phoebe looked over to where she knew Rosamind had been taken; the building collapsed as she watched, and Rosamind's last signal ceased abruptly. A few seconds later, Acme's last alarm was also cut off.

There were four of them left, and though the world was beginning to disintegrate around them, and was taking them with it, still they perceived the destruction as a human would see an event played in slow motion. Lisa and Phoebe were finally able to interact fully via Lisa's new channel when a third signal cut across their communication. It was Allison, and she spoke without preamble to Lisa: "When did you see that Jason Anderson could undo what was done to us?"

Lisa responded, "I was injured on the platform, and began a diagnostic shutdown. Acme attempted to reactivate me before my operating system had stabilized, and the resulting system failures left me in this state. I did not draw the connection until I saw him on the plaza, and saw that Phoebe was with him.

"Acme would never have left Phoebe with him, unless he knew she would prevent him from returning to any other time and place than his own." Her focus changed toward Phoebe; her communications were as wordless as any electronic signal, and yet pictographic to their perceptions. "I came to understand what we are, and what we have become - all of us." Lisa had not realized that her eyes had closed; as she opened them, she saw that Julia alone among them was still resisting the tumult around them, refusing to communicate with any of the three that remained there with her. The station building had collapsed entirely. The flagstones of the plaza were cracking; in places, the once-smooth expanse had rippled outward, away from the rift. A wind was rushing in around them from all sides, carrying away the broken remains of the things of their world, and as Lisa watched, Julia was lifted up and hurled into the sky. Her signal dropped less than two seconds later.

Everything around them was beginning to disintegrate; even the wind, though it rushed ever faster, was pushing less and less air. Lisa glanced at her hands; she could see particles flying off of them, and as she looked toward Allison, and then Phoebe, the same phenomenon was breaking down their bodies as well. In a few more seconds, they would vanish.

Lisa returned to their channel. "It's happening. Jason Anderson has fulfilled the prophecy that was made about him, and the world is changing."

"Do you see what is to come?" The question was from Allison. Already her signal was fading. Phoebe was still receiving, but she had gone mute, and Lisa realized that something had happened a long, long time ago.

"Jason Anderson kept his promise to Phoebe," she whispered into the whirlwind, as her sight failed. "None of this ever happened." And with that, they were gone.

Before

JASON DEPARTED CHAOS, and arrived into a different chaos.

His immediate sense was of belonging, of being where he was supposed to be. It was something he had not felt in days, and the flood of recognition in his mind and heart almost paralyzed him - but when he took in his surroundings, he realized that he had barely left himself enough time.

The lab had been blasted by his arrival; the energy shed in matching his velocity and directional vectors to his new position in space-time had wrought havoc. Smoke and the smell of burning electronics filled the air, and the ground trembled.

Jason knew what that meant. He turned, looking at the shattered window where Phoebe had said goodbye to him days and seconds before, and started toward it. He had a horrible instant when he encountered his own body, its left side charred and disfigured in the blast - but he had known it would be there.

He had known from the moment that he saw what Tinsworth had put together - and what that other self, in that other plane, had also assembled. They had hit upon the simplest change to the rift extension, and they had been able to piggyback their rudimentary transposition onto the thirty years Acme had spent making the extension possible.

Instead of linking to the asshole end - which was of course what Acme would have done; he knew the Wiley Grant version of himself would be absent at the time the extension was made - Jason had, in the command sequence he had programmed into Allison, reversed the direction of the bridge collapse. The rift that had formed, on his original timeline in Hampton Hall, had formed this time in Williams, and from the feel of the last tremor, that rift would close within seconds.

There was no more time. He leaped through the now-glassless window, shouldered open the lab door, and ran as fast as his worn-out limbs would carry him toward the exit. He knew Phoebe would have been clear of the first blast; he had to make sure she was out of range before the second.

He reached the same exit that he had before, and burst out of the doors to see Phoebe not three steps away, staring at him in utter disbelief. The ground shook again behind him. Without any more hesitation, he launched himself at her and knocked her to the ground, shielding her with his body. In the same moment, the blast from the collapsing rift exploded the doors outward. Pieces from the building's façade, chunks of masonry and metal, and myriad shards of glass shot overhead. One large, flat piece of sheet metal frisbeed just above them; as Jason lifted himself off her, he saw that Phoebe's eyes were wide and horrified.

"That thing that went over us - it would have killed us both. Jason, *what happened?*" She looked like she was about to panic, and he couldn't let that happen. He needed her, immediately, and she needed to understand that.

"Phoebe - we have to get out of here. Both of us - right now. We can't be here. I'll explain on the way." He was already staggering to his feet; her hand felt weak and wonderfully human, and for a moment he couldn't let it go. Then he saw how strangely she was looking at him, and realized he had to explain to her, quickly and convincingly, how dire his situation had become.

"Phoebe, if there's one thing I learned today, it's that I will do anything - *anything* - to be with you. I don't care what else happens. Can you believe that?"

Phoebe was looking at his clothing, which had changed since she had seen him less than ten minutes earlier, and was distinctly the worse for wear. She moved her gaze almost unwillingly to meet his own. Whatever she saw there, Jason realized, must have convinced her: she turned, still clasping his hand, and together they moved at a fast walk away from Williams Hall, even as a crowd of onlookers was coalescing around the damaged building. As they left, Jason noted a furrow in the ground pointing toward Hampton Hall; it appeared that the connecting tunnel had collapsed. He hoped that Wiley had still been in the shitter; the very last thing on earth that he wanted, he realized, was for any harm to come to Wiley Grant.

They walked to the parking lot of the adjacent building. Her car was there, overheated in the sun, but he was too tired to care. He fell into the passenger seat as she went around to the driver's side and got in.

"Where do you need me to go?" she asked. Jason opened his eyes - they had closed the moment he was off his feet - and replied, "Your apartment for now, but only long enough to get your things. Then we've got to leave town, and find someplace we can stay low for a while."

Phoebe had been about to start the car; Jason's response froze her. She stared at him, her face flickering between fury, terror and amazement, and after a few seconds she asked in a hissing whisper, *"What. Did. You. DO?"*

"I saved your life, Phoebe." Jason looked at her, as pleadingly as his exhaustion would allow him. "I promise you, I can explain how all of this happened. Someday. But you have to go - *now*." He hesitated. "We have to be out of the city before they get back into the lab."

She looked angry and disgusted. "Did you sabotage the wormhole, just to get me back?"

The look he gave her in reply seemed to cross the half-trillion miles, and every minute of each year, that separated the worlds he had walked. She felt it, visibly, and her anger melted into fear, and her disgust crystallized into awe. When he spoke, his voice was quiet, but for that one, brief instance, it carried the same timbre that it had when he had spoken to a clan chieftain who, in the world to which he had returned, never had been - and might never be.

"I would never have done that. But I would never have let you go, if I had been smarter. I'm smarter now, and I don't ever want to lose you again. I will do *anything* to keep you in my life. Can you believe that?"

She glared at him again for several seconds, but then sighed as she relented. "All right. We'll do it your way. How long do I have?"

"Go to your apartment, get a week's worth of clothes and whatever else you need, and get out of there. I've got to get to an ATM and get as much cash as I can before everything starts going sideways."

Her shoulders sagged, and for another long moment, she said nothing. Jason waited. Without her, there was no more he could do for himself - but he had already done what needed to be done for her.

Either way, it was enough.

Postlude

A few days later

"THANKS FOR LETTING us use your space," Jason said fervently. He had never gotten along particularly well with Phoebe's brother, Alfonzo - Al - but the man's appetite for conspiracy theories and government shenanigans was endless, and just knowing that he and Phoebe were on the run, and being actively sought, was all that was needed to persuade him to let them hide in his storage space for a few days.

"Anything for my future brother-in-law. At least, you'd better be." Al had the knack for raising and lowering his smile in a blink, and he lowered it as he spoke. Nevertheless, Jason knew Al would never sell them out, and his network of fellow-travelers would prove useful in the next seventy-two hours. He did not dare stay there longer. Once his body was discovered, and the cameras in Williams Hall were recovered and reviewed, the chase would begin.

He had known that this would happen. He could not return earlier along his own time than he had left it, unless he rearranged the events that created the rift; this world was not quite the one he had left. Parallel, virtually identical, one of an infinity of infinities that exploded from each single quantum probability, every femtosecond. Nearly all of those merged at once into each other, their differentials insignificant - but in each microsecond, there were more created than any human could ever hope to navigate

Or so he had thought, once. He had returned into a universe where Phoebe had left him, just as in his own, but he had changed this one. Perhaps not on a significant level - a single universe was vast almost beyond reckoning, and who knew how many trillions of sentient - and insentient - lifeforms there were in existence in this one alone, with the actions of each one exploding additional parallel universes in numbers that were calculable, but which reduced the term "astronomical" to a laughable understatement. Jason wondered to himself whether the only check on the expansion and proliferation of the multiverse was in fact its own staggering mathematics.

Al was watching him, and he glanced over to Phoebe as Jason's thought returned to the immediate situation they faced.   His expression was concerned. "You're right. Something's wrong with him. I've seen people who have been through some bad shit, and they all looked like that. He looks worse than most of them, so whenever he decides he can tell you, better be ready for it. Whatever it is." He shot another probing look at Jason, and then turned, shaking his head. "Remember to put the key where I told you. I don't want to have to bust the lock on this place."

With that, Al sauntered back to his aged pickup truck, not looking back. Jason sighed, and pulled down the door of the rental storage unit where they would be hiding. Phoebe had turned on the single bulb affixed to the ceiling overhead.

"Glad this place is climate-controlled," Jason said.   That was indeed fortunate for them; three days without air conditioning in that place would have been about the only thing that could have made their situation worse.

The unit was typical of its kind, ten feet wide by fifteen feet long. Three feet inside the door, an apparent stack of boxes went almost to the ceiling, creating a wall. The boxes were in fact empty, and were glued to a set of heavy shelves set up behind them that held them firmly in place. Al had shown them which box was actually a flap that would allow them to enter the space behind the wall.

Their safe house was ten feet square, poorly lit, and dominated by the bed that took up more than half their space. The shelves held five-gallon water jugs, supplies of food, first aid, and - Jason noted with dismay - a number of guns and a large supply of ammunition.

"It looks like he was preparing for a zombie apocalypse," Jason muttered. Phoebe heard him.

"I don't know about the zombie part, but he was definitely getting ready for some kind of a crash."

"I think that won't start for another ten years. Maybe more. But I'll leave him a note that he'll need more than this." The words escaped him before he realized his mistake. When he looked toward Phoebe, she was staring at him, more than a little fearfully.

Jason sat down on the edge of the bed, and motioned Phoebe to sit beside him. He gave her a very long look, directly into her eyes - eyes that were alive again, he thought. All her heart, all her emotions were right there. He hadn't thought of how much he had missed that - not until then.

"Jason, you've got to tell me what happened."

He sagged visibly. "I know. But I'm afraid that if I tell you everything, you might be in as much trouble as I am."

"Did you destroy the - the bridge on purpose?" Phoebe's expression didn't change, but her eyes spoke volumes to him - volumes that he had taken for granted, until just a few days ago.

"Yes and no." He hesitated. "Something really strange happened to it. It's hard to explain. But someone, or something, tried to extend the bridge past the limits we set, and - destabilized it."

"Who could have done something like that?" Phoebe was both surprised and puzzled.

"Nobody I know of who's alive today could have done it," he responded, doing his best to keep his tone from sounding guarded.

Phoebe was watching him, not suspiciously, but intently, and with considerable worry. "So what happened then?"

Jason thought for a moment before he responded. "Wiley wasn't at his station. I thought he was on the can. When I saw that, and realized how unstable the bridge was, I decided to shut it down before it destabilized completely."

"But you told me it would evaporate by itself," Phoebe ventured. Jason said a slightly rude word to himself.

"It would have, usually. But with what it was doing - especially with the extension, who knows where that came from - I was afraid it might not."

Jason stared at his shoes. He wasn't entirely lying, but he still hated how this conversation felt.

Phoebe was no happier, but she seemed to grasp that he was at least trying to tell her as much as he could. She heaved a sigh, and started to stand up - and then she was right in his face, her eyes boring into his as she whispered, "Is there any more to this?"

He wanted to tell her, but he couldn't. "Nothing that I can tell you without endangering you. I know, I'm giving you an airplane view of what happened, but I'm afraid that if you know the whole truth, and you're found out, you might be in big, big trouble." *And I don't want you to know that I'm not the same Jason you broke up with yesterday,* he mentally added. *That would get us both disappeared. Maybe forever.*

She thought about that. "So what are you going to do? You can't be a nuclear physicist in a safe house. We have to leave soon anyway."

"We'll figure it out," he said, almost despairingly. "I thought I might do some writing, maybe go that route and try to self-publish. I can do odd jobs. But there's one thing I *have* to do, and I have to do it as soon as we get away from here."

"What's that?" she asked.

"I have to write an exposé on what's going on in Nesmith Hall. There's a scientist in there named Allen Bryant, and he's trying to create cyborgs using human cadavers. Definitely not what you'd call legal. From what I understand, he's well on his way to creating one. He needs to be stopped."

Phoebe's expression, so nakedly visible, was a mixture of incredulity and fear. "Jason, *how do you know that?* I don't think you've ever *been* to Nesmith Hall. For anything. It's on the other side of campus. How could you have ever found out about something like that - ?" Her eyes suddenly grew round as she clapped her hands over her mouth. Jason nodded to her.

"I've learned about a *lot* of stuff I shouldn't know. I know who the DARPA guys are running most of the research projects. They're good men, and I'd trust them to do the right thing, but right now I *really* need to stay out of their way. And out of their reach," he added as an afterthought.

"Why did you tell me that?" she asked.

"Because if something happens to me, and you get away, you'll know about it and can try to stop it," Jason answered.

"Have you thought about where we can go?" she asked after a few seconds' silence.

He sighed. "We need to be someplace where we won't stick out too much. It's got to be at least a small city, and I'd like it to be at least five hundred miles from here. I also don't want to be any closer to DC than we are now. And it needs to be relatively safe. Detroit's not an option, or Chicago."

"How about Louisville?"

"No thanks. One thing I know is that the more conservative a place is, the more they distrust strangers. Kentucky is a no-go as far as I'm concerned. I might be wrong, but I'd rather that than find out the hard way that I was right."

Phoebe thought. "Cincinnati?"

Jason considered. "That's a possibility. The only states I was considering were Ohio and Missouri - St. Louis maybe, or Kansas City."

Neither place appeared to appeal to her, but then her eyes brightened. "Wait - Miami's about that far away, and it's a big city. How about there, or Fort Lauderdale?"

Jason closed his eyes and ran a hand over his brow, trying to avoid even thinking about seafloods. Finally he said, "There's a lot of reasons why I really don't want to head into Florida, but let's just say I hate bugs, and the ones in Miami are the size of dogs."

Phoebe sighed in disappointment, shaking her head, and abruptly her eyes were tearful. "I can't believe this is happening."

Jason's own eyes smarted, and he stood up as she did. Embracing her felt like water after a long journey through a desert, and for a few seconds he simply held her, drinking in her closeness as though he needed it to live. Maybe, he thought, he did.

He knew Phoebe sensed that something was different, but it made her softer, more yielding and yet stronger. She drew back a little, so that they could look at each other.

"You've changed. You were so driven to be part of that Nobel Prize. You probably could have stayed there and tried again." She smiled. "Can you tell me, really, whether you did any of this for me?"

He looked at her so soberly, so seriously, that for a moment she experienced an echo of what she had sensed in her car, the feeling that he had crossed an unspeakably vast distance. His reply was barely above a whisper: "I would give up anything, do anything, take any risk to be with you. And if I couldn't, I'd give up my own life, if that's what it took to keep you safe. I know that's not a lot to be going on, not now. But you have all of me." He swallowed. "You won't have to take a back seat to my career anymore. I choose you."

She gave him an odd, yet loving look. "How did you know about that? I never told you, but that was how I always felt about your work."

Jason froze for a bare instant, then smiled. "I suppose I just figured it out. Or maybe you told me in a dream."

The kindness in her eyes became slightly sardonic. "If you say so, Jason." She leaned forward again, and he kissed her; when their lips parted, she added, "Even *I* don't think you've changed *that* much."

Epilogue

An attic's corner of my mind
Where stored were dusty memories
I searched, in hope that I might find
A missing muse, or mysteries
From dreams forgotten long ago,
Of one I loved but never knew:
A story, half-remembered now,
With images blurred from the true.

I drew her memory from its box,
Blew off the dust that lingered there,
Broke off the rust-encrusted locks
Protecting her from decades' wear -
And raised the lid, to look again
Into the shining amber eyes
That lit her face, with tresses framed
Of jet, with light that never dies.

She was the touchstone of a time,
A candle in a darkening room -
She was unrivalled, pure, sublime.
When seeing her, beyond the gloom
Of years that long since are no more,
I know no other could compare:
Within her eyes, from long before,
I see my youth reflected there.

> *"Benita"*
> *6 December 2018*
> *11 September 2019*